059127

W9-AND-550

Grant, Andrew,
1968-

Run.

$26.00

DATE			

By Andrew Grant

Even

Die Twice

More Harm Than Good

RUN

RUN

A NOVEL

ANDREW GRANT

 BALLANTINE BOOKS | NEW YORK

Copyright © 2014 by Andrew Grant

Published in the United States by Ballantine Books,
an imprint of Random House, a division of Random House LLC,
a Penguin Random House Company, New York.

BALLANTINE and the HOUSE colophon are
registered trademarks of Random House LLC.

LIBRARY OF CONGRESS CATALOGING-IN-PUBLICATION DATA
Grant, Andrew
Run : a novel / Andrew Grant.
pages cm
ISBN 978-0-345-54072-0
eBook ISBN 978-0-345-54074-4
1. Technology consultants—Fiction. 2. Computer industry—Fiction.
3. Corporations—Corrupt practices—Fiction. 4. Betrayal—Fiction.
5. Trade secrets—Fiction. I. Title.
PR6107.R366R86 2104
823'.92—dc23   2014017537

Printed in the United States of America on acid-free paper

www.ballantinebooks.com

9 8 7 6 5 4 3 2 1

FIRST EDITION

Book design by Barbara M. Bachman

FOR MY BROTHERS:
RICHARD, JIM, AND DAVID

RUN

*O*N A USUAL MONDAY MORNING, I'D BE THE FIRST TO ARRIVE.
The gate, which was little more than a hinged version of my client's
corporate logo—the name AmeriTel splashed across the globe with
three multi-colored electrons spinning inexplicably around it—would
still be closed. Mine would be the only car in the parking lot, except
for the night-shift security guard's—a pink 1959 Cadillac Eldorado Se-
ville, all tailfins and chrome—which the management made him leave
in the farthest corner from the door. The official reason was that the
car took up too much space. My guess was the fact that it left their
bland German status symbols in the shade had more to do with it. But
anyway I'd pass the guy, dozing in the otherwise deserted reception
area—a double-height triangular wedge driven between the two functional wings of the building like the central tip of a "W," and crammed
with van der Rohe and Le Corbusier in the hope that the smell of
money would impress the visitors—and head to the narrow second-
floor office I'd requisitioned for the duration of my project. I'd check
on the progress of all the new reports I'd left running over the weekend. I'd catch up on email. And I'd line up the jobs I wanted to nail that
week.

It wasn't rocket science, but it worked for me.

Until *that* Monday.

I knew something was up when I couldn't park in my usual space.
It had been taken by a black S-Class Mercedes. Another black Benz was
tucked in next to it, and a trio of BMWs was lined up farther along the
row. It made the place look more like a funeral home than an office

building. But five big-hitters at work before the first pot of coffee was normally brewed? A sure sign of crisis. Something new and nasty must have hit the fan over the weekend. Not that I was surprised. Everyone knew AmeriTel was struggling. They wouldn't have hired me if they weren't having problems. It's just that I was expecting a more general kind of trouble to have surfaced. Something that had pushed the whole corporation another step closer to the abyss. Not something aimed at me, personally.

The security guard wasn't half asleep that morning. He was fully awake, waiting near the foot of the stairs with Simon Wakefield, the Chief Operating Officer—his boss, several levels removed—lurking behind him.

"Good morning, Mr. Bowman," the guard said as I approached. I was surprised. I hadn't realized he even knew my name. "Would you come with me, please?"

"Why? What's wrong?"

"Mr. LeBrock's waiting for you in the boardroom. He'd like to see you."

"I know where the boardroom is. I don't need an escort. But why does he want to see me?"

"I don't know."

"Simon?"

Simon Wakefield shrugged and looked away.

"OK, then. I'll just check on my computers, and I'll be along in a minute."

"No, sir." The guard shook his head.

"What do you mean, no?"

"Mr. LeBrock wants to see you in the boardroom right away, sir." He started to look a little flustered and tried to gesture subtly at Simon Wakefield. "Mr. LeBrock said I was to take you directly there the moment you arrived."

Their little reception committee seemed slightly overdramatic— wouldn't an email or a text have done the job just as well?—but there didn't seem to be much point in arguing. There was nothing to gain by getting the security guard in trouble. Or landing him in the hospital. He wasn't a small guy, and the stress of the confrontation—minor as it was—already had his chest heaving. And Roger LeBrock was the CEO of AmeriTel. I'd known LeBrock for fifteen years. We'd worked together before, and he was the one who'd brought me in when the first potholes started to appear in his latest road to riches. If anyone could explain what was going on that morning, LeBrock could. And he was apparently waiting for me on the second floor, so I wasted no more words on his lackeys and started up the stairs.

THE BUILDING'S ARCHITECTS HAD been opposed to individual offices. They believed shutting people off from their co-workers discouraged communication, and that putting nameplates on doors fostered elitism, so the entire place was designed to be open-plan. That was fine in theory. And the sense of light and space was very attractive to prospective tenants. But the problems started once the people moved in. Human Resources needed privacy for interviewing new employees, they said. A large alcove at the far end of their section was converted into three separate rooms. And within a week, their director was unofficially but permanently ensconced in one of them. The same thing happened in the Sales area. And Marketing. And Customer Service. And as for the CEO? The boardroom—the whole of the second floor above the reception area—soon became his private domain.

Roger LeBrock was sitting in his customary spot at the far side of the boardroom table—a custom-made granite triangle, cut to match the peculiar shape of the room—when I walked in. He was wearing his signature black and blue Prada, from his glasses to his shoes. But even so, he didn't seem his normal self. He looked thinner and somehow slightly deflated, a shadow of the grinning man who was shaking hands with Bono and Hillary Clinton and Steve Jobs and a dozen others I vaguely recognized in the photographs on the glory wall behind him.

"Marc!" He stood and moved closer to shake hands. "Good to see you. I'm glad you're here. How was your weekend?"

"Busy. But good. Yours?"

"It was fine." He tried to smile but only managed to mobilize one half of his face. "Now, please. Sit. There's something we need to talk about."

"Aren't we waiting for the others?" I gestured to the three sets of papers piled up on the other side of the triangle.

"I don't think so." He returned to his chair and waited until I was seated. "They have things to attend to."

As he spoke, the lower lid of his left eye started to tremble. Very slightly. I'd seen it do that once before. Years ago, when he'd brought me in to run numbers for him at a meeting in St. Louis. He'd been trying to revive a deal that was in danger of going south. And on that occasion, I'd known for certain he was lying through his teeth.

"That sounds ominous."

He tried his smile again, with even less success.

"There's no point beating around the bush, I guess, Marc. You knew we were facing some pretty serious challenges when you came on board. I was pretty candid about that, wasn't I?"

"Where's this going, Roger?"

"And it's not just us. The industry as a whole is facing the biggest shakeout in its history. The landscape's changing faster than ever before. Soon it's going to be unrecognizable."

"I know all this, Roger. Save it for the shareholders. What's your point?"

"The point is, the efficiencies you've helped us to identify? We're really happy with them. They've made a tangible difference. But now we're in the final stretch, and things are different. We have to make some tough choices. Choices we're not happy about making. But this is business, Marc. Our own personal happiness doesn't factor into it."

"The final stretch?"

"You know what I mean."

"The bandwidth auction?"

"Of course. It's a watershed. Win or lose, everything'll be different."

"And you're not confident of winning? After all the time you've spent in D.C., glad-handing the stuffed shirts and bullshitting the White House committees?"

"Ask me at noon tomorrow." He shrugged. "Then we'll know our fate. One way or the other, the guessing'll be over."

"There's no guesswork involved. Just a finite number of known outcomes, and I've helped you plan for all of them. The work I've done for you—the customer behavioral analysis, not the boring cost-saving stuff—it makes you unique. Even if you come out of the auction empty-handed and have to sell the company, it'll be worth five times what it was before I started. At least. No one can match the kind of insights I've given you. They're gold dust. They put you light-years ahead of everyone else."

"AmeriTel will be worth fifteen times that, if we win."

"You've got to keep some perspective, Roger. The other players are way bigger than you. There's no shame in being outbid by a crew with deeper pockets. Especially if it's the usual scenario where the winner pays too much and ends up bankrupt."

"I'm not paying too much. I'm not a moron. I just don't like to lose. And the bottom line is, I don't want to lose—the company, or the extra money we'll make if we stay in the game."

"Are we in Death Valley yet? Has your bid gone in?"

"We're putting in a revised bid this morning. The deadline's five pm, eastern."

"So isn't this a conversation for tomorrow?"

"No. Not really. I'd like to get the decks cleared now."

"What does that mean?"

"It's like I said. Tomorrow's a watershed, Marc. Either way, after tomorrow we're going to have a very different kind of company on our hands. We're going to have very different support requirements, going forward. And that's where those difficult choices I mentioned come in."

"Difficult choices? Such as?"

"Look, Marc, this isn't easy for either of us. And I want to be straight with you, right from the start. We've been extremely happy with the work you've done for us. We'll be happy to recommend you to anyone. We'll make sure that everything that's due to you gets paid without delay. There might even be a couple of bonus clauses we can activate. But as of this morning, the reality is—your contract? It's being canceled."

My contract is *being canceled*? Great use of the corporate passive, I thought. All those brave words about being straight with me, but he still couldn't take responsibility for the six inches of steel he'd just plunged between my shoulder blades. I thought about calling him on it. I thought about my wife, Carolyn, who'd encouraged me to take the contract. She was a ten-year veteran of AmeriTel and a fixture at the place—unless she didn't fit in with the new corporate support requirement landscape bullshit, and had been bulleted, too. And then I thought about my weekend, which had mostly been spent there at AmeriTel instead of at home with her. Again.

"Difficult choices? I've got news for you. You need a new dictionary, my friend. Because you're confusing *difficult* with *stupid*. Have you got any idea how much money you're setting fire to, letting me go? How many opportunities you're going to miss out on?"

"I understand you're frustrated." He clasped his hands and placed them on the table in front of him with all the practiced sincerity of a TV preacher. "You're brilliant at what you do, and I truly respect that. But try to look at things from our perspective. We're facing a time of unprecedented change. We need to trim our cost base to the bone. And we need our operations to be as lean and agile as they can possibly be."

"And there's no room for me in that picture?"

"I'm afraid not. Look, this day's dawned a little sooner than you or I expected, but we always knew it was coming. That's the point of using consultants, right?"

"If you think that, you're even more stupid than I realized. You want to cut costs? How much do I cost you?"

"I'm sorry?"

"You're firing me to save money, so it's a fair question. How much do I cost you?"

"Marc. Be reasonable. I don't have your contract in front of me. I can't comment on the details. Only on the overall principles we're trying to adhere to—"

"Nothing."

"What?"

"I cost you nothing. I take a percentage of everything I save you. And a percentage of everything extra you make, based on my ideas. Keeping me costs you nothing. Fact. And firing me will lose you money. Fact."

"It's not that simple, Marc."

"It is that simple. Without my analytics you won't know where your inefficiencies are. And you won't know where to aim your new products. If you're worried about cost, firing me is the last thing you should do."

"Your initiatives have been very successful up to now, sure. That's why we're paying you, and why I said we'd be happy to endorse your work. But here's the real problem: What you do is make recommendations based on the past. Now, a lot of your insights are fascinating. And those grenades you hit us with early on? Like that sales guy you found running an escort service on company time? Dynamite. But if things haven't already happened, how can you analyze them? You see? You're rooted in *history,* Marc. We're not. AmeriTel's entering a new era. We need different thinking. Future thinking. Radical transformation, not a way to milk the most out of the status quo."

"If you don't understand your history, you're doomed to repeat your mistakes."

"Oh, that old chestnut. Maybe it holds water for countries or governments or whatever. But not for the telecommunications industry. We're moving too fast for that."

"You're moving fast, no doubt. But in which direction? Straight over the cliff? How can you tell? If you can't measure, you can't manage. And without me, you can't measure. Not as well as you can with me, anyway. I think I've proved that."

A large frown spread across LeBrock's face, then he nodded.

"You're right," he said, quietly, after a moment. "Everything you've done here has been first class. If I've given you the impression we have a problem with your work, I apologize. If I've given you the impression we have a problem with you personally, I apologize. And if I've given you the impression this subject is up for debate, I doubly apologize. Because it isn't. It's done. I wish it hadn't panned out this way. But my job's not to do what's nice. It's to do what's right for the company."

I didn't reply. I was back to thinking about the previous weekend. Something had struck me. Maybe my time hadn't been completely wasted, after all. Especially if that's the way they wanted to play the game.

"Come on." LeBrock stood and held out his hand once again. "We've worked together before. I know we will again. Let's part as friends. And think of Carolyn. How would she feel if you were dragged out of here in handcuffs?"

"Speaking of Carolyn, how about her job? Is she safe?"

"If we win this damn auction tomorrow, yes. I guarantee it. If we don't—I won't lie to you, Marc. I can't promise anything. But I'll do everything I can to make sure Carolyn's looked after."

"You better." I took his hand. "I'll hold you to that. And good luck tomorrow. For her sake, at least."

"Thanks. I appreciate your understanding. Oh, sorry, there's one other thing. The stuff you left in the office you were using? It's been boxed up. It's being shipped to your home. Simon Wakefield insisted. Security falls under Simon, so I couldn't really argue."

"And the computers?"

"Were any of them yours?"

"One of them. One of the new notebooks."

"Then it'll be in the box. You'll have it by lunchtime."

"And the company computers? Just out of interest."

"Simon's already set the IT boys to work on them. Stripping them down. Wiping the discs. Getting them ready for whatever tomorrow brings, I guess. With the level of access you had, you know we couldn't just leave them lying around."

I nodded. Wiping the computers clean was fine with me. I'd put a lot of effort into building those databases. If I wasn't going to be there any longer, why should anyone else benefit from them?

THE BOARDROOM DOOR CLOSED behind me, but I didn't start down the stairs right away. I wasn't trying to delay my departure, though. And I certainly wasn't trying to capture a lasting memory of the place. AmeriTel honestly didn't mean that much to me. It was just that for the first time since I started my contract there, I didn't have an urgent objective in mind. A burning task to complete, or meeting to get to. I could take my time. Do what I wanted. Not what the company wanted.

And now that I realized how little they valued what I'd been doing, I was glad to be free of them.

I heard a rattling sound below me and when I looked down I saw a janitor wheeling a cleaning cart toward the exit. For one crazy moment I was tempted to call out to him and hitch a ride, since I was being thrown out with the rest of the trash. Then it struck me, I'd never seen the guy before. When I'd started working there, the cleaning crew had all been women. Thinking about it, they'd had different-colored uniforms, too. Blue. Not green. The original company must have lost the contract, somewhere along the way. I wondered what else could have changed without me noticing. The water coolers? The coffee machines? I wasn't sure.

The realization kept me rooted to the spot for another moment or two, shaking my head at the irony. I make my living by seeing what no one else even knows is there. I use my analytical tools to peek beneath the skin of companies and make sense of whatever's hidden beneath. Here, I'd missed the simple things that were in plain sight. But at least I wasn't the only one who was out of touch. When I finally reached the parking lot I passed a pair of IT technicians making their way in with a portable degausser and a couple of cases of other equipment. They must not have started work on trashing my old machines yet, as LeBrock said they had. And they were from a different contractor, too. One with shabby coveralls and a name and logo I'd never come across before. Some kind of bargain basement, Mickey Mouse outfit, no doubt. Which meant the penny-pinching had spread all the way to business-critical systems.

AmeriTel must have sunk deeper into the mire than I'd thought.

All things considered, I was lucky to be out of the place.

WHEN THE GOING GETS TOUGH, THE TOUGH GO SHOPPING.

I left Carolyn a voicemail telling her to ignore any office gossip she might hear—plus a promised to give her the full story over dinner—then headed to one of my favorite spots in the world. The TL Gallery. It's owned by a friend of mine, Troye (that's Troye with a silent "e," as he's always quick to point out to new acquaintances) Liptak. The place is only five miles from my house in terms of distance, but more like five light-years in terms of contents. On any given day you could rely on Troye to have at least one Picasso. A couple of Miros. Maybe a Dalí. A Richter. A Matisse or two. It's like having a world-class art museum in the neighborhood, except that if Troye thinks there's a chance you might buy a piece, he'll take it down from the wall and let you hold it. He'll honestly stand there and put a ten, fifteen, maybe twenty million dollar painting right in your hands and let you drool over it for as long as you want. Forget the Met, or any of those other famous museums. The TL is the place to go if you want an up close and personal encounter with art.

Troye was wearing one of his more restrained outfits that day—a lemon-yellow three-piece suit, a green shirt, and a pair of black and white correspondent shoes. He watched me come in, then after a few seconds he levered himself off the pillar he'd been leaning against and ambled across the floor in my direction.

"My goodness." He swept a curtain of bleached blond hair away from his face before leaning forward and subjecting me to one of his trademark overenthusiastic hugs. He felt like he might have gained a couple of pounds since my last visit, but even after all the years I'd known him I would have struggled to guess his age. The cosmetic surgeon who'd raised his cheekbones and sharpened his nose had made that impossible.

"Marc? Is it you? Where on earth have you been hiding?"

"It's me. You know how I am. Busy, busy, busy. But I haven't been hiding. And I never stay away for too long."

"Yes, you do. I thought you'd forgotten about me. Or found someone else to relieve you of your excess cash. I thought maybe you'd become a car nut. Or worse, one of those antiques guys. I was thinking of closing the place down, I was so worried."

"Well, I'm glad you didn't. What stopped you?"

Troye took a step back and spread his arms.

"I couldn't bear to leave my babies. Although, if you wanted to take one of them home with you in exchange for an obscene sum of money, that would be perfectly fine. Are you in the mood for buying today, Marc? Or are you just here for a looky-lou?"

"To be honest, Troye, I'm here to relive a memory."

"You've had bad news?"

I nodded.

"You need a Roy moment?"

I nodded again. I hadn't gone there with any realistic intention of buying a painting, that day. What I needed was to revisit the scene of my greatest life-affirming moment to date. Because the TL is the place where—after ten years of aspiring and getting by with poster-store copies—I'd bought myself a genuine Lichtenstein. It's only a small one. It's not the most critically acclaimed. But it's the most valuable thing I've ever owned. And I don't just mean in terms of the price tag.

"You and Roy, you're still soul mates?" Troye asked.

"Always will be."

I never had the chance to meet Roy Lichtenstein while he was alive. I'm not related to him. But somehow I feel closer to him than to almost any other human. I felt that way the very first time I saw one of his paintings—or at least paid any attention to one—which wasn't until I was thirty-two years old. I was on a business trip to Chicago and a client took me to a product launch he was hosting one evening at the Art Institute. The presentations were boring so I slipped into the store—the galleries were all closed—and came face-to-face with an enormous cartoonish print of a distraught woman talking on the phone. The image totally captivated me. But it wasn't the bright colors that drew me in. Or the bold shapes. Or the woman's words, spelled out in a speech-bubble above her head. It was the way Lichtenstein painted. How he took an intangible concept and made it visible through dots and lines. Because it struck me, that's exactly what I did. Only in my case, the dots and lines weren't stenciled in. They were the ones and zeros I harvested from my clients' computer records.

"Your bad news—is it serious? Is anyone sick?"

"No. It's just a project I was working on. It got canned. The guy I was running it for? He's the head of AmeriTel. I was halfway to saving his company, and the asshole pulled the plug on me."

"AmeriTel? Sounds familiar. Is that where your wife used to work?"

"It's where she still works. We were there together, for a while. And now I'm not."

"Ouch. That has to hurt."

It did hurt. But nowhere near as much as Lichtenstein must have been hurt back in 1963, when a newspaper published an article reviewing his work. The critic's verdict? That Lichtenstein was the worst artist in America. And this wasn't a small-time regional rag the guy was writing in. It was the *New York Times*.

"Other people have had worse to deal with," I replied. "Don't worry about me. It's water off a duck's back."

It was the way Lichtenstein responded to the setback—to the reality of what happens when people don't understand what you're doing—that really cemented my connection with the guy. And appropriately—given my utter lack of talent when it comes to painting—it had nothing to do with his art. It was his attitude. Because Lichtenstein didn't fold. He didn't hide under a rock. He just kept on swimming against the tide, letting the vitriol and abuse wash over him until his critics began to take him seriously. Until they were forced to recognize his genius. To concede that he brought something new and unique to the table. And that's exactly what I did, when I showed my then-boss my first attempt at an analysis tool and got laughed out of his company for my trouble. I dug deep, and when I got the product right, I sold it to his biggest competitor.

I thought Troye was about to ask me something else, when I heard the door scrape open behind me and instead he excused himself, no doubt anxious to greet the new customers. I wandered farther into the gallery, glancing at the exhibits on the walls and weaving my way through a cluster of waist-high sculptures until I came to a painting that caught my eye. It was a view of a city at night through the rain-swept windshield of a car. But it wasn't the main part of the image—the other vehicles and buildings and pedestrians and streetlights blurring together into a rushing mass of streaking lines—that intrigued me. It was one tiny detail. The car's instrument panel. It grabbed me because that first product I designed—the one that was initially ridiculed, but eventually set me on the path to my own Lichtenstein—was based on the concept of a car dashboard. I'd chosen it because I wanted something that anyone could intuitively understand. Something that made visual sense, not a forest of numbers and charts you'd need a degree in statistics to decipher.

I've done more complex stuff since then, but I was still proud of that original system. Under the hood it used some hard-core algorithms—it had to, given the way it boiled a whole business down to just five key pieces of information—but on the surface it looked like a bank of round, retro-style dials, freshly ripped out of a hunk of Detroit's finest heavy metal. The dials had numbers around the edges. Needles that moved. And the best part? Backgrounds that changed color depending on how things were going. Green meant you were OK. Red, it was time to worry. Amber, there could be a problem, so take a second look, if you've got the time.

"Are you having a moment?" Troye had snuck up behind me. "I can see your reflection. You stand in the corner grinning to yourself, you look like an insane person. What's the matter with you?"

"Oh, nothing. I just like this picture, is all."

"Like it enough to buy it?"

"Well, no, but . . ."

"I knew it. You are turning into a car guy."

"No, I'm not." I was distracted for a moment, thinking about the racing car Lichtenstein had been hired to paint in the seventies, when he wasn't a geek anymore. "It's just that this picture—it reminded me that the future's going to be pretty damn bright, after all."

"It did? How? Tell me. Then I can enlighten my other customers. And then lighten their wallets . . ."

I tried to find the words to explain what I was thinking, but I was actually a little embarrassed. The truth was, I'd been imagining what my life would look like if it were broken down across those original five dials. My key indicators would be, what? My relationship with my wife? That would be green, definitely. Carolyn was smart and beautiful, and—having put a couple of garden-variety bumps in the marital road behind us—we were as solid as a rock. My friends? Green, again. I'd always had my fair share. Family? Amber, I guess. But there was nothing I could do about that—we didn't have kids, my parents were dead, and I had no brothers or sisters. Finances? Green. Leaving Ameri-Tel early was going to hurt me a little, but the long-term damage would be minimal. And finally, my career. On the face of it you'd think, red. I'd just been fired, after all. But over the weekend, I'd had an idea. My biggest one yet. So big that when I was finished with it, I wouldn't be looking back at buying my first Lichtenstein. I'd be looking forward to my second. Maybe even my third.

Cash wasn't an issue, the way it had been when I quit my job to perfect my first product. Now, there were only two things I'd need. Time to develop the idea, which I suddenly had in spades, thanks to Roger LeBrock. And raw materials to experiment with, which in my line of work meant data. Huge volumes of data. And I had that, too. On a pair of rubber-coated memory sticks. They were in my pocket. I'd clipped them to my key chain the previous night, on my way out of AmeriTel's office. There hadn't been any particular reason to keep them, at the time. The data was a by-product of another project I'd been working on. I'd just thought it was too good to waste, the way a carpenter might feel about a hefty offcut of oak or mahogany. But now, taking the memory sticks seemed like a stroke of genius. They were going to change my life. I could feel it.

"Sorry, Troye." I gave up on the explanation. "You'll have to spin your own bullshit. I've got to go. I need to strike something while the iron's hot . . ."

I'D THOUGHT IT WOULD ONLY TAKE TEN MINUTES TO GET HOME from the gallery, but I was wrong. The route I ended up taking was twice the distance I'd expected. And it took three times longer than it should have, due to a jackass in a silver Audi who'd pulled out of Troye's parking lot in front of me. He'd seemed eager enough to get on the road, but then hesitated before every turn and dawdled through each junction as if he were happy for every other car in the county to pull out in front of him. He was so indecisive I couldn't understand how he'd made up his mind to leave his house in the first place. Maybe I should have felt sorry for him. He'd probably been drifting aimlessly around all morning, ever since the breakfast-time rush hour had left him in its wake like a piece of automotive flotsam. But since he was all that stood between me and the work I was raring to begin—and because he stayed resolutely in my way right up to my street—I couldn't help cursing him instead.

I turned into my driveway and for a moment I thought the silver Audi was already there, ahead of me. Then I realized it was Carolyn's car. A silver BMW, which cast Troye's crazy theory in its true light. Me, a car guy now? Hardly.

CAROLYN HAD THE DOOR open before I was halfway up the front path, and even from that distance her presence lit up the entrance to our home. She was wearing the navy blue suit I'd watched her set out the night before—at least I assumed it was the same one, because there's no way to adequately compare clothes on a hanger with clothes that Carolyn's wearing—and her hair was still pulled back in the severe style she uses for the office in the hope that people don't see *blond* and think *stupid*.

"You're home early, gorgeous." I leaned down to kiss her, and imagined how she'd look with her hair set free and the suit replaced by a bathrobe. Or by nothing at all . . .

"Where have you been?" she demanded, pulling away from me and breaking the spell. "I was worried. Why didn't you answer your phone?"

I followed her inside and took my phone out of my pocket. It showed twelve missed calls and three voicemail messages. A four-to-one ratio. And I knew from experience—coming from Carolyn, that spelled trouble.

"Are all these from you?"

She glowered.

"I'm sorry, sweetheart. It was on silent, I guess. I had a meeting with LeBrock, first thing. It was a surprise one. An ambush, really. It didn't go too well, and when I came out, I must have just spaced turning the ringer back on."

"I can't believe you." She turned and headed for the living room. "Why are you always so inconsiderate?"

"Be reasonable." I followed her. "I had other things on my mind. Like being shit-canned by one of my oldest friends. When's that ever happened to you? How about a little sympathy?"

She moved to the chair farthest from me and sat down, brushing a stray hair from her cheek and then crossing her arms and legs.

"I did try to call you. I left you a message. Didn't you get it?"

"Of course I got it. And when I tried to call you back, you'd disappeared. What was I supposed to think?"

"I don't know. Maybe that having been stabbed in the back, I needed a little time to recover? That I'd fill you in tonight, like I said in my message?"

"Leaving me to get the news tonight, when it was cold? When you were done *recovering* from it? I should be the first one you tell, Marc. The one you talk to about things like this."

"You were. You are."

"We should have talked then. Right away."

"We couldn't."

"Why not?"

"You were working. You didn't answer your phone. I guessed you were busy."

"You could have come and found me."

"No, I couldn't. I was shut down. Thrown off the premises."

"Then you should have kept calling till I picked up. I'd have dropped everything and come to you."

"Would you? Are you sure?"

She looked away without replying, so I took the chair closest to hers and leaned forward.

"Sweetheart, let's not fight over this. What's done is done. The smart thing is to draw a line and move on. Plus, I've had a great idea. I'm dying to tell you all about it. Do you remember—"

"Where did you go?"

"What about my idea?"

"I want to know where you went."

"When I left AmeriTel?"

"Yes, when you left AmeriTel. Who did you talk to?"

"Oh, I see where this is coming from. This isn't about supporting your husband. It's about protecting your career. You're worried about the fallout. What my contract being canceled might do to your reputation. You wanted to get to me first, to make sure I didn't run my mouth."

"That's ridiculous!"

"What do you see when you look at me, Carolyn? Tell me."

"I see my husband. Same as always. Why?"

"I don't think you do. I think you see a problem. Something to be *handled*. A potential banana skin on the path to your next big promotion."

"That's not fair," she snapped, but the spattering of pink that began at her neck and spread to her cheeks said otherwise.

"Well, I'm sorry. But that's how it seems to me."

"Only because you always see everything in black and white, Marc.

You don't get the gray areas. Everything has to be either right or wrong in your little world. But real life? It's more complex than that. I can be worried about you *and* my career, believe it or not. Two things. At the same time. Equally. And there's absolutely nothing wrong with that."

"If they were equal, maybe you'd be right. But they're not. You know what? I sometimes think you'd have been happier if you'd married AmeriTel instead of me."

"What does that mean?" She added a sharper edge to her voice. "You think you don't get enough attention? Because how could I give you more? You're never here."

"Neither are you. That's my point. You need to get your priorities straightened out."

"No, I don't. There's nothing to straighten out. I value my marriage. To you. And I value my job. At AmeriTel. I work extremely hard at both. I need both. I shouldn't have to pick between them. It's not a competition."

"I'm not asking you to pick. I just think it says a lot about your priorities when you spend more evenings at the office than you do at home."

"That's temporary. We're still a finance manager down, after Melanie Walker's accident. Which is hardly my fault. And I never wanted to work at AmeriTel in the first place, remember. I only went there as a temp. Then I had to stay when you got fired—the first time—and needed someone to support you while you were busy becoming mayor of nerd-central. My dream job went out of the window. I sacrificed it, for you. It was too late for me, by the time you were back on your feet. Don't blame me for making the most of what I was left with."

"It was me getting back on my feet that got us this house. Your car. All your fancy clothes. Your—"

"So your work is more important than mine?"

Not this again . . .

"Not more important, no. Just different."

"Don't patronize me!"

"I'm not."

"You are. You've never valued what I do. I thought, if we worked together for a while? If you saw firsthand what I did? But no. Minute one, what did you do? Found a corner to hide in. Locked yourself away with your computers. Started poking into people's private lives. And let me tell you, when the computers are the only ones doing the networking, not the people, something's very wrong."

"I networked, plenty. And I wasn't hiding in that damn office. I was *working*. Doing the job they hired me to do."

"Maybe. But not anymore. And now they're keeping me and letting you go. And you just can't handle that."

"That's nonsense. I've—"

"You know what?" She erupted from her seat. "Forget it. Just stop talking. I'm sick of the sound of your voice."

"Suits me." Her footsteps thundered across the room and up the stairs. "I'm bored with listening to you, anyway."

WHEN IN DOUBT, MAKE COFFEE. THAT PRINCIPLE'S ALWAYS PAID dividends for me. I've broken through more conceptual logjams standing in front of my old Cuisinart and watching the murky liquid drip hypnotically into the jug than through doing anything else. It's a charmed activity for me, magically summoning the solution to my current problem out of thin air, and that day things seemed no different. The pot was no more than half full when I heard soft footsteps creeping up behind me.

"Let's not fight about this, Marc." Carolyn's voice was quiet. Her face was very pale, and her eyes glistened with dampness. "Please. I'm sorry you lost the contract. I honestly am. I guess I was feeling a little embarrassed, still working there, and thinking about how it was me who pushed you into taking the job in the first place."

"It's no biggie, sweetheart. I'm over it already."

"I honestly thought it would be good for us, to work together. In the same place, anyway."

"It was. It was great."

"Did you like it? Really?"

"Of course I did. And thanks for coming home early today. I know you were worried about me, sweetheart. I appreciate it. I'm sorry I wasn't here when you got back."

"You're really OK about it? Losing the job?"

"I was pissed at the time, I'm not going to lie. It was mainly the way LeBrock told me. He can be a pompous prick at times. Sending the security guard to summon me. Then trying to bury me in a bunch of management-school double-speak. You know the kind of thing? I'm so good and so valuable he's got no choice but to go ahead and terminate me. The asshole."

"Roger's not an asshole." The angry pink swept back into her cheeks. "It's not his fault. The company—it's a house of cards, waiting to fall. The whole industry is."

"You're on LeBrock's side now? What happened to being sorry I got thrown under the bus?"

"I'm not on his side." She clenched her fists, then slowly released them. "There are no sides, Marc. I'm just saying, things are complicated. There's a lot going on."

"I know exactly what's going on. I'm probably the only one who does, after all the analysis I've done. And let's be clear, the whole industry isn't in trouble. AmeriTel is. And AmeriTel's problems are LeBrock's fault. His, and the spineless imbeciles he surrounds himself with. Like the new CFO he brought in. Michael Millan. Have you met him? He's a complete cretin. If you ask me, you're crazy, too, if you keep working there."

"Now you're telling me where I should work?"

"No. I just think you're wasting your talent. AmeriTel doesn't deserve you."

"Because of what happened to *you*?"

"Because of the state the company's in. Plus, the bandwidth auction's tomorrow, and AmeriTel's going to lose."

"It might not."

"It will. And then it's just a question of who the company gets sold to. And how long after that till your contract follows mine down the toilet. You'd do better jumping now, before the job market gets flooded with washed-up telecom people."

"Funny you didn't say this before." She clamped her hands on her hips, tipped her head back slightly, and pretended to sniff the air. "What's that smell? Oh? Could it be sour grapes?"

"No, it couldn't."

"No." She released her hair from its ponytail, shook her head a couple of times, then tied it back up again. "You're right. We're not going to argue. We have a whole afternoon together for the first time in how long? Months? And a whole night to follow. We should put them to better use, don't you think?"

"I guess . . ."

"The question is, where to start? How does a pitcher of million-dollar margaritas sound to you?"

I was torn. A pitcher of margaritas sounded extremely good to me. Not just because I'm a fan of Mexican cocktails, though. More because of the effect tequila has. On Carolyn. Tequila usually leads to a whole host of pleasurable possibilities. But on the other hand, there was my new project. My head was so full of ideas for it—colliding into one another, multiplying, racing away in a hundred different directions at once—I was literally feeling dizzy. I was on the verge of suggesting a rain check—at least till that evening, to give me time to get a few initial simulations up and running—when I saw the expression on her face. It brought back an echo of an old childhood saying. Something about living to fight another day . . .

"Great idea." I was careful to keep the reluctance out of my voice. "How about La Pasadita?"

La Pasadita is the closest Mexican restaurant to our house.

"I was thinking Zapatista's. They use better tequila."

And are much farther away . . .

"All right, Zapatista's." I paused to calculate the extra journey time. "Do you want to head over there right now? Or change first?"

"You change, if you don't want to go in your work things. I'm going as I am. There's something I need to drop off at the office on the way."

"Oh? What?"

"Something you might have brought home by mistake?"

"What do you mean?"

"Something you brought home from AmeriTel. I need to take it back. To keep you out of trouble."

"How can I be in trouble? They can't fire me twice. And I didn't bring anything back. I didn't have the chance. They threw me out on my ass, remember? My office was sealed. They're sending my stuff back by messenger, later today."

"That's not quite true, is it, Marc?"

I felt my temper start to flare at the implication, but then I remembered the memory sticks nestling in my pocket.

"What are you talking about? Of course it's true."

"I don't mean anything physical." Carolyn's eyes stayed on my face, searching for the lie. "Or anything with any real value, even. But Simon found out you downloaded some data over the weekend. A lot of data."

"So?"

"There was no sign of it in your office, Marc. It wasn't in your database. There were no discs. No hard drives. No memory sticks. Nothing. So, whatever you copied the data onto, you must have it with you. You probably forgot, with all the drama this morning. I thought if I could jog your memory a little bit, you could just give it to me, and I could return it on the way to the restaurant. Draw a line under the whole thing. Save any unpleasantness further down the road."

I slid my hand into my pocket and took hold of the key ring that the memory sticks were attached to, but I just couldn't pull it out. I couldn't move forward on my new project without data to work on, and I had no way of getting hold of more from anywhere else. Not the kind of authentic, real-world data I needed to prove my new concept. Not in large enough quantities. Not after AmeriTel had stabbed me in the back. And that realization gave birth to another nasty little thought.

"Was it your idea to ask me for the data back? Or did someone send you to get it? Simon Wakefield? Or was it LeBrock?"

"It was my idea, Marc. It's a serious thing—stealing confidential data. I'm trying to keep your chestnuts out of the fire. A little gratitude wouldn't be out of place."

"How did you find out about this supposedly missing data?"

"Roger told me."

"LeBrock told you I had it?"

"He figured you must, since there was no sign of it in your office."

"When?"

"When what?"

"When did LeBrock tell you?"

"I don't know. This morning. After Simon told him."

"What time this morning?"

"I don't know. Do you think I look at my watch every time I have a conversation?"

"Was it before the meeting you were in when I tried to call you?"

"No. Of course not."

"Did LeBrock pull you out of the meeting to tell you?"

"No. It was later. I was back at my desk for an hour, but then Roger called me upstairs and I had to cancel . . ."

Her voice tailed off, and she started to trace a circle with a drop of water that had formed on the countertop.

"Cancel what, Carolyn?"

"A performance review with Mike Atherton. One of my direct reports."

"What time was it scheduled for?"

"Eleven."

I pulled out my phone and took another look at the records of the calls I'd missed that morning. The first one had been at 11:07. I held the phone out for her to see.

"You didn't reply to my voicemail. You didn't try to call me during the hour you were at your desk. But you did call seven minutes after LeBrock started whining to you that I'd taken some data. And then you called another eleven times."

She didn't reply.

"What's going on, Carolyn? Why are you doing LeBrock's dirty work for him?"

"I'm not. I didn't call you in that hour I had at my desk because I was mad at you. That's the truth."

"You were mad at me? What for? I'm the *victim* here!"

"Marc, have you taken a single moment to think about how this makes *me* look? I didn't just encourage you to take that job. I went to Roger and I begged him to give it to you. I vouched for you. I put myself on the line for you. And what happened? You skulked around the office like a vampire, afraid to be seen in daylight. Upset the few people you bothered to come in contact with. And got terminated less than halfway through your contract. At least you get to walk away. I'm the one left with egg on her face."

"It's not egg, Carolyn. It's horseshit. A ton of it got dumped on my head. And all you can worry about is whether any splashed on *you*? Gee, thanks for the sympathy."

"That's not *all* I'm worried about. I've told you, I don't live in a single-track universe, like you do. But it's one of the things I'm worried about. Of course it is. Don't you understand me at all?"

"No. I clearly don't. And after what LeBrock did to me, I don't understand why you're backing his plays, either. You should be standing up for me, not running that bastard's errands."

"You've got this whole thing ass-backward, you idiot." She threw up her hands in frustration. "I'm trying to help you. Not Roger. Not AmeriTel. *You*."

"You're lying. You're just trying to squirm back into favor with LeBrock. What happened? What was the deal? You come home and get the data from me, and he makes sure your halo doesn't get tarnished?"

"No." She smoothed her skirt over her hips then clasped her hands in front of her, as if she was about to pray. "Getting the data back was my idea, I swear. You don't know what's at stake here."

"Then why don't you tell me what's at stake, Carolyn? Because from where I'm standing, this whole thing stinks. You seem pretty damn desperate to keep LeBrock happy, and I'd like to know why."

"Roger's furious. He's talking about calling the police. Think what that would do to your reputation, Marc. You'd never get another contract, ever again."

"And you're so worried about my employment status you're prepared to entice me with an afternoon in the sack to get LeBrock's data back for him? What a dutiful employee you are, Carolyn."

"You make it sound . . . dirty." She moved in close, a loose strand of her hair tickled my cheek, and a delicate wave of Chanel No. 5 wafted over me. Then she placed a hand on my chest and slowly worked a finger in between the buttons of my shirt. "What's wrong with an afternoon in the sack with your wife? Most husbands would welcome it!"

"Maybe. If they felt like it was their wife's own idea. But if she was being pimped out by the guy who just fired them? Not so much. No, thank you. Count me out."

Carolyn stepped back, eyes ablaze, body rigid with anger, and for a moment I thought she was going to punch me. Then I thought she was going to burst into tears, which would have been worse. But in the end she just turned on her heel and stormed away, leaving me frustrated and alone in a lingering cloud of her perfume.

*S*HE WAS BLOND. SHE WAS BEAUTIFUL. AND SHE WAS DOOMED.
The tragedy was etched into her face as she slipped from her lover's grasp and plunged backward into the abyss, their fingertips an agonizing inch apart, a single tear escaping her piercing blue eyes, the drama of their entire lifetimes captured in that single pivotal moment.

I didn't know her name. Her age. Where she lived. If she had a job. Whether she survived the fall. But I did know what she was thinking: *I SHOULD HAVE KNOWN I'D NEVER HANG ON TO A GUY AS GOOD AS JEFF.* Lichtenstein had written it in a speech bubble when he created her, back in 1964. That was all the information he'd given us, apart from the title. *The Break-up.* And I knew that because Troye had written it on the appraisal, back when I bought her.

"Is that how you picture us?" Carolyn took me by surprise. I hadn't heard her come into the study behind me. "Are you Jeff? And is she me? I always wondered."

"No, I'm not Jeff." I turned to face her, and struggled to keep the dismay from showing when I saw she was still wearing her office clothes. "You're not her. And I resent the implication."

"But that's where you were, right? This morning. When I couldn't reach you? I was frantic, and you were at the gallery."

"Right. I like it there."

"You lose your job, and instead of talking to your wife, you go look at stupid overpriced cartoons. Don't you think that's just a little bit messed up, Marc?"

"You're jealous of a painting? Is that what this is about? Because that's ridiculous, Carolyn."

"I'm not jealous." Her tone turned icy. "And I wouldn't call it a painting, either. I just think you'd relate to me better if I covered myself with dots and stood motionless against the wall."

"You don't think we relate well enough? Seriously? What does that even mean?"

"I get that this is difficult for you, seeing as you only understand things that don't have a pulse. I realize it must be hard, not having any friends, to grasp the concept of listening to another person. And I know it might not get the needles spinning on your precious geek-ometer. But I really, really need you to stop. Take a moment. Open your ears. And hear what I'm telling you."

"If you have something to say, say it. No need to insult me first."

"For goodness' sake, do you not understand? Do you need me to send an email?"

"What? I don't know what you want."

"The data, obviously." She held out her hand. "Give it to me."

"What is it with you and that damn data? Why don't we just forget about it, and go in search of tequila instead?"

"No." She shook her head, definitively. "We're not going to forget about it. I need you to give it to me. Right now. As your wife, Marc, and after everything we've ever been through together, I'm asking you. Please. I need you to do this one, simple thing for me."

I wanted to help her—really—and not just because of the thunder in her eyes. But before I could figure out how, I was hit by a vision of Roger LeBrock, standing behind her, pulling her strings. And he wasn't just asking me to pass back some data. He was asking me to pass up a golden opportunity—maybe a once-in-a-lifetime opportunity—to create something truly amazing. I could understand why *he* wouldn't care about that, but what about Carolyn? What earthly reason was there for my wife to side with him?

Then it struck me. All Carolyn could see when she thought of the data was base metal. The same thing everyone else could see. The vision of the gold it could become was still in only one place. Inside my head. She should have trusted me—I was annoyed that she didn't—but if I explained to her what I was planning, I knew she'd soon understand.

"If your man Roy was going to paint what happens next in our lives, what would he call it?" Carolyn broke my train of thought. "*The Kiss* what? How many of them did he do? *Forty-seven*? Or *The Break-up Two*?"

"What are you talking about?"

"I'm telling you to make a choice. Give me the data you stole, and we'll go forward, together. Refuse, and you'll lose me as sure as Jeff lost that bimbo on the wall behind you."

"You'll walk out over a bunch of someone else's data? You haven't even let me tell you what I need it for, yet. If I could just—"

"That's your decision?" She turned away, then stopped. "I'm really disappointed, Marc. But you've made your choice. Now live with it."

"Wait. Come back. Let's start this conversation again. Talk things through properly."

She strode the whole length of the hallway, then paused with one hand on the front door handle, breathing heavily. For a moment she was transformed into the girl I'd fallen in love with at college, all those years ago. Lost. Out of breath. An air of bewilderment adding spice to her beauty as she blundered into my lecture theater. My pulse spiking dangerously before she realized her mistake and retreated from the room.

Back then, it had taken me two days to track her down. And another three to conjure an opportunity to speak to her. But now, before I could say another word she yanked open the door and walked out of our house, not bothering to close it behind her.

"You bastard, Marc." She fired her parting shot without even turning her head. "You selfish, miserable bastard. You have no idea what damage you've done."

*T*HREE MONTHS AFTER MY FIRST CAR DASHBOARD PRODUCT launched, I brought out an even better, premium version. One that featured real-time updates. It was a big improvement. Customers loved it. I made a lot more money as a result. But as I stood in my kitchen that afternoon, listening to Carolyn's tires crunching angrily across the gravel on our driveway, I couldn't help but picture how my life would look now if it was displayed on the upgraded system. The "marriage" needle would be moving before my eyes, winding back from green to amber. But no farther. Not all the way to red. Maybe I'd been wrong about our issues. Maybe they weren't as far behind us as I'd thought, but our marriage was fundamentally strong. It would survive. Carolyn would be back, once her rage had burned itself out. I mean, she'd literally left the door open. How much more symbolic could she have been?

I had no idea how long Carolyn would be gone—she'd never done anything as extreme as this before—but it made sense to take advantage of the time she'd given me. Especially now that there'd be no tequila-fueled distractions in my path. So, I went to my study, pulled out the memory sticks, and fired up my computer. I was excited. I didn't know if I could really turn my vision into reality, but if I succeeded, it would be nothing short of the Burj Khalifa of analytical tools. It would etch my name into the competitive intelligence landscape forever. But to change the game that dramatically—whether you're talking about architecture or software design—you need to build on solid foundations. I knew that how I approached these first steps was absolutely critical. And that by leaving me in peace to concentrate, whether she'd meant to or not, Carolyn had done me a huge favor.

Like most big ideas, mine was actually incredibly simple. The seed had been planted in my mind at AmeriTel's headquarters over the weekend, when I was putting the finishing touches to a new report I'd created. The report contained a ton of dynamite information, but my heart sank when I pictured myself presenting it to AmeriTel's board. It would be the same old story—their two-minute pretense of paying attention, followed by increasingly feeble attempts at disguising their boredom while one vital detail after another sailed over their empty heads. The anticipation was weighing me down until it gave way to a momentary fantasy—the thought of walking into the boardroom with a cappuccino in my hand instead of a sheaf of handouts saying, *Nothing to worry about this week, guys,* and then just leaving. Because it struck me: Ultimately, most people don't give a damn about details. Busy people, anyway. They just want confirmation that things are OK, or a warning if they're not. I'd known that instinctively when I created the *Car Dashboard* system, but now I thought, why not take it a step further? Why not take it all the way to its logical conclusion? What if I put an attention-grabbing object in the office of every director and every manager in the country? It could be anything. A glass sphere. A sculpture. A football-team mascot. The frame around the obligatory family photograph. And with no human interaction at all, the whole thing would change color, foreseeing the future like a twenty-first century oracle.

I pictured a CEO's office: A meeting in progress. Four or five of the company's top people sitting around a table, arguing. A crystal globe in the center, glowing softly. The whole thing a warm, reassuring green. Then it changes to red. The debate stops, mid-sentence. They know they have a problem. But where do they go to uncover the source? What can give them the exact information they need to fix things before it's too late?

One thing will be able to. And one thing only. My new software.

Like most ideas that don't seem complicated on the surface, mine was going to be fiendishly complex when I stripped it down to the nuts and bolts. But that knowledge only encouraged me. I actually have a version of JFK's words from 1962 in a frame on my wall: *We choose to do things not because they are easy, but because they are hard.* So, I did what I always do when I'm starting something new. I glanced up at that quotation for inspiration. Then I rolled up my sleeves and started pounding on the keyboard.

IT TOOK ME JUST over four hours to come up with a first pass for the basic algorithms I figured I was going to need. Some parts were taken from products I'd created before. Some parts were new. They were cobbled together into a very bare skeleton, and it was going to take weeks more work to even get close to fleshing the whole thing out. But the first step had been taken. Now it was time to run the initial batch of tests, which would tell me what to do next. This is where the data's needed, so I plugged in one of the memory sticks. I drained it dry, and was about to add the files from the second when I paused. I'd already given the system hundreds of millions of bytes to chew on. That was enough at this early stage. More would just slow things down. It was time to cross my fingers and roll the dice.

When you click the mouse and set a prototype running, you don't just trigger a program in a computer. You trigger a series of emotions in yourself. And they always go the same way. First, elation, that you've taken a tangible step toward your goal. Then anticipation, because you'll soon see how big that step is. And finally impatience, because once the machine starts to run, there's nothing for you to do till it spits out its results. Depending on the complexity of the job, that can take anything from a few merciful minutes to several torturous hours.

This job was a large one. It was going to take a while.

To distract myself, I generally use the time to think of a working name for the project. I got up from my desk and a stream of random titles floated through my head as I made my way through the house in search of coffee. *Avenger* came to mind, as I mulled over the events of the day. Or *Backstabber,* I thought, picturing Roger LeBrock's lying face. Maybe *The Towering Inferno,* looking ahead to AmeriTel's inevitable fate. But then, when I reached the kitchen and saw a dirty mug

Carolyn had left on the countertop, I had a flash of inspiration. *Traitor.* She'd always wanted me to name a project after her. What better time to make her wish come true?

I picked up Carolyn's mug, uncertain whether to put it in the dishwasher or throw it in the trash, then I saw what was inside it. The dregs of black coffee. Normally Carolyn took her coffee white. She only skipped the milk when she was particularly stressed. Or if we'd run out. I looked in the fridge, and found two cartons. One was half full, the other unopened. Both were fresh. That meant she must have been really suffering as she waited for me to get home.

How many times had I come in and found her sitting on the stairs, overcome with anguish? It was always something trivial—a ding in her car, a disaster in the kitchen, buyer's remorse over another extravagant purchase—but the words would come tumbling out so fast it often took a while to understand what she'd actually done. I never cared, though. Seeing her smile chase away the tears as she unburdened herself made anything forgivable. Until that day, when the mold had been broken.

I replayed Carolyn's last words in my mind, wishing I'd been smart enough to say something before she'd walked out, and the idea of talking to her prompted another thought: After she left I'd gone straight to the study to start work. I didn't take the time to switch my phone off silent. What if she'd been trying to call? Wanting to patch things up, but put off by my failure to answer?

I whipped my phone out of my pocket, terrified of finding a screen full of missed calls. And when I saw there'd only been one, I somehow felt even worse. I hesitated for a moment, then—like a wounded man desperate for the coup de grâce, even if it had to be self-inflicted—I hit the Voicemail key.

The message began with several seconds of silence. Had she called my number by mistake? I pictured her phone lying unattended in her purse, and her going about her business with no desire to speak to me and no knowledge that the line was even open. But then, as my thumb was reaching for the *End* button, I heard Carolyn's voice. It was shaky, like she was struggling to keep her tone neutral, and her words were brief. She wanted to meet. To talk. To see if we could put things right.

She suggested a time and a place, and I almost dropped the phone in my haste to check my watch, suddenly convinced I was already too late.

The restaurant she'd named was a half hour away. She was going to be there in twenty minutes. I headed straight for the door. And hoped there wouldn't be too many traffic cops in the area that night.

*C*AROLYN HAD PICKED A RESTAURANT WE'D BOTH BEEN TO BEFORE, but never together. It was French. Or had aspirations of being French, anyway. But as far as I could remember, the theme was set more by the decor—huge images of the Eiffel Tower and Arc de Triomphe clumsily stenciled in wild colors across every inch of wall space—than by the menu. Or the standard of cooking.

If the place wasn't too firmly wedded to its chosen geographic region, that suggested another possibility to me. It made me hopeful margaritas would be available. I wondered if that had factored into Carolyn's thinking. And whether bringing the car was a mistake.

Maybe I should have risked the extra few minutes it would have taken to call a cab?

THE FIRST VEHICLE I SAW when I pulled into the restaurant's parking lot was Carolyn's silver BMW. There's no way she'd have driven if she'd foreseen a heavy night's drinking for the two of us. My sinking heart told me I'd gotten a little ahead of myself with the scope of my reconciliation plans. A nice meal together was a more realistic target. A glass of good wine. A shared drive home—we could leave the Beemer and collect it tomorrow—with maybe a stop at a liquor store en route. One that sold the right tequila. The kind they have at Zapatista's.

I saw Carolyn the moment my eyes adjusted to the candle-fueled pseudo-Parisian gloom inside the cavernous restaurant. She was sitting in a booth diagonally opposite the entrance, about three-quarters of the way back. She never liked to sit with her back to the door, so she spotted me right away, too. She waved, and I set off to join her without waiting for a hostess to escort me.

My smile grew broader as the distance between us shrank, but when I came close enough to see Carolyn's eyes it was clear that any warmth I felt would be more than canceled out by the frostiness of her stare. I slid into place opposite her. And despite everything I'd wanted to say since our last unpleasant exchange—and all the zingers I'd imagined myself unleashing in the car, driving over—I couldn't summon a single intelligible word.

"Hi" was the best I eventually managed.

"You're late." Carolyn took a sip from a barely touched glass of red wine. "I was about to leave."

"I'm sorry. I'm glad you waited."

"Are you?"

"Of course I am. I didn't keep you waiting on purpose. I jumped in the car the second I got your message."

"You did? Why? Where had you been?"

She stormed out, then starts grilling me about where I've been?

"Nowhere." I resisted the temptation to throw the question back at her. "I was at home. Working. You know how I get."

Carolyn stared at me for a few seconds, then her expression softened.

"Sorry. Let's start this over. First of all, thanks for coming."

"No problem. Thanks for asking me."

"And second, I think there are some things we need to talk about. No surprise there, right?"

"Not really. What's on your mind?"

"You are, Marc. You and me. And whether that still adds up to *us*."

"Of course it does. Why would you doubt that?"

Carolyn looked away. A waitress began to approach, but she scurried away when she caught my wife's expression.

"I want *us* to make it, Marc," Carolyn answered, facing me again. "I really do. More than anything. But that's not going to happen on its own. It's going to need a little help. There are going to have to be some changes."

"OK." I nodded. I was willing to negotiate, if that's what it would take to bring her home. "What kind of changes?"

"Take working at AmeriTel as an example. When we were there together. Or supposed to be."

"This again? I've already agreed, Carolyn. Your work is fantastic. I appreciate what you do. I see how everyone values you. I—"

"No. I'm not talking about work now. I'm talking about you and me. How we were."

"How we were what?"

"Right. What were we? We're supposed to be a couple, but we sure didn't act like one. We weren't like Alison in Sales, and Ian in Engineering. Or Imogen and Glynn. Or—Anyway, the point is, what did we ever do together? We didn't drive to the office together. We didn't even have lunch together."

"Yes we did."

"How many times? Once? On your first day? That's hardly the sign of a deep and meaningful connection between us."

"It was more flexible, to drive separately. It's not like we couldn't afford the gas. And you like to eat at your desk."

"Only because I have no one else to eat with! No one who's not trying to stab me in the back, or get in my pants, anyway. Of course I wanted to eat with my husband. And I didn't want things to be *flexible*." She spat the word back at me. "I wanted them to be better. I wanted us to be closer. I wanted us to carve out a few minutes a day to *talk* about what's important to me, since I don't get to *do* anything I care about anymore."

The waitress attempted another approach, saving me from having to respond, but Carolyn waved her away.

"We have the potential, Marc. We complement each other. Where you're strong, I'm weak. Where you're weak, I'm strong. But for us to work, we have to be close. We have to mesh with each other. Do you understand?"

I nodded, stunned by the ferocity in her voice.

"We have to be like this." She held out her hands and laced her fingers together. "See? That's strong. But if we pull away, this is what happens." She pulled her hands apart and held them up, palms vertical, fingers stiff and separate. "We're left as two isolated, spikey individuals. And I don't want that."

"I don't want it, either." I wished the waitress would come back with the wine list, because I clearly had some catching up to do.

"Good. I'm glad. But it'll take more than words, Marc. We'll have to work at it. Hard. Both of us. And I need to know, are you up for that?"

"I am. Absolutely. I love you, Carolyn. You know I do."

"I love you, too. And to prove I'm in this for the long haul, I've brought you something."

She rummaged in her purse and pulled out a small parcel.

"Go ahead." She passed it to me. "See if you like it."

The package contained a key ring–size Swiss Army knife. Carolyn knew I loved them. The intricacy. The craftsmanship. But this one was extra special. Because instead of being finished in the signature red, both sides were shaded with tiny, beautiful Benday dots.

"I don't think it's copied from an actual painting or anything. But it looks Lichtensteiny to me. And I wanted to apologize for being rude about your picture. It's never going to be my cup of tea, but I understand how important it is to you, and I respect that. No more nasty comments. I promise."

"This is amazing. Thanks, sweetheart. It's perfect. I love it. I just wish I had something for you in return."

"Aren't you going to put it on your key ring? See how it feels in your pocket?"

"Sure." I pulled out my keys and pried open the tight spirals of the main ring, ready to slide the knife's smaller one into place. It was tricky, but the gap was almost wide enough when I became aware of Carolyn's face. She was staring at me.

"What? Am I doing it wrong?"

"No, you're doing fine. But what's that? I haven't seen it before."

I looked down at the key ring and took a quick inventory. House keys—front door, back door, windows, filing cabinet. One key from AmeriTel—for a drawer in the desk I'd been using, which I could now throw away. My Jaguar's key, with its shank folded neatly back. And the memory stick I'd decided not to use, earlier.

"Is that why you bought me the knife? To set me up?"

"Is that the stick with the AmeriTel data on it?"

"No."

I wasn't lying. Not technically. Because it wasn't *the* stick. There were two.

"The stick's at the house, then?"

Her use of the words *at the house,* not *at home* was starting to ring warning bells.

"Do we have to talk about this again? I thought we were changing."

"We are. You're right, Marc. Let's not get sidetracked. I've agreed to change, to be more understanding about your interests. But what about you? What are you going to change?"

"I could be more supportive of your interests, I guess? Like theater. I used to love watching your shows."

"You never came to any."

"I did. And to the parties. Remember after *Much Ado,* at college? That was the first time we—"

"It was *Merchant of Venice. Much Ado* was the one your parents came to."

"Oh. Yeah. Still, it was fun."

"They hated me. They couldn't have made it any clearer. And anyway, the acting ship sailed long ago. I've been out of the game way too long."

"Not necessarily."

"I have. Trust me. OK, what else?"

"I don't know. There's nothing obvious, or I'd have changed it already. But I love you, Carolyn. I'm happy to change anything you want me to."

"Well, you could develop a little self-awareness, for a start."

"Self-awareness? About what? Could you be more specific?"

"This should really be coming from you, Marc. It doesn't work if I have to direct you. But honestly? I think this is all part of a larger problem. Your lack of openness."

"I don't even know what that means."

"It means you're holding things back from me. Bottling them up. Not sharing. Keeping secrets, even. I guess it's hard, given how much time you spend alone. Not having many friends probably doesn't help. I do try to make allowances, but even so . . ."

"Wait a minute. I have friends!"

"Whatever. But the point is, the way things are, it makes me wonder if I can really trust you."

"Of course you can trust me. Ask me anything. I'll tell you the truth."

She toyed with her wineglass for a moment, then nodded.

"OK, then, Marc. I'm sorry to come back around to this, but I think you're lying to me about the memory stick. I think that one right there—that's the one you stole from AmeriTel. I'm right, aren't I?"

"Carolyn, I've got lots of memory sticks. Dozens. You need to stop jumping to conclusions. And why are you all worked up about this? Just let it go. I don't work at AmeriTel anymore."

"But I do. And you didn't answer my question."

"Right. Because the subject's closed."

"Give it to me, damn you!" Carolyn launched herself at me from across the table, sending silverware, serviettes, and her half-full wineglass flying in all directions.

A wave of embarrassed silence washed over the restaurant and the two of us were left tugging at the key ring like brats in a schoolyard while everyone else sat and stared.

"Let me have it!" Carolyn's face was pale, like she was deathly sick. "Please, Marc. You don't know how important this is to me."

"You don't know how important it is to me. You wouldn't listen, before. So this is what it comes down to. You told me our marriage and your job were equally important. You told me there wasn't a choice to make. Well, I'm telling you there is. And you have to make it. Right here. Right now."

Our eyes were locked. Our fingers were locked. Every other person in the place was staring in our direction. The seconds ticked by. Neither of us gave ground. Murmured comments began to ripple from nearby tables. Carolyn tugged harder, and without warning a kind of howl spilled from her lips, more animal than human. Then she let go. Grabbed her purse. And ran out of the restaurant.

THE JOURNEY HOME PASSED in a blur. It was like I'd been driving on autopilot, my conscious brain kicking in only when I reached my own street and a woman emerged without warning from the raised stretch of woodland that borders the road, waving her arms wildly and nearly finding herself under my wheels. She claimed to want directions to a pharmacy, and was very unhappy when I told her there were no stores of any kind within five miles. She seemed to have trouble grasping my words, making me think the kind of pharmaceuticals she was looking for wouldn't be available over the counter anyway. And as soon as I had disengaged myself from her and started to move again, I was almost hit by two guys in a Mercedes who had picked my driveway—the only break in the tree line for a couple of hundred yards—to make a three-point turn.

Despite the time I'd spent at the restaurant I hadn't actually eaten or drunk anything, so my first port of call at home was the kitchen. I was vaguely thinking of ordering Chinese when my eye fell on Carolyn's mug, still sitting on the countertop. I wasn't happy with the way she'd behaved that evening, but that didn't stop me worrying about her. Or wondering if I'd been too harsh, accusing her of only wanting the memory stick to appease LeBrock. Maybe she *had* been looking out for me? So when I pulled out my phone it was Carolyn's number I summoned from the directory, not a take-out service.

Her phone rang. And rang. But she didn't answer. Eventually I was dumped into her voicemail, and as I listened to the bland generic greeting—she hadn't bothered to record one of her own—I couldn't help wondering if she'd seen the call was from me and ignored it on purpose. That was all it took to send the pendulum swinging back the opposite way, so when I heard the beep I followed the anonymous announcer's instructions, and I left a message. Not a very pleasant message. But when—if—Carolyn listened to it, even she would have to acknowledge the change. Because I certainly didn't hold anything back that time.

———

STANDING IN THE KITCHEN with my absent wife's discarded mug in one hand and an unanswered phone in the other, I realized I don't usually spend much time in the house on my own. Not unless I'm doing something specific, like working or watching a game on TV. Then, I'm only really aware of the room I'm in. But for the first time I was conscious of the entire, empty structure massing around me. Six thousand vacant square feet. Each one emphasizing Carolyn's absence. The fact that I'd done nothing to stop her leaving. And had failed to convince her to come back.

I needed to distract myself. Urgently. But how? Work was out. The computer wouldn't be ready yet. Food? I dumped the mug, wandered into the dining room, and decided I wasn't hungry. There was a TV in the living room, and another in the den, but nothing I wanted to watch. There were books in my study, but nothing I wanted to read. I wasn't tired. I didn't want to exercise. Of all the possibilities our home had to offer, nothing seemed interesting. And nothing could distract me from wondering where Carolyn had stormed off to.

Her words from the afternoon started to ring in my head. *How does a pitcher of margaritas sound to you?* So I crossed the room, opened the liquor cabinet, and smiled at the irony. There'd been tequila in the house the whole time. One bottle we'd already started, and another still in its box. What if we'd just got drunk, together, instead of arguing? And with that thought in mind, I did another thing I don't normally do. Fixed a drink for myself. Then another. And another. And I'm not sure how many others after that . . .

NEVER KICK A MAN WHILE HE'S DOWN *MY PARENTS USED TO SAY.*
It's a shame no one ever urged the hangover I had the next morning
to show the same restraint. It had already been to work on my head and
my stomach before I woke up, replacing my brain with molten lava
and filling my gut with swamp water. Then, once I was conscious, it
moved on to my heart, waiting till I'd reached out across the pillow in
search of Carolyn to smack me with the memory of why she wasn't
there.

I staggered to the bathroom and once the urge to throw up had
subsided, I dosed myself with Advil then headed downstairs in search
of caffeine. But when I reached the hallway, all thoughts of coffee were
put on hold. I stopped dead in my tracks. Because the front door was
standing wide open.

My first thought was that Carolyn had come home. My heart raced,
and the pain and sickness were forgotten as I called her name and ran to
the kitchen. I pictured her standing at the stove, humming as she
cooked something delicious for breakfast. Sitting by the French doors,
reading one of the historical novels she loves so much. Even striding
around the room, brandishing a random utensil and looking to reignite
the fight over the memory sticks. Anything would be better than her
not being there at all . . .

There was no answer to my call. When I reached the room, it was
as empty as it had been the night before. I shouted again, louder, and
went to check the dining room. It was deserted. As was the living
room. And the den. I even looked for her in my study. Then I won-

dered if she could be upstairs, in one of the spare bedrooms. I started back along the hallway, and two other thoughts crossed my mind: If she was back, her car would be in the driveway. And if she was in the house, why had she left the door open?

Maybe she'd gone outside to get something from her trunk? She hadn't taken any luggage with her, but she could have bought clothes or overnight things after she left. I diverted to the doorway and looked out. My Jaguar was where I'd parked it yesterday. But there was no sign of Carolyn's Beemer. Only the tracks it had left in the gravel when she'd sped off.

What about a taxi? Maybe she'd continued drinking, and had taken a cab home? She'd always been responsible that way. And because the trip was unplanned, she may not have had much cash with her. She could have come inside to get enough to pay the driver. I went all the way to the street to see, but again, there was nothing.

I stood at the end of my driveway, deflated, suddenly aware of the pain in my head, the cold pavement beneath my bare feet, and the wind tugging at my pajama top. I saw that I'd misaligned two of the buttons, causing it to gape open around my stomach. And then a question popped into my mind, far more hurtful than the embarrassment or the physical discomfort. The last time Carolyn had left the front door open, she was leaving me. Temporarily. What if this time she'd only been here to collect her things before leaving again, permanently? How deeply had I been asleep? Could she have sneaked in and dismantled our marriage without me hearing her?

I hurried back to the house and shut the door behind me. Then I took the stairs two at a time, ignoring the throbbing between my temples. All our suitcases were still in the spare-room closet, so I moved on to Carolyn's dressing room. I couldn't be sure nothing was missing, because who could memorize every single outfit his wife owns—especially one as devoted to shopping as Carolyn—but there were no obvious gaps. What else would a woman need if she was going away for a while? Underwear? I checked her drawer, and it was full to overflowing with tiny scraps of colorful lace. Bathroom stuff? I looked, and the cabinet was crammed with all kinds of feminine things, the way it usually was.

I had to face facts. Carolyn's things were here, but she was still gone. I moved over to the bed, fighting the temptation to crawl back under the covers and wait for the disappointment to pass me by. But before I could lie down I realized that an ember of doubt was still smoldering away at the back of my mind like a warning beacon, barely visible through the mist.

Something else was wrong.

It had to do with something I'd seen. When I was looking for Carolyn. Something had been disturbed, or out of place. Not up here, though. And not in the kitchen. Not in the dining room. Or the den. In my study! Suddenly the picture in my head was as clear as day and I was out of the bedroom before I even realized I was moving, heading back downstairs.

I hurried to my desk, sat in front of my computer, and stared at the screen. It was dark and lifeless. For most people, this wouldn't be a problem. But it was a major red flag for me. Because the first thing I always did when I set up a new computer was to disable its ability to sleep. It's an old quirk of mine. When I'm working I often have to pause to figure out a problem—often for thirty or forty minutes straight—and it drives me crazy if I have to wait for the machine to wake up when I'm finally ready to continue. So, there was no way the computer should have been dormant like this. It should have still been running my tests from yesterday, or waiting for me to review the results, patiently filling the screen with a succession of digitized Lichtensteins. Unless—could there have been a power outage when I was lost in the tequila haze?

I hit the space bar, and the computer came back to life. That was the last thing I was hoping for, but it did actually make sense. A hiccup in the electrical supply wouldn't have restored the computer's ability to sleep. Only a manual reset could do that. And more alarmingly still, there were no test results for me to view, and no indication my new program was running in the background. I was lost for an explanation. But as I sat and stared at the inert Home screen, my confusion began to unravel itself into something much more straightforward. Worry.

I pulled the keyboard closer to me and checked the computer's directory. There was no sign of my new program at all. It had completely vanished. As had the data I'd imported. The memory stick had disappeared, too, from the port on the side of the machine. To lose the program was bad enough, but my only copy of the data as well? That would be a disaster.

Then, a moment's reprieve. All the data wasn't missing. I hadn't used the files on the second memory stick, had I? But what had I done with it? My sluggish mind was blank. It took a real effort to recall details of the previous night. And out of the murk I dredged up—nothing.

That was the answer. Nothing. I hadn't done anything with the memory stick. I'd left it on my key ring. The key ring I'd put on my desk when I checked that the tests were still running. And now there was no sign of it, either. There was just my keyboard, and the monitor. Other than those, the glass surface—and the wooden floor that was visible through it—was completely bare.

Hopes for Carolyn's return were suddenly replaced by another, altogether more sinister explanation for the door being open when I came downstairs earlier. My stomach turned over. I looked up at the wall above my desk, neurotically checking that my Lichtenstein was still there.

Then I reached for the phone and dialed 911.

*I*N A FEW MINUTES' TIME, THERE'D BE ARMED MEN IN MY HOUSE.
I'd never imagined myself having to call the police. In fact, like
most people, I'd never given the police much conscious thought at all.
Ever since I could remember they'd just been a hypothetical, intangible
presence. Sometimes unwelcome—like when a guy breaks out a joint
at a college party, or when your speedometer creeps a few miles-an-
hour north of the limit on the freeway—but usually reassuring. Like a
safety net. Only there's a big difference between being vaguely aware
of something that's there to catch you *if* you fall, and finding out how
it feels to crash face-first into the mesh.

MAYBE ARMED MEN HAD ALREADY been in my house that morning? If
I was right, and someone had stolen my prototype, they'd have had to
break in to get to my computer. And what kind of burglar breaks into
a house, knowing the owner is inside, without being armed? I couldn't
believe I'd been there all along, asleep, and oblivious. It reminded me
of my favorite TV show from a while back. *Deadwood.* Set at the height
of the gold rush. In those days, if someone stole your stuff you were
free to cut their throats and have their bodies eaten by pigs. Today, I
had to wait for a couple of government clock-punchers to show up and
take care of business for me. It made me feel irrelevant, like a redun-
dant spectator on the sidelines of life, and I didn't like it one little bit. I
began to wonder if I'd been too hasty, refusing point-blank when Car-

olyn suggested we should keep a gun in the house after a spate of break-ins in the neighborhood the Christmas before last.

MAYBE ARMED MEN WERE still in my house? The thought hit me as I finished making the coffee I'd neglected earlier. The front door had been left open, after all. Could that have been deliberate? Could the intruders have left it that way in case they needed to make a quick exit? They could have heard me moving around, and taken cover to avoid a confrontation. Like cornered animals. I never did check the spare bedrooms upstairs. Or the closet in the hallway. Or the laundry room, or . . .

I heard a noise behind me. Someone was trying a door handle. Trying to get in? Or out? I spun around and saw two people outside, on the rear deck. Both were women. Both were younger than me—maybe in their early thirties—and both were wearing nondescript pant suits and flat shoes. I stepped back, momentarily panicked, then the obvious realization hit me. It was the police. These women were detectives. For some reason I'd been expecting uniformed cops. I relaxed, and one of them motioned for me to open the door. That was a whole other problem, though, due to the missing keys.

"Well," the taller detective said when I finally managed to retrieve the spare set of keys and wrestle the door open. "That was quite an adventure."

"I'm sorry about that. The keys . . . My regular ones are missing . . . I couldn't remember . . ."

"Is that coffee I smell?" the second detective asked, cutting me off. "Pour me a big mug, no cream, no sugar, and we'll call it even. Do that, then maybe go put on clothes, and we can get started."

WHEN I RETURNED, five or six minutes later, the detective who'd asked for the coffee was sitting at my kitchen table, leaning back comfortably like an old friend who'd popped round to shoot the breeze. Her gray jacket was draped across the back of her chair. She had dark hair—

almost black—that hung down below her shoulders, curling in slightly at the tips, and contrasting sharply with her crisp white blouse. Her colleague, the taller one, had cropped blond hair that stood up in sharp little spikes. Her suit was dark blue, and its cut was a little more flattering. She didn't have a wedding band, but from the way she was leaning against the fridge, looking like she'd be happier somewhere else, she did seem to have an attitude.

"That's better." The sitting detective smiled. "It's an old rule of mine. If I can't be in pajamas, no one can. Now, let's get this show on the road. Introductions. My name's Detective Hayes. This is my partner, Detective Wagner. You're Mr. Bowman, right? May we call you Marc?"

She didn't wait for an answer.

"You called 911 this morning? Said there'd been a break-in? And property had been stolen?"

"Right. I did."

"OK. Well, we're very sorry about what's happened to you, Marc. But the good news is, Detective Wagner and I are here to help. Why don't you start at the beginning, and tell us exactly what happened? In your own words. Take your time. And don't leave anything out."

DETECTIVE HAYES TOOK A notepad out of her purse when I began talking, but she didn't write anything down. About halfway through my account she started tapping the paper with her pen, and by the time I'd finished I could see from her expression that her idea of sympathy was very different from mine.

"Thank you, Marc." Hayes tipped her head back to take a final swig of coffee. "I'm getting the bare bones, no problem. But there are a couple of things you could help us straighten out. Like, the front door. You found it wide open, before, you said. Why's it closed now?"

"Why's it closed?" I repeated. "Because I closed it. Obviously."

"You closed it? According to you, someone opened that door to gain illegal access to your home, but you went ahead and closed it? It never crossed your mind that we'd need to examine it?"

"Oh. No. It didn't. Look, I'm sorry, I'm new to this."

"New or not, you should be capable of using some common sense. Instead, you completely contaminated the scene. How are we going to recover any evidence? You destroyed all chance of that. And with no neighbors inside a hundred-yard radius, the canvass will be a fool's errand, too."

"I'm sorry. It just didn't occur to me. And it wasn't till later, after I closed the door, I realized anything was missing."

"So what *did* you think? The door had been open all night, and that seemed *normal*?"

"No. I thought . . ." I stopped, not ready to admit what was going on with my marriage. "I didn't really know. I didn't think it was anything bad, though."

"Is there a reason you might not have been thinking straight this morning?"

"No. Of course not."

"Do you live here alone, Marc?" Wagner spoke for the first time. She had her hands in her pants pockets now, and her head was tipped to one side, making her look slightly menacing. "This feels like a big place for one person."

"No. There are two of us. Me and my wife, Carolyn."

"And where is Carolyn, Marc? Can we speak with her?"

"She's away right now." I felt my face begin to glow.

"Away?" Wagner echoed.

"Working. She's an exec at AmeriTel. They're bidding for a chunk of wireless bandwidth right now, from the government. It's a huge deal for them—make or break, actually, billions are at stake—and they're finding out the results today. That's all they've been thinking about for months. Things have been crazy around here."

"So, where *exactly* is she?" Wagner's patience was clearly running low.

"D.C." I hoped that sounded plausible. I didn't want to get caught lying to the police. Not just to save face, anyway.

"When did she leave for D.C.?"

"Yesterday."

"What time yesterday?"

"I don't know exactly. Afternoon."

"When will she be back?"

"I'm not sure. Soon, probably. AmeriTel's going to get creamed."

"Tell me again what's missing." Hayes suddenly leaned in toward me.

"Two memory sticks, a set of keys, and a computer program."

"How do you steal a computer program?" Wagner was scowling.

"You copy it." I was surprised she didn't know. "It's easy."

"It's not like stealing, say, a valuable painting? You don't need the original. Just a copy?"

"That's right."

"Then the original program's still on your computer?"

"No. It's gone."

"How's it gone?"

"The thieves must have deleted it. Securely. I can't recover it."

"So you touched the mouse and the keyboard and whatever else, as well as your front door? You're a forensic nightmare, Marc."

"Of course I touched them. How else could I be sure the program's missing?"

"Here's what I don't understand." Hayes was frowning. "Why delete the program after copying it? Why attract attention to what they've done?"

"I don't know."

"You see, Marc, in our experience, criminals don't usually try to draw attention to their crimes."

"I don't know why they did it." My voice betrayed a little of the annoyance I was beginning to feel. "I don't know how criminals behave. Or think. Unless, maybe, they wanted to set me back? To give themselves a head start? To get the product to market ahead of me?"

"This program, it's valuable?"

"You could say that. My whole future depends on it."

"Valuable, as in a big insurance claim is on its way?"

"Of course not. It's intangible. And it's not finished yet. It's not even a fully-fledged prototype. It's so new, if it were a fetus, not even the Pope would lose sleep over it."

"But you kept a copy for yourself, right? You can load it up and keep on going?"

"No. But I can rebuild what I've lost. That's not the point. It—"

"Who knew you were working on this thing?"

"No one."

"What about your wife?" Wagner asked. "The mysteriously absent Carolyn?"

"I told her I was starting something new, but nothing specific. She didn't know how big it's going to be."

"Really? Your whole future depends on this one, mega-important thing, but you don't even tell your wife?"

"I started to, but there wasn't time to go through all the details. I'm saving that till she gets back."

"You didn't keep it from her because you think it's *your* future, not *hers*?"

"No. Listen. I swear. It's for both of us."

"There's no bad blood between you two?"

"None."

"Are you certain?"

"Absolutely."

"Because your front door shows no signs of being forced . . ."

"No. Never. There's no way in hell Carolyn's involved with this."

"Has anything else suspicious happened lately? Strange people hanging around the neighborhood? Anything like that?"

A bead of sweat broke out on my forehead as I recalled the woman asking for directions and the guys in the Mercedes, last night. They hadn't just been hanging around the neighborhood. They'd been hanging around my house. Right before it was burglarized. And right when Carolyn had made very sure that I wouldn't be there.

"No." I swallowed my uneasiness. "Nothing I can think of."

"Who else had a key?" Hayes asked.

"Well, we have a part-time housekeeper, Ramona. She has one, of course. And so do our neighbors, the Frankels. In case there's a problem when we're away."

"Write down their details." Hayes pushed her pad toward me.

"The keys, and the memory sticks," Wagner said, as I scribbled the names and numbers. "When did you last see them?"

"Last night, before I went to bed."

"You left the keys next to the computer?"

"Yes. With one of the memory sticks. The other was still connected to the computer."

"In your study?"

"Yes."

"Show us."

PRETTY MUCH EVERY NEW VISITOR follows the same routine the first time they enter my study. First they stare at the Lichtenstein. Then at the Eames lounge chair—I have a limited-edition white ash and cowhide version with a matching ottoman, which is a bit of an eye-catcher. Then at the shelves full of computer books, which most people would sooner poke their own eyes out than read. Then finally at the desk, which is made of glass so thin and so pure it makes the computer stuff look like it's floating on air. But the detectives didn't do any of that. They just took three paces into the room, stopped, and turned to face me.

"No keys," Hayes said. "And no memory sticks. We can see that."

"But what about the program?" Wagner asked. "It's invisible. Intangible. How can we tell if it's here?"

"How could a thief tell it was here?" Hayes raised her hands, palms upward, exaggerating her incredulity. "If Marc didn't tell anyone . . ."

"Spyware," I suggested. "On the computer. One of my competitors must have infected it, somehow."

"Oh, you think they saw the earth-shattering genius of your new project, even at its pre-embryonic stage, and ran straight over to steal it while you took a nap?"

"I guess."

"This spyware, it's like a virus, right?" Hayes' expression screamed, You idiot. "It works over the Internet?"

"Usually."

"But if these rivals were monitoring your new program over the Internet, why didn't they steal it over the Internet? Save themselves a lot of time and trouble?"

"I don't know."

"Don't you have anti-virus software?" Wagner asked.

"Of course I do."

"Then why didn't it pick up this spyware?"

"It must be something new. The hackers are always one step ahead."

"And the hackers with their new virus picked you, even though no one knew you were working on this product? Not even your wife?"

"You must be in a tough business." Hayes rolled her eyes. "Competing with clairvoyants."

"If I had all the answers, I wouldn't need you guys. Look, I thought you were supposed to investigate, and find out this stuff. Not just dump it back on the victim and start making insinuations."

"Insinuations?" Hayes repeated. "I don't think so. Back to the kitchen, Marc, where we can sit. I want more coffee, and you need to hear some home truths."

WAGNER TOOK A MUG this time, but she still declined to join Hayes and me at the table.

"You know when we first got here, we told you we were here to help?" Hayes pulled her hair back and tucked it behind her ears. "Well, I've listened to the story you've spun, and honestly? It's up to you to help yourself."

"I don't understand."

"Why did you call us, Marc?" Wagner asked. "I want the truth."

"The break-in. The thefts. Why—?"

"Filing bogus reports." Hayes shook her head. "Wasting police time. These are serious things. If that's what you're doing here, Marc, you're going to bring a lot of heat down on yourself."

"Wait a minute. You think I'm making this up? Because I closed my own front door? And used my computer? Seriously?"

"There's no smoke without fire, Marc." Wagner looked smug. "Ever heard that? Well, we have a different version. Do you know how ours goes?"

I didn't respond.

"What we say is, there's no tequila without bullshit." She crossed to the garbage can and pulled out last night's empty Patrón bottle. "Someone laid this soldier to rest. You? Last night? On your own?"

"How did you . . ." Then it dawned on me that leaving a pair of detectives unsupervised in the house while I changed my clothes hadn't been the wisest thing to do. "Forget that. Yes. I had a drink last night. But not the whole bottle. It was already three-quarters empty."

"Any witnesses to that?"

Carolyn might have confirmed that the bottle had been opened, if I'd known where to find her. But it was fifteen hours since I'd seen her. And she might also have mentioned it was considerably more than a quarter full when she last set eyes on it.

I shook my head.

"Anyone see you working on your new program?" Wagner asked. "Or with these memory sticks?"

A couple of people did know about the memory sticks, obviously. But asking them would hardly be in my best interests, given how I came by the contents.

I shook my head again.

"I don't know what your deal is." Hayes paused. "Maybe you're trying to scam your insurance? Or maybe you're late with some work deadline, and you figure you can dodge a bullet by claiming your computer's been messed with? But whatever it is—and I honestly don't care—it's not going to fly. You're better off getting in front of it now. Trust me. Just tell us."

"Once this goes to paperwork, our hands'll be tied." Wagner leaned in close and a chunky silver necklace jolted loose from the collar of her blouse, its stylized "J" swinging toward me like a tiny scimitar. "There'll be zero wiggle room. It'll generate a ton of trouble, and that trouble will all land on you. Whatever kind of mess you're already in, you'll make it a hundred times worse."

"Is that what you want? Or would you prefer to be sensible?" Hayes didn't make it sound like a question.

Alarm bells were ringing in my head. These two thought I was lying. If I took back what I'd said—which actually would be a lie—they'd take it as proof. They said they'd turn a blind eye, but what reason did I have to trust them? It would be easier to charge me with wasting police time or some bullshit like that than to catch whoever had stolen my program.

"You're sticking to your story?" Hayes feigned shock. "Seriously?"

"It's not a story. It's the truth."

"So if we take your computer to the lab, they're going to find a new spy virus lurking on it?"

"What do you mean, take my computer? You can't take my computer. I need it."

"Oh, but we can take it, Marc. You opened that door when you reported your program stolen. And if the lab doesn't find a virus, meaning you've been jerking us around and wasting our time, you're going to be in a whole heap of trouble. Why not be smart? Admit you've been hosing us the whole time."

And walk straight into a trap? I was damned if I did, and damned if I didn't. I couldn't work without the computer. And I couldn't work if I was in jail. If they even took me to jail. Maybe I could trust them not to. It was a gamble. But if I lost, going to jail—even overnight, waiting for the charges to be dropped—would bring a host of problems with it, down the road. Could I afford that? Carolyn had been right about one thing yesterday. The importance of reputation for consultants. You can't expect people to share their corporate secrets with you if you're under a cloud of suspicion. Even a stupid, unjustified cloud.

I was chasing my tail, going round and round in paralyzing circles, when the fog in my head cleared for a moment and I realized the answer was right in front of me. Well, en route to me, via messenger. Because I didn't need that specific computer. Any computer with a high enough spec would do. And there was one on its way to my house as we spoke, courtesy of AmeriTel. In fact, it should have arrived yesterday, making the whole point moot.

"Detectives, you're right." I suppressed a smile. "Be my guest. Take the computer. I'll help you carry it to your car, if you like . . ."

CAROLYN WAS STILL MISSING. THE DETECTIVES HAD TAKEN MY computer. And I was left alone again, with nothing but questions for company.

Who had broken into our house? Where had they gotten the key from, if that's what they'd used? Were they the same guys I'd seen outside the night before, right after Carolyn had lured me away? How had anyone known I was working on something new? And what were they going to do with the files they'd stolen?

In fact, following the detectives' visit there was only one thing I could be sure about: I was in a race. Someone was trying to beat me to market on the back of my own idea. They had my prototype. And they had my test data. I felt like a character in a Western, sucker-punched in a bar fight and left to watch helplessly as the faceless villain rode away on my horse.

There's only a handful of people in the country who do what I do, and I know them all, to a greater or lesser degree. The competition gets a little fierce sometimes—a couple of the guys have monstrous egos— but I couldn't imagine any of them going to these lengths to steal a march on me. And there was a self-defeating aspect to the whole thing, as well. Anyone who announced a product based on my concept would be outing themselves as a thief. I daydreamed for a moment, reveling in the fantasy of publicly unmasking whoever had sandbagged me. Then I pulled myself back to reality. I had a job to do. And to do it, I was going to need the right tools. I took out my phone and called Ameri-

Tel. It was time to find out what had become of the equipment they said they'd return.

It was Roger LeBrock who'd made the promise, so I tried his number first. It rang for what seemed like half an hour, then dropped me into voicemail. I left him a message—without wasting the effort it would have taken to keep the irritation out of my voice—then moved on to Simon Wakefield. I couldn't reach him either, so I tried his deputy. Then the IT department's helpdesk number. And finally, the switchboard. I got no answer from any of them. Surely the whole company couldn't have been told to blackball me? Then another explanation popped into my head. The clock had crept past noon. The bandwidth auction would be over. AmeriTel might have sunk without a trace.

I opened the browser on my phone and searched for news. There were plenty of stories about AmeriTel on the business pages. But they weren't reporting a disaster for the company. They were shouting about a triumph. AmeriTel had trounced its competitors—its bigger, richer, better-connected competitors—and walked away with the plum allocations in four of the five major auction categories.

The news was nothing short of miraculous. To do well in one category would have been a coup. But in four? The stress had been etched into LeBrock's face yesterday. He'd obviously been pouring his lifeblood into AmeriTel's bid. At the time I'd thought he was showing the defiance of a dead man walking. But now it looked less like honest exhaustion and more like he'd sold his soul.

The news also explained why no one was answering the phone. They'd be too busy celebrating. The people who, till yesterday, I'd been working alongside. Who now had a rich future. People I should have been happy for. And if I'd still been there, raising a glass with them, I would have been happy. But instead, all I could think of was LeBrock's parting shot. *We don't want you anymore.* He was setting sail for the promised land with all his buddies, but there was no room on board for me.

And what about Carolyn? There was room for my wife. She'd be at AmeriTel now, caught up in the collective euphoria of cheating the corporate hangman. Dodging the noose and hitting the jackpot instead. I wondered who she was with. Who was getting her drinks. Re-filling her glass. Watching, as her gorgeous eyes lost a little of their sharpness. Wondering, as her sweet laugh gained an extra few degrees of warmth.

It should have been me she was with. But my wife had turned her back on me for the sake of an errand she'd been sent to run. For a few gigabytes of surplus data. Which I'd lost, anyway. How would things have played out if I'd given in to her demands? Would we be together now, somewhere fancy, all black tie and cut crystal? Tangled up in the sheets of a five-star hotel, the way we'd toasted her last few promotions? Or hopping on a plane to Europe, as we'd done after my first product had sold?

Maybe we'd have been together. But maybe not. Carolyn would have gone to LeBrock, anyway, to hand over his prize like a well-trained errand girl. And would she have come back to me again? I was beginning to wonder. The way she'd reacted yesterday, I was beginning to suspect I'd only seen the tip of the iceberg. And I'd been so certain our marriage was solid, too. Bombproof, in fact. I'd have sworn the needle was firmly in the green. But now? I wouldn't even have put money on amber.

I slipped my phone back in my pocket. My appetite for news had dried up. I needed something to distract myself. For a crazy moment the thought of more tequila crossed my mind. Carolyn would be drinking. She'd probably be three sheets to the wind by now. I could join her in spirit, if not in body. And I knew there was another bottle of Patrón in the cupboard. I remembered seeing it last night. Still in its fancy presentation box. I'd actually flirted with the idea of opening it, when the first one had run dry.

I made it as far as the dining room doorway before sanity prevailed. I paused, still tempted, then returned to the study to look for the spare keys for the Jaguar. A bit of distance between me and the house would be good. And if I could get into town, I'd have access to the one thing that life has shown me to be the equal of alcohol when it comes to providing consolation.

Pizza.

Plus, my hangover had finally passed, and I was starving.

MY LOCAL ENOTECA WAS ONLY TEN MINUTES AWAY. THE FOOD was great. And because I went there at least once a week—to take a break from my computer screen, or just to avoid cooking for myself when Carolyn was working late, especially following a debacle involving an egg and a now-replaced microwave oven—my Jaguar could practically find its own way there.

I pulled out onto the road, and right away I was stuck behind another driver. He was dawdling his way along, braking at every pothole, slowing me down, just like the idiot in the Audi had done yesterday. Only this guy was in a black, aggressive-looking Infiniti SUV. My hopes rose as we neared the end of my street, until I saw we were going the same way. Then something occurred to me. As we'd approached the intersection I'd put my turn signal on before the Infiniti guy had, even though I was behind him. Yesterday, hadn't the exact same thing happened with the Audi? I thought back carefully, and yes, I was sure of it. Normally I doubt I'd have noticed anything as trivial, but I guess the shock of the break-in and the grilling from the police had made me more observant.

Or more paranoid?

The same thing happened again at the next intersection. Once or twice, and I wouldn't have been convinced. But at every turn, two days running, with two different cars? I reached for my phone to call the police, but stopped before I even dialed the nine. If they didn't believe me about the break-in, why would they take this seriously? Some guy driving too slowly in front of me? Big deal. They'd think I was wasting their time again. Or that I was crazy.

Maybe I *was* losing it. I needed to get a grip. Fast. So I looked at the situation like it was a problem with my work. What would I do if a program wasn't behaving the way I expected it to? I'd run tests till I could determine what was going on. As we approached the next stop sign I signaled left. The Infiniti signaled left. There was no other traffic, so it pulled out without delay. I waited till it was beyond the point where it could easily swing back around, then I steered right and hit the gas pedal. Hard. The supercharger howled. The Jaguar lurched forward in a hail of gravel. And I kept my foot down till I was safely round the next bend.

After a quarter of a mile I spotted a gas station on the right-hand side. I remembered it had a small grocery store attached to it, with a parking lot tucked away at the back. I checked the mirror. The Infiniti wasn't in sight, so I turned in. I followed the narrow driveway around the side of the building and slid the Jaguar into a space between a pickup truck and a delivery van. Then I ran into the store and found a spot next to a magazine stand where I could keep an eye on the road.

I'd been there maybe ninety seconds—not long enough to be distracted by the tales of teenage pregnancy and celebrity indiscretion, anyway—when I saw the Infiniti. It was traveling even faster than I'd been and, to my relief, it kept going, leaving me farther behind with every second that passed.

For a moment I basked in a glow of euphoria—I'd proved I wasn't nuts, and I'd outsmarted whoever was following me—but the feeling was swiftly replaced by worry. Why would anyone want to follow me? And what if the guy in the Infiniti hadn't been fooled by my trick? What if he'd followed me inside the store? Or ambushed me in the parking lot? What would I have done then? I had no idea. And how long would it be till he realized he'd lost me, and doubled back to look for hiding places? I hurried to my car, not wanting to be caught in the open.

I paused at the exit from the gas station, suddenly unsure which way to turn. Continue to the restaurant? Return home? Or head somewhere else? To some random location, where I'd be less likely to be found?

I didn't like the idea of running and hiding. And why should this guy in his macho car make me change my plans? I should say *Screw him*, and go get my pizza. But now that the thrill of the chase had ebbed away, so had my appetite. Unless—maybe I'd want to eat later? Maybe I should get some food and take it home, just in case.

Home. Was that the key to this thing? The same day I'd been followed from the gallery by the Audi, someone had broken into my home. And if the door had been left open because I'd disturbed the intruders before they found everything they'd wanted, could they be looking for a second chance? Was that why I'd been followed again today? To make sure the coast was clear? They could be ransacking my place even as I sat there worrying about my dinner options.

I turned for home, but the questions kept on coming. What if intruders were in my house? What would I do? Confront them? I didn't know how many there'd be. They'd probably be armed. Even if they weren't, what were the odds they'd just roll over and surrender if I told them to? Zero. I was stupid if I thought I could deal with this alone. I needed help. But from where? The police? I could hardly count on them to believe me. Not after our last encounter.

Photographs. If I could get close enough to take pictures with my phone I could email them straight to the detectives. They couldn't ignore me then. The key would be to park where I'd be out of sight and sneak up to a window. It wasn't rocket science. But doing it without getting caught would be far from straightforward.

I slowed down, hoping to buy a few extra minutes' thinking time. The road narrows at that point, snaking around stand after stand of broad trees. It gave the impression of driving through a small forest, rather than the kind of residential district favored by lawyers and Wall Street bankers. For miles at a time the worn pavement with its faded yellow lines and low, crumbling stone walls on either side were the only signs of human habitation. The tranquility usually reminded me why I'd chosen to live in the area, myself, but that day was different. It just made me feel isolated, until a dirty brown Ford Escape appeared in front of me. At the same moment another car—a black Volkswagen sedan—closed right up from behind. Three, maybe four seconds passed with me at the center of our little convoy. Then the Ford lurched to the left, turning hard then slamming into reverse so it completely blocked the road. I had to stand on the brakes to avoid smashing into it. I heard a screech from behind me, and saw the Volkswagen had carried out exactly the same maneuver. It had ended up sideways, inches from my trunk, sandwiching me in like the cross bar of a capital "H."

"Turn off your engine and toss the keys out of the car," a harsh metallic voice ordered. The Ford driver had opened his window. He was holding a shotgun, and was pointing it right at me.

How could this be happening? They must have mistaken me for someone else . . .

"Turn off your engine," the guy repeated. "Toss out the keys. Do it now."

I forced my shaking hand to slide the gearshift into Park, hit the window button, pull out the key, and drop it onto the blacktop. I risked a glance in my mirror. The passenger in the Volkswagen also had a shotgun trained on me. His driver was sheltering behind the front wing, gripping a black pistol in both hands and holding it out in front of him.

What were they going to do with me?

"Good," the guy said. "Now, hands behind your head. Fingers laced together. Go."

I did what I was told, then closed my eyes. I was waiting for the boom. The splintering windshield. The glass shards and shotgun pellets tearing my flesh, burying themselves in my face and chest. But when I did hear a sound, it wasn't what I expected. It was another vehicle. Approaching from behind. Stopping. And not driving away again. Its motor continued running, and that filled me with hope. Surely whoever it was would call 911? And whoever these guys with the guns were, surely they couldn't be psychotic enough to murder me in front of a witness?

I OPENED MY EYES AND SAW THE TWIN BARRELS OF THE FORD driver's shotgun still staring back at me. His passenger had a pistol, which he was aiming at my chest. The two guys in the Volkswagen hadn't lowered their weapons. But the newcomer—a man, tall, maybe in his mid-forties, with a manila folder in one hand—had climbed out of a white panel van and was walking straight toward me.

What was wrong with the guy? Couldn't he see the guns? Didn't he realize he was stepping into the middle of a war zone—probably making a bloodbath all the more likely—when I needed him to keep his head down and call the damn cavalry? I was thinking I should shout a warning, but he'd arrived alongside my door before I could form a word.

"Marc Bowman?" The man leaned down toward my window.

I was too surprised to answer.

"Is your name Marc Bowman?"

Still speechless, I nodded.

"I'm Jordan McKenna." He pulled a leather wallet from his jacket pocket and flipped it open to reveal an identity card. A photograph of his frowning face was set against a pale blue background next to an eagle clutching an olive branch in one talon and a bunch of arrows in the other. The bird was half hidden by a shield and surrounded by the words US DEPARTMENT OF HOMELAND SECURITY. Then came confirmation of his name, a narrow bar code, an expiration date about two years away, and a gold data chip. "I'm sorry to detain you this way, sir, but I have a very important question to ask. Mr. Bowman, do you have any weapons of any kind in the vehicle? Any weapons at all?"

"No. No weapons. Absolutely not."

"Good. In that case, you can put your hands down. OK. Now, there are some things we need to talk about. Is it all right with you if I get in the car?"

I nodded.

Agent McKenna reached down and picked up my key, then gestured to the other cars. The Ford moved first, maneuvering until it was parked neatly at the edge of the road on the opposite side, facing us. Then the Volkswagen tucked in behind my Jaguar and turned on its flashers as if we'd broken down and it was there to shield us against oncoming traffic.

"Nice car." McKenna slid into the passenger seat, closed the door, and placed the key on the central armrest. "You should see the crap we have to drive around in. Anyway, I don't suppose our rental issues are a big concern of yours, so let's get down to business. You already confirmed your name, and as for your profession, you're an IT consultant?"

"Correct."

"And you're currently working on a contract at the AmeriTel corporation?"

"Yes. Wait, no." I felt like a swarm of butterflies was loose in my head. "I was working at AmeriTel. But yesterday they canceled my contract. I was let go."

"AmeriTel cut you loose? Yesterday?"

"That's right."

"Why?"

I gave Agent McKenna a brief rundown of my conversation with LeBrock and his grand vision for a Bowman-free AmeriTel. Marc-Bowman-free, anyway. I didn't mention there was evidently still room in the company for my wife.

"OK. That's good." McKenna's expression remained neutral. "Now, I'm going to take a wild guess and bet you're a little curious about what's going on here?"

"If you bet your house on that, you wouldn't be left on the street."

"All right. Well, I apologize for the drama. But believe me, it's necessary. We've been watching AmeriTel for a while now and we have some serious concerns. I can't go into those right now—National Security—but the fact they fired you puts you in a better light. And it makes me hope you might be willing to help us. How do you feel about that?"

I felt like all the air had been sucked out of the car and for a moment I struggled to catch my breath. I'd been working alongside traitors? Or terrorists? And Carolyn still was? After what had happened yesterday I was no fan of LeBrock's, but I still couldn't imagine him in bed with al-Qaeda or some other bunch of murderous bastards. But if it wasn't LeBrock, who was the rotten apple? Or was there more than one?

"Mr. Bowman?" McKenna touched my arm. "What do you think? Can you help us?"

"I don't know. I'd like to, but I'm not sure what I can do. I was only there for a few weeks, and I was a consultant. Not an employee. Never a real insider. And they won't talk to me now. They won't even let me back on the premises."

"I understand. But don't worry about that. Don't try to second-guess anything. Just listen to my questions, and answer as many as you can. If you're not sure about anything, just say. Remember, I only want facts. I don't want you taking any shots in the dark."

"OK. I'll try."

"Excellent. I appreciate it. I'd like to start with a bunch of photographs." He opened his folder and revealed a stack of color eight-by-tens. "These were taken over the last couple of weeks. I'd like you to look through them and tell me if you recognize anyone."

Each of the pictures showed at least one AmeriTel employee. A few had been taken in the company parking lot, and the rest at local bars and restaurants. I identified them as fully as I could, but didn't see anything suspicious. Not until the last one, anyway. And even then my concern had nothing to do with anything that could interest Homeland Security. The image did make my blood run cold, though. Because the last photograph showed Carolyn, at lunch with a guy called Karl Weimann. One of my competitors. And the last guy in the world I wanted her talking to.

Ten years ago Carolyn had been all set to leave AmeriTel. An acquaintance was starting a hot new theater cooperative in New York, and had offered Carolyn the chance to trade her desk for the stage. It was a dream come true for her. The only thing she'd really wanted, ever since high school. But at the eleventh hour, the opportunity had fallen through. Twice shy, Carolyn had resigned herself to life in the commercial world. She'd worked hard, hoping that the trappings of success would outweigh her disappointment. *It just wasn't meant to be,* she said.

Except that fate wasn't to blame for what happened. I was. I'd just been fired. Without the money Carolyn was bringing home from AmeriTel, I'd never have been able to finance my first product. So, knowing that Renée Weimann—Karl's wife, and part of our social circle at the time—had matching aspirations but far greater experience, I gave her the inside scoop on the theater project. Long story short, Renée was asked to join the cooperative. Carolyn was left to climb the corporate ladder. I founded my company. Bought my Lichtenstein. And lived in constant fear of Carolyn finding out the truth.

Had Karl Weimann let the cat out of the bag? The detectives' insinuations about Carolyn's key suddenly seemed sickeningly plausible.

"What's wrong?" McKenna asked. "You've gone quiet. Did something in the pictures ring a bell?"

"No. It's just—that's my wife in the last one. I wasn't expecting to see her."

"Oh, of course. It had slipped my mind, her working at AmeriTel. But please, don't worry. Your wife's not in any kind of trouble." He slid the pictures back in the file and snapped it closed. "Now, tell me. Has anything odd happened since you left the company?"

"It depends what you mean by odd." I sketched out the basics surrounding the Audi that had tailed me, the break-in, the visit from the two detectives, and the Infiniti I'd just dodged. "In fact, I was heading home now because I was worried someone might try to break in again."

"I can see why you'd be concerned," McKenna said, opening the door. "But don't worry. We can help you with that." He slid out, went over to the Ford, had a word with the guys inside it, then turned and got back in my Jaguar. The other driver moved off, turning sharply to avoid a battered silver Avalon—the first car that had passed us the whole time we'd been sitting there—and sped away. "My guys are going to your place now. If anyone's there who shouldn't be, they'll get a nasty surprise."

"Oh. OK. Thank you."

"We'll catch up with them in a minute. In the meantime, there are a couple of other things I need to ask you."

"Sure. What do you need to know?"

"The stuff that was stolen. Your list. It's pretty short. You didn't leave anything out?"

"No. I don't think so."

"Like, for example, what was on those memory sticks?"

"Oh. Nothing important. Just some data files. I was going to use them to test my new product."

"Where did these data files come from?"

This was awkward. From what I'd heard, the Fifth Amendment didn't carry much weight with Homeland Security so I glanced at McKenna to see what I could make of the man. He looked calm and assured and in good shape, like he'd be equally happy working in a bank or climbing a mountain. His face was tanned, disguising the lattice of fine lines around his eyes, and his dark hair—about an eighth of an inch long—was showing the first signs of gray around the temples. Not the kind of guy you'd cross the street to avoid. But not the kind you'd pick a fight with, either.

"It's OK." McKenna smiled at my less-than-subtle inspection. "We're on the same side. I'm not looking to jam you up. And I have bigger fish to fry than you, believe me. I just need to have a complete picture of what's going on. Such as this data. What was it, exactly?"

"Communications records. Details of landline calls. Cellular calls. Texts. Emails. IMs. Web searches. That basically covers it."

"Where did they come from?"

"AmeriTel."

"I mean, who made all these calls and emails and so on?"

"Oh. Anyone, I guess. Anyone who uses AmeriTel's network. That's potentially their whole customer base. Hundreds of thousands of people."

If the scope of that community fazed McKenna, he didn't show it. "What about AmeriTel's own employees, at their HQ?"

"Of course. Them, too."

"Why did you collect this data, in particular?"

"To run some reports the CEO wanted. But then he changed his mind. And then he canned me. I thought, why let it go to waste?"

McKenna was silent for a moment.

"Is that a problem?" I said. "Have I screwed myself? Because if I've broken some kind of rule, it wasn't on purpose. I swear."

"No." He shook his head decisively. "Don't worry. Like I said, I'm not trying to trip you up. Believe me, if I were, you'd know."

T

HE CAR MCKENNA HAD SENT ON AHEAD WAS WAITING FOR US when we pulled into my driveway a few minutes later. It was sitting in the spot where Carolyn usually parked, and the thought that I'd allowed—even indirectly—someone else to take her place made me feel a twinge of disloyalty. And a little sadness, too, as if it turned her temporary absence into something more permanent.

The two guys who'd recently been pointing weapons at me were out of their car and moving toward us before I brought the Jaguar to a stop. The one who'd been driving was carrying a small, ribbed aluminum case. McKenna joined them for a brief huddle, then turned and motioned for me to follow them to the front door.

"Have you changed the locks yet?" he asked, as I fished for my spare key.

"No. I haven't had the chance."

"That's the first thing you should do when your keys are stolen. It's basic common sense. You need to get on it, right away, before you leave the house again. And this time, get a lock that's more practical. And less pretty."

"Why? Is this one no good?"

"It depends what you want it to do. If you want it to keep criminals out, then no. Look at it. You could pick it in, what? Fifteen seconds?"

"Really? You think it was picked? Is that how the thieves got in?"

Normally the suggestion that my house was so insecure would have horrified me, but at that moment it filled me with hope. Because if the lock had been picked, it meant the thieves hadn't used Carolyn's keys.

"It's possible." McKenna knelt and examined the keyhole. "But I doubt it."

"Why? How can you tell?"

"We'd need to have the forensic guys check it out to be sure." He took a pen from his pocket and pointed to the metal bezel with its tip. "But you see this part? It looks pristine. If it had been picked, I'd expect a deep scratch here, and a smaller one here. I'm guessing someone got hold of a key. And since yours is missing, you'd be dumb to take any chances."

"Well, OK." I opened the door and tried to hide my disappointment. "Thanks for the advice. As soon as you've seen what you need to see, I'll call a locksmith."

McKenna headed down my hallway with the other two guys trailing in his wake. Each of them glanced into every room they passed, but it was my study that held their interest.

"Is that real?" McKenna was staring at the Lichtenstein.

"It is."

"Interesting."

"Very. It's one of his less well-known works, but there are a couple of features that—"

"It's interesting because it tells us the people who broke in were professionals. They had discipline. They came here with a specific target in mind, and that's all they took. Amateurs would have stolen the painting. They wouldn't have been able to resist. The question is, how did these guys know you had what they wanted? Did the police have any theories?"

I hesitated, reluctant to throw Carolyn under the bus. But when I saw the look in McKenna's eye I knew I couldn't risk lying to him.

"The detectives thought my wife might have tipped someone off."

"Hence your reaction when you saw that photograph. But what do you think? Do you agree with them? That your wife is involved?"

"I didn't at the time. I assumed I'd been hit with some kind of spyware."

"Either way's possible, I guess." McKenna's words carried less conviction than I'd have liked. "Mind if we look around and see if we can throw any light on it? What about the computer itself? Where have you got it hidden?"

"Oh, the computer? Didn't I tell you? The police took it."

"No, you didn't mention that. Why did they take it? Did they say?"

"To look for the spyware. They figured it must have been something pretty advanced, given my virus protection hadn't picked it up. They wanted to see if their lab could identify it."

"Smart move. We'll check in with them, see if they're making any headway." McKenna shot a glance at one of his guys, who immediately left the room. "Our labs have more experience with malware, so it could be they'd rather kick it over to us. In the meantime, let's take a look at the usual suspects. Have you got a landline phone?"

"A cordless one, on top of there." I pointed toward a wooden filing cabinet in the corner of the room.

The guy with the aluminum case covered the distance in a couple of strides and picked up the handset. He slid the cover off the rear compartment, pulled out the battery, and started to root around inside the body of the phone with short stubby fingers that looked extremely unsuitable for the job.

"Looks like an old one." McKenna grimaced. "Does it work OK? Or has it ever had to go for repair?"

"It is pretty old, I guess. I couldn't tell you when I bought it. But it works fine. Never had a minute's trouble with it."

"And it begins." McKenna directed my attention back to the guy with the phone. A tiny silver disc, about the size of a hearing-aid battery, was nestling in the palm of his hand with a pair of skinny red wires with neatly soldered ends poking out between his fingers.

"Wait. What is it? A—"

McKenna cut me off with an urgent waggle of his index finger. Then he nodded to his guy, who tossed the disc on the floor. It landed near my feet, and McKenna mimed a stomping gesture to me. I hesitated, then stepped forward and crushed it under my heel.

"Seriously?" I felt a shiver dance down my vertebrae. "A bug? In my phone? How long had it been there?"

"Impossible to be sure." McKenna shrugged. "It's old technology.

Been around for years, but people keep using it because it works. It's pretty basic. It only gives you audio, and it has a limited range. But it gets the job done."

McKenna's guy opened his case and took out a shiny black box about the size of an iPhone. He flicked a switch on its side, then brought it over to the bookcase.

"We call it a sniffer. It picks up radio waves." McKenna spread his arms wide. "If anything else is transmitting, this will find it."

The guy reached the end of the top shelf, pausing next to each book in turn. He moved down a shelf and started in the opposite direction. This time he made it less than halfway along before I heard a high-pitched squeal. The guy switched the machine off with his thumb and started to gently ease the nearest book away from its neighbors.

"Are those all about computers?" McKenna looked incredulous. "You could fill a technical library with them."

"Nearly all of them are." I was on the defensive. "It's my job, remember."

"Have you read them all?"

"Of course. Some of them several times."

"Really? Because a couple look a little dusty. Oh, hang on—I think we have another winner."

The second guy had unearthed something from between the books. Another device. It was made of white plastic, about the size of a box of matches, and a narrow wire about eight inches long with a sliver of glass at the end was sticking out from one of its narrow sides. As I watched, the guy snapped the wire and slipped the remains into his pocket.

"This one you can't just buy at RadioShack." McKenna made a circle with his thumb and forefinger, held it to his eye, and peered at me. "It's video. And did you see how small the lens was? It's a lot more sophisticated. We're going to take it with us. If we catch a break we might be able to trace where it came from."

"Someone was watching me? In my own office?" For the first time I was glad Carolyn wasn't here. She'd have freaked.

Unless Carolyn was the one who'd planted the camera.

"I'm afraid so. But I'm not surprised. Video increases the value of the intel tenfold. And it would be very sloppy to rely on a single device. If it were me, I'd have placed at least four in a room like this. In particular, I'd want one covering the desk. I presume that's where your computer usually is?"

"Yes. But there's no other furniture anywhere near the desk. Where would you plant it?"

"Maybe in the light?" McKenna suggested.

McKenna's guy held the sniffer up, but it remained silent.

"What about the desk lamp?" McKenna asked.

The guy tested it, but again came up dry.

"There isn't anywhere else," I said.

"There is one place," McKenna countered.

"Where?"

"How long has that been there?"

"What?"

"The painting. Do you ever take it down? Store it when you're away? Have it cleaned?"

"No. Never. It hasn't been moved since I bought it. And no one ever touches it besides me."

Unless . . . Carolyn had always hated that picture. And if Weimann had revealed the role she'd played in me buying it . . .

"It's in the perfect position." McKenna pointed to the painting, and then my desk. "We have to check it."

"No." I stepped forward, as if I could somehow protect it from something that might have already happened. "No way. Please."

"We have no choice," McKenna said. "But would you feel better if you did it yourself?"

McKenna stepped back, out of the way, and his guy handed me the machine. I lifted my arm, and swept it along the bottom edge of the frame. I was praying for silence. The thought of someone vandalizing my Lichtenstein—inserting things into it, using it to spy on me and maybe Carolyn—made me sick.

I moved the machine all the way to the right-hand side without triggering an alarm. My arm trembled with relief. Desperate to be done, I swept back the other way, faster, about six inches higher. Still no sound. I kept on going, back and forth, higher and faster each time, until I'd reached the top of the painting. And uncovered nothing. I laid the device down on the desk—gently, as if there was a danger it would trigger itself out of spite if I banged it around—pushed my chair back with my foot, and sat down without a word.

THEY GAVE ME A MOMENT to collect myself, then McKenna's guy shook my hand, put the sniffer back in his case, and left.

"You've been through a lot today, Marc." McKenna took a business card from his pocket and held it out to me. "If you need to talk about anything, here's a number for someone you can trust."

"No, thanks. I'll be fine. I'll talk to my wife when she gets home. Or to a friend. I'm seeing a couple of them for lunch tomorrow. Old friends. Good listeners."

McKenna shook his head.

"Sorry, Marc, but you can't mention this to your wife. Or anyone else. There's too much at stake. If you need to talk, call the number on the card. OK?"

"I guess."

"Good. And I'm going to leave you my card, as well. I doubt you'll have any more trouble, but if anything does happen, I need you to call me right away. Night or day."

"OK. Thanks."

"Remember, call *me*. Not those detectives you met. Our resources are far superior. And we're dealing with something way above the locals' pay scale here."

"Understood."

"Excellent. Now, I have just one other thing. That AmeriTel data we talked about? I'd still like to take a look at it. So if any of it shows up anywhere—any other old memory sticks, computer discs, email attachments, whatever—call me. Immediately. It's important."

"I will. Absolutely."

"Great. In that case, I'm done here. I'll get out of your hair."

———

THE AGENTS' TIRES CRUNCHED across the gravel, more cautiously than Carolyn's had done yesterday, but an unwelcome reminder of her departure nonetheless. I glanced at my Lichtenstein, still relieved that it hadn't been violated—by her, or anyone else—but my eyes were playing tricks on me. Instead of the blond woman's face, I saw my own. I was the one falling into the abyss. Losing the love of my life? Or even my grip on reality?

What the hell had just happened?

Why was McKenna so interested in the AmeriTel data? LeBrock had been desperate to get it back, too. And what about Carolyn? Was it the data everyone had been after all along? I'd thought my work was the target. But if it wasn't, why was Carolyn dining out with Weimann, my old rival?

More to the point, why was my wife dining out with another man? How naive had I been?

*N*ORMALLY, I CAN'T STAND DEALING WITH MUNDANE HOUSE-
hold crap.

Cleaning, gardening, plumbing, electrical work—I leave Carolyn
to find people to take care of it. But without Carolyn, and after a night
without a wink of sleep—when the house was alive with creaks and
groans, as if the structure itself were mourning her absence—I had no
choice but to get on the case myself.

Two cups of strong coffee, a Google search, and one conversation
was all it took to hire a locksmith, and he was parked on the driveway
unloading his tools before another hour had passed. It seemed like he
knew his business, although whether Agent McKenna would think the
ridiculously expensive Centurion Elite he installed would be secure
enough, I hadn't a clue. It didn't look any more substantial than the old
lock, to me. And given the guy's constant, annoying attempts to make
me admit I was doing the work because I'd caught my wife cheating
and kicked her out, I was certain I wouldn't be employing him again
anytime soon.

The locksmith was clearly putting two and two together and getting fifty—at least I hoped he was—but his faulty logic did spark
another thought that was actually useful. I didn't want Carolyn to
come home, find the locks had been changed, and jump to the wrong
conclusion. I was tempted to call her and explain, but didn't trust
myself not to confront her about Weimann. Not yet. It was a conversation that called for a cooler head. So, I sent her a text. And I was

deliberately vague about how my keys had come to be lost. I didn't think she'd see me sleeping through a break-in on my first night alone as evidence of increased awareness—of myself, our marriage, or anything else.

THE IDEA OF SEEING old friends for lunch was a welcome distraction from the events of the last couple of days, but as I was driving to the restaurant I found myself struggling to decide how much to tell everyone about my new situation. Vincent—the oldest of our group—had come through a tough childhood, and talk of the police and burglaries could quickly put us on the opposite sides of an argument. Jonny—who seemed to start a sickeningly successful new business every fifteen minutes—was ultra-competitive. He always wanted to show how he had the best watch or the fastest car. I could just imagine him seeing my brush with Homeland Security and raising me an encounter with the CIA. And Sally-Anne—the only woman—worked in telecoms, just like Carolyn. Their paths crossed pretty regularly at industry functions, and I wasn't sure I wanted our personal problems leaking into my wife's professional world.

WHAT A WASTE OF TIME, worrying about people's feelings, I thought, getting back into my car exactly forty-six minutes after we were due to have met. Talk about an exercise in futility. Because not one of my *friends* had shown up. And not one had called to cancel. They'd just left me to sit on my own at our usual corner table, trying to deflect the waitress's pity and avoid eye contact with the smirking twenty-somethings at the bar.

None of my *friends* had taken my calls, either. I had to make do with a muddle-headed text from Sally-Anne trying to convince me they'd thought I wouldn't want to meet, following what had happened with AmeriTel. I didn't know which was worse—being stood up, or realizing that my problems had become nothing more than grist for the local rumor mill.

—

THE EIGHTIES CHANNEL PROVED a much better companion on the drive home than any number of fair weather friends, and by the time I pulled into my driveway I was feeling a lot more focused. Work was what I needed next. Something to reconcentrate my mind. But ironically, I was dependent on something else that wasn't there. My computer. Either of my computers, in fact. I was tempted to head into the city and buy another one—you can never have too many—when I spotted a business card wedged between my front door and the frame. I went to investigate, hoping it would be from the messenger who had my delivery from AmeriTel. But instead, it was from the police. On the back there was a handwritten message, signed by Detective Hayes:

Mr. Bowman—please call me ASAP re yr computer.
Important!!! Thx.

I took the card inside with me and tried to call the detective, but was routed through to an administrative assistant who wanted to schedule a time for me to come down to the station house in person. She claimed not to know if I'd be able to take the computer home with me afterward, but her tone was evasive. My inner cynic was alerted, and when I hung up I was left with no confidence I'd be getting my hands on my property any time soon. So, unless I fancied a long drive to the store, my only other option was to try AmeriTel again.

I called the same sequence of phone numbers as yesterday, and with each failed attempt I felt a little more of my newfound enthusiasm drain away, only to be replaced with frustration and anger. The final straw was the conversation I had with an idiot on the IT helpdesk who insisted my things had already been delivered. I didn't actually beat my head on the desk at the end of the call, but believe me, I was close.

I really wasn't looking forward to schlepping all the way to the city, parking, and dealing with the crowds and the salespeople and everything else that computer shopping entails, but I didn't see that I had a choice. Not unless I wanted to be unemployed for the rest of my life, or remain trapped in the AmeriTel/police department's telephonic equivalent of *Groundhog Day*.

I grabbed my jacket and made my way back down the hallway, but stopped when I drew level with the dining room door. A tempting thought had popped into my head. I didn't need to go to a store to buy a computer. Why not just order one on my phone? And if I didn't have to drive anywhere, it wouldn't matter if I had a little something to drink. You could argue it was a little early in the afternoon to really cut loose, but these were special circumstances. And it had to be after five somewhere in the world . . .

I crossed to the liquor cabinet and reached for the Patrón. A second bottle of tequila. A second day without Carolyn. That seemed like a reasonable ratio. Until I started wondering where she was. Because that opened the floodgates to a cascade of darker questions. Who was she with? What she was doing? And had she only betrayed me for a paycheck? Or for personal reasons, too?

I pulled the fancy presentation box from its shelf, but when I tried to open it I saw the seal at the top had already been broken. It had been hacked through, clumsily, by a small, thin blade. And inside I heard something rattle, metal against glass.

I carried the box to the table, holding it at arm's length as if it might explode at any second, and cautiously opened the lid. The bottle of tequila was still there. It was still full. And, lying next to its neck, jammed up against the cardboard wall, was my key ring. The door key was still attached. So was the second memory stick. And so was the little Swiss Army knife Carolyn had given me two nights ago at the restaurant, before she disappeared.

Seeing the knife triggered a few other memories. I'd done more than just think about this second bottle, after Carolyn had left. I'd gone as far as opening the box, using the new penknife to cut my way in. Not the most efficient tool for the job, judging by the result. And having struggled through such a simple task, discretion had proved the better part of valor. I'd decided on an honorable retreat. I'd closed the box and shoved it back in the cupboard, where it belonged. But, it would seem, without realizing I'd dropped my keys inside.

For what must have been the second time, I returned the box to its shelf without opening the bottle. On this occasion, though, I held on to the key ring. I let it swing from my index finger for a moment, like a hypnotist's charm. Then I closed my fist around it while I thought things through. Its presence seemed significant. It meant I'd lied—albeit unintentionally—to the police, because it clearly hadn't been stolen, after all. And I'd lied to Homeland Security. It meant I'd suffered the expense and inconvenience of changing the front door lock for no good reason. But it also meant I still had test data to work with. On the memory stick. Only half as much as I'd originally had, but enough for the time being.

The next question was, what to do about it? Should I call the detectives, and set the record straight? I could. But what would be the point? They hadn't been burning much rubber since they'd interviewed me. If they heard that the only tangible item I'd claimed to have lost in the break-in wasn't missing, after all, they'd take it as vindication for their low-energy approach to the investigation. Plus, the way they'd treated me so far, they'd probably arrest me for wasting their time.

I could try Agent McKenna, at Homeland Security. He'd said he was above the detectives in the pecking order. He'd been more dynamic, grabbing me off the street and sweeping my house clean of bugs. He had more manpower on display. And he'd made me promise to tell him if any more data came to light. Something to do with his ongoing investigation into AmeriTel. Which meant calling McKenna could conceivably derail some kind of terrorist activity. It could possibly save lives. And, perhaps, land Roger LeBrock and his backstabbing cronies in hot water.

Maybe calling McKenna was the way to go?

The payback would be sweet. Especially in LeBrock's moment of triumph. But don't they say the best revenge is massive success? And Homeland Security would confiscate the data. McKenna would take the memory stick away for examination. I was stymied without it. Losing it the first time was a blow. I couldn't face it a second time, especially if I was the one handing it over and watching it being taken away in an evidence bag. I didn't want to undermine the government's case, whatever it might be, but I honestly couldn't see what information was on that memory stick that McKenna wouldn't be able to get his hands on from somewhere else.

Plus there was my second Lichtenstein to think about. The one I wouldn't be able to buy if I didn't finish my new product ahead of whoever had stolen my prototype.

What about a compromise? McKenna needed the data. I needed the data. Why not share it? He wouldn't agree—if he knew. So why not share it without him knowing? All I'd have to do was copy the files, then call him and volunteer to hand over the original memory stick. Everyone would win. Except perhaps that bastard LeBrock. And I wasn't about to shed any tears over him. Or Carolyn. Perhaps the experience would help her. Show her that picking her job over her husband hadn't been her smartest move. Assuming that was all she'd done . . .

The afternoon was shaping up much more productively than if I'd dived into that bottle of tequila. A plan was coming into focus. First, hide the memory stick. I didn't want it lying around in plain sight in case the detectives showed their faces again. That would be embarrassing, not to mention hard to explain. Second, order a new computer. I couldn't copy the data files without one. And finally, put the rest of the day to good use. Call a few of the people I'd need on board further down the line, as the project built momentum. Finance guys. Marketing. Public relations. And Intellectual Property lawyers, given that the prototype had been stolen.

My so-called friends had been reluctant to be associated with me recently.

But it would be different with the people whose pockets I crammed with cash.

I'D KEPT THE PHONE PRESSED TO MY EAR FOR MORE THAN THREE hours, whetting people's appetites and furthering my plans for world domination. But when I heard tires on the gravel outside, I was on my feet in an instant.

Carolyn?

I ran to the window and saw—a UPS van. A guy in a brown uniform climbed out and after ducking into the cargo bay for a couple of minutes he started toward the front of the house, wheeling a heavily taped movers' box behind him on a little trolley. I opened the door for him and he asked me to confirm my name, and that I was expecting a delivery from AmeriTel. Satisfied, he held out a little touch-screen device and gestured for me to sign. But when I reached out to take it he grabbed my hand and bent it back on itself, twisting my wrist and forcing me to spin around. Then he bundled me along the hallway and into the living room. Red-hot needles shot through my shoulder and into my neck. I pushed back and yelled for him to stop but he just wrenched my arm harder and kept on shoving until he had me down on my knees.

My first thought was that I was being robbed again. It must be the same people from a couple of nights ago. Dissatisfied with their haul, they were back for more. But now they'd chosen a time when I was home. And awake. They'd even confirmed who I was. There must be something specific they were looking for. Something they were sure I was hiding. Something they were confident I could get for them. But would they believe I didn't have a secret stash of valuables? And how far would they go to get what they wanted?

"Homeland Security." The man maintained the pressure on my arm. "Marc Bowman, do you have any weapons on you? Or concealed anywhere in the room?"

Not this again, I thought, after a moment of stunned relief. *Do these idiots not talk to one another? Why have they come back?* And then I was filled with dread. Maybe they knew about the data? That I was holding out on them? I should have reported it straightaway. Keeping it made me look guilty. But that was crazy, surely. The memory stick was still where I'd hidden it, under the section of countertop in the kitchen that had been loosened years ago when Carolyn dropped her mother's old stand mixer on it. There was no way Homeland Security could have found out about that. I was being paranoid again.

"Is Agent McKenna here?" The sound of blood rushing in my ears subsided a little and I realized I could hear other people moving around the room.

"Weapons?" The guy twisted my arm even harder. "Yes or no."

"No. No weapons. But who are you? And what the hell do you want?"

"I'm going to release your arm now. You can slide up onto the sofa, but you must remain sitting. Make no attempt to stand. And keep your hands where I can see them. Understand?"

I nodded, the guy let go, and as I wriggled around and slithered into a sitting position I got my first good look at him. His UPS uniform seemed genuine enough, but on closer inspection I noticed the buttons across his chest were struggling to remain fastened and the pants were maybe an inch too short. Another man was standing behind him, next to Carolyn's hideous antique jardinière, near the doorway. He was wearing a suit—dark gray—with an identity card clipped to his breast pocket. And he had a gun in his hand. I was still struggling to reconcile all this when the two detectives from yesterday walked in. Hayes was first, looking worried. Wagner followed, and she just looked pissed off.

"You're from Homeland Security?" I studied the strangers' unfriendly faces, trying to read their intentions. "Where's Agent McKenna? Have you spoken to him? What's this all about?"

The guy in the UPS uniform leaned down till his face almost

touched mine, and he stared at me as if he were examining an object in a museum to see if it was a fake.

"You think we came all this way to answer *your* questions? Are you new? You better get with the program, pronto, or we're going to drag your pampered ass out of here, away from your comfy house and your fancy car, and introduce you to a whole other world. One so different from what you're used to, you can't even imagine it."

"OK." I raised my hands. "I hear you. And I'm happy to cooperate. Just as long as you are who you say you are. Could I see your ID, please?"

The guy sighed, then pulled out a leather wallet and thrust it at me. The card inside was blue. It showed his photo, his name—Agent Daniel Peever—an eagle, some arrows, the Homeland Security logo, and all the other identifiers I'd seen on McKenna's.

"Satisfied?"

"I can't tell." I handed the wallet back. "It looks like the other agent's one, but—"

"What other agent?"

"Jordan McKenna. He was here, yesterday. Don't you people coordinate at all?"

"You're sure he was an agent?"

"Absolutely."

"What makes you so sure?"

"He had ID. And, I don't know. The way he behaved."

"You're an expert in the way Homeland Security agents behave?"

"Well, no. But he was . . . professional. And respectful. He didn't barge into my home and throw me on the floor. He asked for my help."

"With what?"

"An investigation."

"What kind of investigation?"

"I don't know if I should say. Maybe I should call him? Clear it with him?"

"Go ahead. I'd very much like to talk to Agent McKenna myself."

"His card's in my pocket. Is anyone going to shoot me if I get it?"

Peever shook his head, so I dug out McKenna's card and dialed his number on my cell.

"Put it on speaker," Peever ordered. "This I want to hear."

For thirty seconds the five of us were silent, transfixed by the harsh amplified ringtone that filled the room. Then the call dropped into voicemail.

"This is Jordan McKenna, Department of Homeland Security." The recorded voice was a little distorted, but definitely McKenna's. "I can't take your call right now. If you are personally in physical danger at this time, hang up and dial 911 immediately. Otherwise, leave a message and I'll get back to you when operational circumstances allow."

I turned to Peever in triumph, but he only gestured for me to leave a message.

"Uh, Agent McKenna? This is Marc Bowman. I have some urgent information regarding the matter we were discussing. If you could call me back ASAP, that would be great. Thanks."

"Good." Peever was scowling. "Let's hope he calls back soon. And while we wait, tell me more about him. He just showed up on your doorstep, yesterday, flashing a badge and asking for your help?"

"No. I was driving. Heading back here, actually. He and the other agents intercepted me."

"These agents pulled you over?"

"In a manner of speaking."

"How did they make you bring them here? To your house?"

"McKenna offered to come. I was grateful, actually."

"Why's that?"

"He asked if I'd changed my locks after losing my keys. I said no, and I was worried about the burglars coming back—a weird guy in an Infiniti had been following me that morning—so McKenna came to check the place out for me. And it's a good thing he did."

"Why? *Had* the burglars come back?"

"No. But he found out how they knew about my work. Which is more than *some people* have done."

Wagner shot me a look so sharp it could have sliced the leather I was leaning against.

"What did he find?" Peever's expression was equally uninviting.

"Bugs. Listening devices. Someone had planted them in my study. They'd been watching me while I worked."

"Who had?"

"We don't know yet. One bug was too generic to be any help, apparently, but McKenna took another one with him, hoping to trace it."

"Where were they planted?"

"One was in the—"

"No." Peever took a step back. "Show me."

I WAITED FOR PEEVER'S ATTENTION to return to me from the Lichtenstein, then I pointed to the filing cabinet in the corner of the study.

"The first was over there. In the phone."

"And the others?"

"One other." I gestured toward the bookcase. "Second shelf down, roughly in the center."

Peever stepped in front of me and picked up the phone.

"In the battery compartment?" He turned it over in his hands a couple of times.

I nodded.

He slid the cover off and probed the cavity in the back of the handset with his fingers, just like McKenna's guy had done. After a few seconds he pulled his hand back. He was holding something. A tiny silver disc. A double of the one I'd seen removed from that same phone, yesterday.

How could there have been two? And how could McKenna's guy have missed one of them?

Then another explanation dawned on me.

"Now you get the picture." Peever was smiling, but without any warmth. "Still think your new buddy was *getting rid* of bugs, Marc?"

*P*EEVER SENT THE OTHER AGENT OUT OF THE ROOM AND FOR THE next few minutes I stayed still, pinned to the ground as if the force of gravity had increased by a thousand percent.

When Peever's guy returned, he was carrying a black box, like an old-fashioned transistor radio. He set it at the center of my desk, flicked a switch, checked its display, then nodded.

"OK." Peever pointed to the box. "This thing will block the signal of anything else that's transmitting in here. It means we can talk."

No one said anything, giving me a respite to focus on Peever in the hope of escaping my mental merry-go-round. It struck me that if McKenna would be at home working in a bank, this guy would be better suited to delivering your groceries. He was around six foot, but looked shorter because he was so stocky. His two-day stubble didn't match his swept-back bleached hair, which looked like it had been transplanted from a My Little Pony doll. And neither could deflect attention from the unruly straggle that was escaping from his undone top button.

"Specifically, it means *you* can talk." Peever swiveled around on one heel and jabbed his finger in my direction. "Let's start with your computer."

"Which one?"

"The one the detectives impounded, yesterday. Who knew they'd taken it, aside from yourself? Who did you tell?"

"Nobody. Except for McKenna."

"Not your wife? She doesn't know?"

"No. I haven't spoken to my wife since before the break-in."

"Why not?"

"She's been tied up. With work. Her company won big at—never mind. But why? What does it matter who knew?"

"It matters because your computer's been stolen."

"Stolen?" I almost laughed at him. "No. The police have it."

Peever didn't reply.

"Wait. You mean, it's been stolen from the police?"

"Someone broke into the evidence locker and took it." Peever frowned. "Have you got any idea how much juice it takes to pull off a thing like that?"

"How would I?"

"It takes a lot. Believe me. Which tells us that someone with major-league connections was desperate to get their hands on your computer."

"That's ridiculous." I shook my head. "The only valuable thing on it was my prototype, and that had been erased by whoever broke in here. Which was why I called the police in the first place."

"Maybe that is why you called them." Peever waggled his finger at me. "But you weren't expecting them to take your computer. The detectives' report says you were surprised, and reluctant to let it go."

"Only because I needed it for work."

"That's not the full story, is it? You realized there was something else on the computer. Your problem wasn't what's missing. It was what's still there."

"This makes no sense." I'd never liked people who spoke in riddles.

"Who did you call? Who else is involved? One name. Give me one name—one that leads somewhere—and it'll go a long way toward making things easier on you."

"I don't know what you're talking about."

"Have you ever seen the movie *Titanic*, Marc?"

"Yes. I guess. But what the hell does that have to do with anything?"

"You know what happens at the end, when the ship's hit the iceberg? It's going down, and one of two things can happen to the passengers. They can get on a lifeboat. Or they can drown. Well, I'm the guy who decides if you get on a lifeboat."

"I still don't know what you're talking about."

"Do I need to draw you a picture? What am I wearing?"

"A delivery guy's uniform."

"Correct. And you didn't hesitate when you saw me at your door, because . . . ?"

"I was expecting a delivery."

"Two for two. Only there's something you don't know. Your delivery came already." He tapped his watch. "Earlier, when the detectives were here, waiting to break the news about your first computer being stolen."

"My delivery came? Then where's my stuff?"

"At the police lab."

"What the hell? Why? And if they opened it and interfered with my private property without a warrant—"

"We had no need to open anything." Hayes' voice sounded thin and shrill after Peever's booming foghorn. "Not to know what was inside. The contents are listed on the waybill."

"What did you think, Detective?" Peever turned to her. "One computer disappeared before your lab could take a look at it. And someone went to elaborate lengths to hide another one from you altogether."

"I thought, this looks like bullshit. And it smells like bullshit. And in my book, that makes it bullshit. In other words, probable cause. So we impounded the computer. Sent it to the lab. And told them, this time, get on it right away."

"But I didn't hide anything!" I caught myself almost shouting.

"You did." Peever was emphatic. "You mailed the second computer to yourself."

"The one I was using at AmeriTel? No. I didn't mail that."

Peever pulled a computer printout from his pocket and handed it to me. It took a moment to scan the form, but when I found the shipper's details I saw my own name and address. At first I was baffled, but then it hit me. Those bastards at AmeriTel. They'd done it that way to make me pay for the shipping instead of them. They wouldn't even pick up the tab for returning my own property after they'd fired me.

"This isn't right. I know how it looks, but—"

"It was very smart." Peever pretended to applaud. "The perfect way to hide something. To make sure it wasn't here when the detectives came the first time, in case they snooped around. Or at your office, in case they looked there."

"Look, I didn't mail that computer." I could feel the heat building in my face. "But even if I did, so what? It's just a computer. Who cares who mailed it? Ask Roger LeBrock. The CEO of AmeriTel. I wanted to bring the computer home with me, Monday, after I was fired, but LeBrock wouldn't let me. He insisted on shipping it. Talk to him. He'll confirm it."

"Maybe we will." Peever sucked his lower lip for a second. "But things move on. Who shipped the computer isn't the issue anymore. Remember, Marc—the lab's seen it. They know what's on it. Therefore, *I* know what's on it. And if you want a chance to save yourself, you need to tell me who put it there."

"Who put what where? There are lots of applications on that computer. Dozens. Some are very specialized. Maybe—"

"It's not an application we're interested in, Marc."

"What, then? I can't remember every piece of software on every computer I've ever owned! But whatever's caught your eye, I'm sure there's an innocent explanation."

"Really?" He passed me another piece of paper and a pen. "Read that. Then start writing. I want names."

CONCLUSION: THE PRESENCE OF A MALICIOUS PROGRAM CAN BE CONFIRMED ON THE COMPUTER EQUIPMENT PRESENTED FOR EXAMINATION. NO NON-MALICIOUS PURPOSE FOR THE PROGRAM CAN BE IDENTIFIED. NO EXAMPLES OF PROGRAMS WITH SIMILAR OR RELATED STRUCTURE, METHOD OF CONCEALMENT, OR METHOD OF PROPAGATION HAVE BEEN OBSERVED BY U.S. AUTHORITIES TO THIS DATE. AS THE FULL EXTENT OF THE PROGRAM'S PURPOSE OR CAPABILITY IS NOT YET

KNOWN, AND DUE TO THE EXTREME HAZARD IT
APPEARS TO REPRESENT, ALL POSSIBLE MEASURES
SHOULD BE TAKEN TO ENSURE ITS CONTAINMENT.

I passed the paper back to Peever.

"This is your big discovery? My computer had a virus? Big deal. Computers pick up viruses all the time."

"True." He folded the paper and tucked it back into his pocket. "But it's all about context. What kind of virus? What kind of damage could it do? Who could it hurt?"

"It's a new virus. Your report confirms that. Which means no one knows. So why aren't you trying to find out, instead of harassing me?"

"You're—"

"Wait a second." I was starting to join some dots. "It makes total sense for there to be a virus on that computer. I bet I know exactly what it does. It's spyware."

"And who would be getting spied on, in this scenario?"

"*Me,* of course. Detectives, remember *why* you took the computer from here? To get your lab to search for spyware! I figured that's how whoever stole my prototype had known what I was working on."

"That's true," Hayes admitted.

"Did they find anything out, before it was stolen?"

Hayes shook her head.

"I'd junked that idea when I thought my study had been bugged. But if it hadn't been bugged, then someone must have been using spyware. And if they were using spyware on one of my computers, they'd be using it on both. Right?"

"A plausible theory, based on the facts. The ones in the open, anyway." Peever spoke with the confidence of a guy who knew he was about to turn up a fourth ace. "But you're missing a piece of the puzzle."

"I'm not—"

Hayes' cell started to ring, breaking my chain of thought. She excused herself, and withdrew to the hallway to take the call.

"You saw the lab report." Peever's grin had hardened. "But I talked to the guy who wrote it. There's a difference between what he'll commit to on paper and what his gut's telling him. And guess what? His gut had a lot to tell."

"You're putting me through all this because of a guy's gut?"

Hayes stepped back into the room before I could continue, and Wagner started for the door before her partner opened her mouth.

"That was my lieutenant." Hayes looked paler than before. "Something's come up. Family emergency. Can you guys take it from here?"

"Absolutely." Peever ushered her toward the door. "Go. Do what you need to do."

He waited until the detectives had left the room, then turned to me.

"It's back to context, Marc. If you were a small-time nerd, and it looked like you'd picked up a nasty disease from a porn site after your mom had gone to bed one night, we wouldn't be too worried."

"Don't call me a nerd, just because I work with computers. I'm an entrepreneur, and someone's trying to steal my invention."

"Raw nerve? Don't be so touchy. I'm not calling you a nerd. And if we genuinely believed you were being ripped off, we'd probably help you. But when I talked to the lab guy, he painted a different picture. He believes we're dealing with a whole different kind of malware, here. Über-sophisticated. Way more complex than something to log a few key strokes or steal a couple of passwords."

"How complex? What does it do?"

When you're in a hole, stop digging. I know that. But I couldn't help myself. My professional curiosity had kicked in.

"Stop deluding yourself, Marc. Faking ignorance isn't going to help you. Your only mileage is to talk to me. Our cyber guys are on this, twenty-four/seven. When they figure it out, it's all over for you. Your value will be gone. The window to help yourself is very, very narrow. And it's closing all the time."

"This makes no sense. You don't know what this virus does, but you're convinced *I* do?"

"Yes. Because of the context. Who you are. Where you work."

"A regular guy? Who works in a regular office? Or did until Monday, anyway. Now I don't work anywhere. Not after I was fired, and the police department lost one of my computers, and you took the other."

"Except you're not a regular guy, are you, Marc? You're a highly trained computer—not nerd, I know you don't like that word—let's say, *expert*. An *expert* who had unrestricted access to all of AmeriTel's systems. And AmeriTel? That isn't a regular office. Take away the desks and chairs and boring telecom stuff, and what have you got?"

I didn't reply. There were lots of things I could say about AmeriTel. None of them were flattering. Especially the ones connected with Carolyn or LeBrock. But I couldn't see how any of that would be relevant to Homeland Security.

"AmeriTel hosts a top-level ARGUS access node." Peever looked me straight in the eye. "You had a direct line to the largest national security database the world has ever known."

His words hit me like a tree trunk falling on my chest. Because what he said was true. Special equipment made a record of every phone call, text message, email, Web search, and online purchase AmeriTel's customers ever made, and relayed them to a government data-storage center in Utah. The place was new. It was state of the art. And it was enormous—five times the size of the Capitol building. They'd had to extend the boundary of the town where it's located to contain it. And it could store so much data they'd soon have to think up new names for the volumes involved. They were already working in yottabytes— 1,000,000,000,000,000,000,000,000s of bytes. There isn't even a word for a higher magnitude.

Why hadn't I put two and two together on my own? I remember arguing with Carolyn over ARGUS when I first heard rumors about it, before she talked me into working at AmeriTel. There was initial resistance from a few civil-liberty groups, but all the telecom networks are hooked in now. And after Peever mentioned it, everything made much more sense. ARGUS was the cyber equivalent of a nuclear missile bunker. It was the last place the government would want a trained computer technician to be loose with an unidentified, aggressive virus. And if Homeland Security thought I was involved in an attack against it, I was in for the devil's own job convincing them otherwise.

"I see we're on the same page, at last." Peever was gloating. "This is your last chance to do yourself some good. Give me a name."

"I can't. You don't understand. I don't have anything to do with ARGUS. The node's in a secure room. I've never even been—"

"Marc, I'm disappointed." He cut me off. "I thought you were smarter than that."

I'D NEVER UNDERSTOOD IT WHEN I TURNED ON THE TV AND SAW people who claimed to have done nothing wrong being led away by the police, heads bowed, hands cuffed, bodies meekly compliant. Why didn't they shout their innocence from the rooftops? Fight for their freedom? Force the officers to drag them into custody, kicking and screaming every inch of the way?

Now I know. You fall under a kind of spell. The immediacy of the situation is at such grotesque odds with the truth that your brain just can't process it. Your emotions are no help—they're overwhelmed with the stress. So you shut down. You regress to a childlike, naive, unquestioning state. And rather than rebel against authority, you cling to anything that resembles it as a last desperate defense against the chaos that's consuming you.

I walked out of my house flanked by the agents and they waited, one on either side, as I fumbled for my keys and robotically locked the door. Being arrested by Homeland Security was by far the most extraordinary thing that had ever happened to me, but even as it played out I somehow clung to my mundane rituals—trying the handle to make sure it was properly secure, checking there were no windows open or lights left on. I almost walked to my Jaguar, still on autopilot, but Peever gripped my arm and diverted me past the UPS van he'd parked on the driveway when he'd arrived.

The agents had left their other vehicles on the street, out of sight of my house. They had a pair of nondescript sedans—a silver Ford and a dark blue Dodge—and a white panel van. The van was covered with pictures of seafood and had a logo for a company called Guttman Lobster and Crabmeat on the side. They were different models and colors, but it was basically the same configuration that McKenna's team had used. Except there was a pair of agents sitting in the Dodge. McKenna had deployed all his people to apprehend me, but Peever had come at me with only one guy to back his play. Incongruously, given the circumstances, I felt a little insulted.

Peever ushered me into the back of the Ford. He climbed into the driver's seat and fired up the engine. The other agent got in next to him. Then the van pulled away from the curb and Peever followed, so close it was like we were attached. The Dodge moved off too, making us the meat in a tightly packed law-enforcement sandwich, and the three vehicles tore down the center of the long, winding, tree-lined streets of my neighborhood so fast that any normal driver would have been arrested for it.

I kept waiting for Peever to say something, but he stayed absolutely silent. As did the other agent. I figured they were trying to trick me into starting a conversation so I'd incriminate myself, somehow. Like McKenna had tricked me with the bugs in my study.

Wait. *McKenna had tricked me?* How did I know that? I only had Peever's word for it. Peever claimed McKenna had his guy pretend to find the first set of bugs, as a cover to plant his own. But who was to say Peever hadn't pretended to find the second set, to discredit McKenna? Or to plant more? What they'd done with the phone wasn't a million miles from pulling a dime out of a kid's ear, and the two guys' performances had been equally convincing.

I was still weighing the odds when a small sports car—a Mercedes SLK, in red—shot out from behind a giant boulder at the side of the road. I lost track of it for a moment, then realized it had managed to squeeze into the tiny gap between our car and the Dodge. The Mercedes' hood was alarmingly close. I couldn't see its radiator grill. Or license plate. But I could see the driver. She had long, wavy, blond hair. Richly tanned skin. Scarlet nails. And she was simultaneously applying eye makeup and adjusting her CD player. The lack of a collision suddenly seemed like a miracle.

The woman reached down to swap her mascara for a paper coffee cup, losing a little of her speed and allowing a small gap to open up between her car and ours.

"Watch her," Peever warned his partner, backing off the gas a little himself as we steered into a tight curve.

It was an unnecessary instruction. The agent—like me—couldn't keep his eyes off the woman. It was fascinating, the way she could apparently pay so little attention to the road and yet keep herself out of harm's way. Next she discarded the coffee in favor of her phone, and the only impact was the loss of a little more speed.

Rubber squealed ahead of us and almost simultaneously I heard the hollow, ripping *thud* of one vehicle plowing into another. I pitched forward as Peever hit the brakes, and flew sideways into the foot well. I clawed myself up, winded from slamming into the front seats and desperate to escape the confined space.

Behind us, there was no sign of the Mercedes. Or the Dodge. But ahead, I could see the van. Its rear end had slewed round thirty or forty degrees, narrowly avoiding the trees at the side of the road. Its passenger side was all caved in. The vehicle that had rammed it—a shiny orange pickup truck with huge, knobbly tires—was in front of us, blocking us off. Steam was spilling from its radiator and clods of mud led back to a gap in the wall.

Movement caught my eye. It was a man in black coveralls, running, with a mask over his face. He was heading around the van, to the side that hadn't been wrecked in the collision. Then another man appeared. He was raising some kind of weapon—like a rifle, only shorter and with a wider barrel. A bright flash came from the van, followed by a dull *whump*. The crumpled vehicle rocked on its springs. Peever and the other agent were scrabbling to open their doors. They were raising their guns and aiming at the second man, but I already knew they'd be too late.

"Bowman, down!" Peever yelled, but I was already back on the floor, pressing myself into the musty carpet.

There were three shots, painfully loud, then something shattered—the windshield?—and I felt pellets of glass rain down on my back. A heavy object slammed into the seat behind me, bouncing up against the rear door and hissing malevolently. And within a millisecond of it landing, ten thousand needles were ramming themselves into my eyeballs.

I heard the front doors opening and I raised my head, desperate for clean air, unable to see, my cheeks streaming with tears. There were two muted *bangs*, like someone swatting flies with a rolled-up magazine.

And then there was silence.

*T*HE WORLD FROZE ON ITS AXIS AND REMAINED THAT WAY UNTIL both of the car's back doors were pulled open, jolting the universe back into motion. Hands grabbed my ankles and lifted my legs up onto the seat. Then someone took hold of me under the arms and started pulling me out of the car.

"Marc, can you hear me?" The voice was familiar, but distorted by the ringing in my ears. "Come on. We have to get you out of here. Take you somewhere safe."

How could the police have arrived so fast? Then the penny dropped.

"Agent McKenna?" My feet hit the pavement. "Is that you? I can't see. Why are you here? What the hell's going on? And the other agents? Are they—"

"They're fine, Marc." McKenna was still taking most of my weight. "But we have to get you away. Right now. Come on."

"Wait." I struggled to free myself. "Peever said you're an impostor. Said you were planting bugs in my study, not removing them."

"I'm not surprised." McKenna let go of my chest but straightaway grabbed my right arm. "I can't air too much dirty laundry, but there's a chance Peever's been turned. Think about it, Marc. If we'd had bugs in your house, we would've rescued you before those guys got out of your driveway."

I felt a second pair of hands take hold of my left arm.

"How did you know to act at all?"

"Remember when I told you I didn't think the thieves would come back? I lied. So we've been watching your house. Around the clock.

We saw Peever's crew arrive, and figured they were up to no good. But we couldn't be sure until they tried to take you away. We couldn't let that happen, so we intervened."

McKenna sounded plausible. But Peever had, too. I didn't know who to trust. And my eyes were stinging like hell, which made it impossible to think.

"What the hell did you use tear gas for?" I muttered.

"We had to. So we could pop them with tranquilizer darts. We need them alive, to stand trial. Here." McKenna pressed a piece of damp fabric into my hand. "Use this. Time's the only real cure, but this'll ease the sting a little."

He gave me a moment to dab my eyes, then started to lead me away from the car again.

"Here's another question." He was trying to make me move faster. "When Peever busted into your house, there were two detectives with him, right?"

"Right. The lazy pair who took my burglary complaint."

"They left before the agents drove off with you. One of them took a phone call. About a family emergency."

"That's right. How did you know?"

"Because there was no family emergency. We had her lieutenant make that call. We wanted them pulled before we came for you. A maneuver like this? There's no guarantee things won't get out of control. And we don't want the wrong people getting hurt, if they do."

"And the ambush?" I was struggling to see a flaw in his words. "You staged it? The woman in the Mercedes was part of it?"

"She's one of ours," he admitted.

What he said seemed reasonable. How could he have known about the phone call to the detectives, or the woman in the Mercedes, otherwise? And honestly, I didn't trust Peever. He rubbed me the wrong way. There was something creepy about him. It was no surprise to hear he was dirty. So I stopped resisting and let McKenna pick up the pace.

My eyes were less painful but my vision was still blurred and I was struggling to make out more than the broad outline of the shapes around me. The car they'd dragged me from was the closest vehicle to us. All four doors were open. And behind it the van and the pickup had merged into a single tangled mass, further obscured by the smoke that poured out from beneath it and lapped greedily around its sides.

The agents had picked a good spot for their ambush. The traffic was light, especially in the evening, and the few homes in the neighborhood were hundreds of yards apart. Plus, they were set well back from the street—a relic of the days when privacy was more valuable than conspicuous wealth.

McKenna suddenly tightened his grip on my arm and started moving faster. A moment later I picked up the sound of a siren. A second after that I heard a motorcycle engine coughing into life. Then another one. Small-sounding, and raucous. Trail bikes? Ideal for a getaway on—or off—these twisting, uneven streets. Impressive foresight on McKenna's part.

We were ahead of the bikes, but McKenna made no attempt to wait for them. Instead, he pulled away to his right, wheeling me and the other agent around in a tight arc and propelling us toward a spot where a previous accident had punched a hole in the wall that bordered the road.

The two bikes burst into sight out of the smoke that was leaking from the wrecked van, racing toward us, about six feet apart. The riders were wearing leather coveralls and ducking down low over their handlebars. McKenna raised his arm and fired three quick shots, kicking up sparks from the pavement but doing no visible damage.

We'd gained ten feet when I heard another bike engine start up. It was directly in front of us, on the other side of the wall. It revved hard, then leapt out through the gap in the stonework. McKenna dived to his right, pulling me and the other agent with him. The bike kept coming. I thought it had missed us, but at the last moment the rider stuck out his leg and planted his huge boot square in the other agent's chest. The blow sent him reeling backward—nearly ripping my arm off before he released his grip—then he stumbled and fell, cracking his head against the blacktop.

The first two bikes were on top of us again, coming in from our left. McKenna fired two shots, then shoved me to the ground and dived onto my back as the riders zipped by, one on each side of us. A second later his weight shifted and he pulled himself into a crouch, scanning for the third bike. It was on the far side of the street, diagonally opposite, lining up for another run. This time McKenna found the target with his first shot. The bike's front tire blew. The rear bucked vertically upward, and the rider was flung forward over the handlebars, landing in a heap of twisted limbs and lying inert as the remains of the bike somersaulted over him.

McKenna scrambled up and pulled two black discs from his pocket, each a little bigger than a hockey puck. He pressed down on a recessed section at the center of both of them with his thumb, then threw them in the direction the two remaining bikes had been going. They landed ten feet apart, rattling along the ridged surface of the blacktop and spewing dense clouds of oily black smoke.

"Come on." McKenna grabbed my arm. "Not much time."

I'd assumed he was worried about the bikes coming back, but then I realized the sirens sounded much closer than they had been. And then another thought hit home: If McKenna really was from Homeland Security, surely he'd welcome the police arriving? Why would he be alarmed by it?

We reached the other agent, who'd recovered enough to struggle up onto all fours. McKenna hauled him to his feet and kept on dragging us away from the barrier that the smoke had formed in the road. I tried to hold back, but then I heard the motorcycle engines growing louder again.

"Where—" I started to say, when a car swept around the corner and accelerated toward us. It was the blue Dodge that Peever's people had been using. I expected McKenna to dive to the side again or turn back toward the smoke screen, but he just kept going straight. I took another couple of steps and realized why. I recognized the driver. It was the woman who'd been in the little Mercedes, earlier. Only she didn't have long blond hair anymore. Now it was much shorter, and brunette.

The woman closed to within fifteen feet then swung the car around in a tight arc, tires locked and screaming, ending up sideways on to us. She leaned across and flung open the passenger door. Then a look of horror swept across her face. I turned and saw one of the bikes had

broken cover. It was bearing down on us, trailing little eddies of smoke
in its wake. It seemed to be heading for the injured agent again, but
at the last moment it swerved and the rider slammed his boot into
McKenna's back. McKenna—too occupied with helping his comrade—
was slow to raise his arms. He hit the ground face-first, hard, and didn't
move. The bike slalomed around the rear of the car and kept on going,
accelerating into the curve, but before it disappeared little sparks
started to flash on the ground around it. I heard a rattling sound to my
right, spun around, and saw the woman firing at him with a short black
rifle.

"Shit," she snarled as the rider escaped unscathed. Then she moved,
rifle still at the ready, heading straight for me. "Are you Marc Bowman?"

I nodded, not sure what she might do.

"Good. Now listen. The police are nearly here. They're not briefed
on what we're doing—their security clearance isn't high enough—and
we don't want them finding us with our pants down. We have to move
fast. OK?"

"Who are you?"

"I work with McKenna. Now move! Don't waste time!"

I wasn't sure I believed her rationale about the police, but I did
know one thing: I didn't want to fall prey to the bikes. One look at
McKenna confirmed that. He was still motionless so I started to half
carry, half drag him toward the car. Blood was streaming down his face
from a ragged gash on his forehead and I ended up with plenty on myself as I wrestled him into the passenger seat. The sirens had become
louder still, so I slammed his door, opened the one behind it, and
turned my attention to the other agent. He could move a little faster,
but we were still six feet from the car when the second motorcycle
burst out of the smoke.

"You're nearly there." The woman was firing again. "Just get him
inside."

Her shots rang out behind me, three at a time, over and over, as I
bundled the agent headfirst onto the rear seat. I reached back to shut
the door, then kept on moving, planning to take cover behind the car.

The rifle fell silent. I swung around and saw the woman calmly climbing in behind the wheel. And the rider on the ground, twenty feet away, his bike sliding along the pavement behind him.

Then the woman's expression changed.

"Get in," she shrieked through her open window. "Quick!"

The bike that had hit McKenna was charging in from the rear. I yanked the door handle, opening a gap of maybe six inches. Not enough to fit through. I was too late. The bike was too close. It was almost on top of me. I was going to be crushed against the side of the car. But the rider didn't hit me. He kicked the door, instead, slamming it closed. And he yelled at me before speeding off.

One word.

"RUN!"

I didn't know how to respond, but the decision was taken out of my hands. Because at that moment, with me stretching for a door handle I could no longer reach, two police cars arrived. They'd turned their sirens and roof bars off for their final approach but their headlights cut through the smoky air like shiny steel blades. I froze. But the woman didn't hesitate. She hit the gas and the blue Dodge disappeared into the smoke.

One of the police cars lurched forward in pursuit, suddenly alive in a swirl of sound and colored light. The other stayed where it was. An officer jumped out and started walking toward me, yelling at me to get on the ground.

If his gun had been in its holster, I might have done what he'd said. But it wasn't. It was pointing at my chest. The spell I'd been under since I left my house was finally broken. I was innocent. I was sick of people attacking me. Following me. Breaking into my house. Taking my things. Spying on me. Stealing my work. Accusing me of crimes I hadn't committed. Confusing me with contradictory stories. Shouting at me. Threatening me.

I'd had enough.

So when the last remaining bike emerged from the smoke, causing the officer to dive for cover, I did what its rider had told me to.

I ran.

*T*HE DECISION TO RUN SEEMED WISE FOR ABOUT TWO MINUTES. It's years since I've seen the inside of a gym, and I was feeling the pace before I'd covered a quarter of a mile. My heart was pounding, my legs were heavy, and with every second the dread of hearing a siren or a motorcycle engine grew greater. I'd be a sitting duck if anyone caught up with me. I hadn't passed a single turnoff. The wall on my left had given way to a natural bank. It was steep, and covered in slippery moss. The woods on the right were accessible, but what then? I couldn't hide forever. And the police would have dogs . . .

The road forked, after another quarter of a mile. The town names carved into the dainty wooden signpost were too eroded to read, so I picked at random. I went right, and after five more minutes I heard the murmur of traffic. My heart soared. I was closing in on safety.

I pushed myself faster, approaching a stand of taller trees that masked the intersection with the busier road, then stopped dead. Something weird was going on. Low down, around their pale trunks, the trees were glowing. Red, then blue. I crept closer, and saw a police cruiser parked at the crossroads, its light bar firing LED rays in all directions. An officer was standing next to the car. There was a shotgun in his hand, and his body was stiff with tension.

Trying to run quietly now, as well as fast, I started back toward the fork in the road. But as I approached I saw the same telltale colors lighting up the sky around the final bend. The police were there, too, now. The net was closing. I couldn't go forward. I couldn't go back. So I went sideways, off the road and into the woods.

I ran wildly, crashing through the undergrowth and pushing visions of attack dogs out of my head until I found a narrow path. It merged with a wider one, and then another until it reached a stream. The water was flowing away from the road, so I followed as it meandered through the trees. Then I saw lights through the branches to the right. They were coming from a house. The house itself was nothing special—a poor attempt at a van der Rohe clone—but it would lead to a road. A different road. One that might be on the other side of the police blockade . . .

Brambles snagged my clothes like barbed wire as I fought my way through the scrubby no-man's-land that surrounded the property. I was within touching distance of the rough lawn that covered the bulk of their yard when I heard a dog bark. Then another. They were in front of me. Rushing toward me across the grass. They were small. Black terriers. Not police dogs. Nothing that could hurt me. But still noisy. Lights came on in the house. Would the occupants be armed? This was Westchester, not the Wild West, but I wasn't about to take the chance. And if the owners didn't have guns, they'd certainly have a phone.

I cut back to the stream and pressed on through the woods, moving as fast as I could in the failing light. After another quarter of a mile I saw a second house. It was larger and more traditional. Two floors, white clapboard, screen porches, and turrets. The kind Carolyn was always saying we should buy, as if we needed the extra space.

A light was on in one of the first-floor windows. Anyone looking out would have a clear view all the way from the tree line to the side of the house. There was no cover. I was just as worried about being seen, but the road was calling to me. Plus night was falling fast, making moving through the woods more dangerous. I'd tripped on exposed roots twice in the last hundred yards.

I took a deep breath, and went for it.

There were no brambles in my way this time, allowing me to move faster. And to rush headfirst into a deer fence. The mesh was so fine it was almost invisible. It was too high to jump. Too flimsy to climb. Too tough to tear. But as far as I could tell, it extended all the way around the perimeter. If I followed it on the outside, could I reach the road that way?

I took a dozen steps, then gave up. The undergrowth was impenetrable. I'd never make it without a machete. I was about to turn around and slink back to the stream when I noticed a branch that had fallen from a tree a few yards farther on. It caught my eye because one end wasn't resting on the ground. Something was suspending it, about two feet in the air. I pushed on and saw what was holding it up. It was the fence. It wasn't broken. But it was weighed down to a height that could easily be climbed.

The stretch of open ground was even wider than it had seemed from a distance. There was a vegetable garden to the right, backing onto what was probably the garage wall. To the left, half a dozen flower beds were separated by fancy rustic-brick paths that branched out like the veins in a leaf. Farther round the side of the house, I could see a large pond—probably a natural extension of the stream I'd been following. And beyond that, screened off from the house by a wattle-weave fence, was an aboveground pool. A little low-rent for the neighborhood despite its fancy cedar-wood sides, but in-ground pools are banned around there due to the high water table. It's the same where we live, which is why Carolyn refuses to have one.

I reached the corner of the house and began to creep across a semi-circular area of paving that fanned out from the side door. Beyond it the ground fell away and a curving brick path led down to a thicket of tall bushes. A wide gate nestled at the far end. And there was no sign of red and blue lights on the other side.

My right foot reached the path, and I froze again. A car was approaching. It was close. Its headlights cut through the bushes, sending thousands of points of light dancing toward me up the path. I willed it to keep going, but the crazy patterns grew calmer. The car was slowing down. And then it stopped, right on the other side of the gate.

I turned and ran, desperate to be back in the woods, and the house door opened. Light spilled out like a physical barrier, so I dived for the end of the fence. Then I crabbed across to the side of the pool and threw myself against its base, fighting to control my breathing.

There was no other sound, except for the car engine on the other side of the bushes. Didn't pools usually have motors to circulate the water? Heaters? Equipment to keep them running? Maybe this one was empty. Could I hide inside? I started feeling for a way to pry open the cover, but all my hands settled on was a two-inch, flexible hose leading to an abandoned pool vacuum.

I crawled back to the fence and peered around the end. A man— short, with gray hair and a camel raincoat—was standing with his back to me. He closed the house door, very gently, picked up a tan leather suit carrier, and started down the path. And then it hit me. The car I'd heard pull up wasn't a police cruiser. It was a cab, coming to pick the guy up. Or a car service. A way out I could have exploited, if I'd been thinking straight. Which was annoying, given that the police were searching for a man on foot.

The old guy had made it five yards when the door to the house opened again.

"Otto!" The woman looked about seventy. She was wearing a pink robe, and her long white hair was loose and disheveled. "You were leaving without saying goodbye?"

"You're awake?" The guy dropped his bag and hurried back up the path. "My love, I was trying not to disturb you! How's your head? Are you feeling better?"

The old couple embraced. Praying they'd take their time, I scuttled back to the pool. Found the pipe. Ran my fingers along its ridged surface until I found the connector. Poked and squeezed and wrestled until it came loose. Then I grabbed the vacuum—a cutesy thing that looked like a whale, about eighteen inches across. I crawled to the opposite corner. And flung the machine as hard as I could.

"Help!" I yelled, a second after it hit the surface of the water. "My daughter! She's fallen in the pond! She can't swim! Neither can I! Please! Somebody! Help!"

The old man didn't hesitate. He ran forward, and his wife followed. I went the opposite way, keeping the pool between us for as long as I could, then making a break for the end of the fence.

I picked up the guy's bag and ran down the path, shrugging off my jacket and turning it inside out as I went. Bloodstains are too easy to recognize. But that thought prompted another. What if the guy had a regular driver, who knew what he looked like? Or what if it was a friend of his, coming to collect him?

Either way, I'd be finished.

Wednesday. Evening.

THE CHAUFFEUR'S FACE REGISTERED SURPRISE AS I STEPPED THROUGH the gate. But he headed for the Town Car's trunk, nonetheless.

"Don't worry about that." I went straight to the rear door. "I'll keep the bag with me."

"Sure, sir." He opened the door for me, but didn't close it after I was settled.

"What are we waiting for?"

"The job sheet said two people, Mr. Schmidt. You and your wife. Going to the Grand Hyatt. Above Grand Central Station. Is that not right?"

"Oh. Well, it was. But my wife? She's sick. She had to drop out. It's a last-minute thing. And I'm actually in kind of a hurry now. There's a couple of people I want to catch up with before they spend too long at the hotel bar, so the sooner you get me there, the happier I'll be."

"Understood, sir."

THE LINCOLN WASN'T THE KIND of car you'd pick to race around those narrow, curving lanes, but the chauffeur still seemed excessively cautious.

"You heard me when I said I was in a hurry, right?"

"Sorry, sir. Can't risk it. Too many police around here tonight."

"Police? Why?"

"They're looking for someone. Homeland Security's involved, apparently . . ."

"How do you know?"

"I got stopped on the way here. They only let me through because I was picking up two people, and the job was booked a fortnight ago."

"Where—"

The blue and red pulsing light that appeared around the next bend answered the question for him. I was heading straight into a trap, but I couldn't tell the chauffeur to turn around. It would be like screaming, *I'm the one they want.* And we were only seconds away from the road-block. There wasn't much time to think.

I pushed my incriminating jacket down onto the floor, then un-zipped the suit carrier. There was a tuxedo in the main compartment, along with a fancy shirt and a paisley bow tie. A pair of patent leather shoes was in the outer pocket. And a pair of silk pajamas in a narrow, central section. But there was no ID. No formal invitation. Not much to work with. And without my phone—I cursed Peever for confiscat-ing it—I couldn't Google to see what events were being held at the Grand Hyatt that week.

The officer stepped away from his car when we were still twenty feet away. He signaled with his flashlight and the chauffeur touched the brake, winding down his window as we coasted to a halt.

"You told me two people." The officer flashed his flashlight at me, alone on the backseat.

"I was booked for two." The chauffeur's shoulders rose a little in a muted shrug, but his hands stayed prudently on the wheel. "His wife's sick, he said."

The officer reached back and pulled open my door.

"Step out of the car, please, sir."

I complied, willing my legs not to shake.

"Your name?"

"Otto Schmidt."

"And where's your wife, Mr. Schmidt? Why isn't she with you?"

"She has a migraine." First I had to account for the absence of my real wife. Now, for someone else's I was pretending to be mine. The irony was killing me. "She stayed home."

"Let me see your ID."

"You know, Officer, I don't have my wallet. I'm not driving, so I didn't think I'd need my license. Everything's pre-paid at the hotel. Except for the silent auction. It's for charity, and I've learned from experience, the only way to avoid leaving a few thousand dollars lighter is not to bring any money with you."

"Really?" The officer didn't join in my forced laugh. "What's your home address, Mr. Schmidt?"

"This is my street." I gestured to my left. "Mine's the first house you come to, that way."

"And your phone number? Let's call your wife. See if she confirms your story."

"I'd rather not disturb her, actually, Officer. Her migraine was wicked bad. Why not call the car service, if you have any doubts? My secretary made the booking, what, a couple of weeks ago."

"Sir, please turn around and place your hands on the car."

"Officer, please. Is that really—"

"Hands on the car. Now."

I turned and leaned, and the officer jabbed my ankles with his foot to force my legs farther apart. He didn't say a word as he patted me down, starting low and working his way up to the collar of my shirt. Then I heard something metallic jangle behind me.

The officer took hold of my right wrist and pulled it down behind my back. This was it. My escape had failed. I felt numb. Then his radio squawked. He stepped away to talk, but after a minute moved back and tapped me between the shoulder blades.

"Sorry, sir. You can put your hands down now. Your wife is at home, like you said. She just called 911 and reported an intruder in your yard. You're welcome to follow me over there, but stay in the car until I give you the green light to get out, OK?"

I sank back into my seat, and the chauffeur started to turn the unwieldy Town Car around.

"What are you doing?"

"Going back to your house. Like the officer said. To make sure your wife's all right."

"Forget about it. You know *the boy who cried wolf*? It should have been the *wife who called the police*. This is the fourth time since Memorial

Day. We'll probably get billed for it. Seriously, don't worry. Just keep going."

WITH THE POLICE BEHIND US, the chauffeur's right foot became a little heavier. I pictured the cop, racing in the opposite direction. Reaching the Schmidt home. Finding the old woman's husband still there. And then what? Jumping back in his patrol car, and trying to catch us? Radioing ahead, to have more cops lying in wait at the Grand Hyatt? Or would they intercept us on the way to the city? And what about the car company? Could they contact the chauffeur, and have him divert somewhere to hand me over?

I wriggled forward in my seat and surveyed the front of the Town Car. It wasn't like a cab—there wasn't a radio or a screen to indicate the next pickup—but the chauffeur must have had a phone. Where would he keep it? *Not in his pocket, please!* I moved a little farther, and breathed a silent sigh when I spotted it lying facedown on the passenger seat.

"Look out! Stop!" I shot my arm out, pointing to the chauffeur's left. He slammed on the brakes. The car shuddered to a stop. And the phone skidded forward on the shiny leather, slipping off the edge and disappearing into the foot well.

"What the hell—"

"Sorry. I thought something ran out. A deer, maybe. I'm coming up front with you. I'll keep watch. Damn creatures are everywhere. They're a menace."

Before he could object I grabbed my jacket and moved to the passenger seat, carefully planting my foot on the fallen phone. At the next bend I allowed the jacket to slide off my knee. Cursing, I reached down to retrieve it. And with it, the phone. I took a quick glance to locate the power button. Then I made a show of refolding the jacket, wrapping it tight to smother any sounds the phone might make as I surreptitiously switched it off.

What should I do next? Continuing to Manhattan was out of the question. So was staying in the Town Car much longer, given the number of police in the area. But where else could I go? Then I noticed the chauffeur glancing down at his instrument panel.

"You know, the fancy dinner at the Hyatt's not till tomorrow. And I'm off the leash tonight." I winked, then gave him an alternative address. "Take me there, instead. It's not far. I'm thinking, a hand or two of cards. A friend of mine has a little place above a restaurant. The kind of place you don't go with your wife in tow . . ."

I had no idea whether there was a card school above the restaurant I'd named. But I did know it was only a block away from somewhere I'd be safe.

Troye's gallery.

ROYE'S GALLERY WAS, OF COURSE, CLOSED.
I stood in front of the building, wondering what to do next and worrying about prying eyes in the darkness around me, when I noticed a car parked in the corner of the gallery's tiny lot. Just one, on its own. A Rolls-Royce. Maybe from the 1970s. Not old enough to be really valuable. Not new enough to impress anyone. But still a classy ride. The kind of car you buy to please your own eccentric taste, not to fit in with the crowd. And given that it was painted metallic gold, only one person's name sprang to mind. Troye's. I moved over to take a closer look and when I saw the license plate—ART-LVR—there was no doubt left. Troye had to be nearby, but where?

I went to check around the back of the gallery in case there was an office entrance. Maybe he was working late. Troye didn't strike me as a paperwork kind of guy, but you never knew. There were two large, evil-smelling Dumpsters crammed into the space below a rusty metal fire escape at the north side of the building, so I crossed to the south and made my way cautiously into the shadows. A single naked light-bulb was burning farther ahead. I hurried toward it. Beneath it was a plain gray door. The faint remains of painted-out graffiti were still vis-ible across its surface. There were no windows, no mailbox—not even a company name marked anywhere—but there was an intercom. I hit the button, more in hope than expectation. There was no reply. I tried it one more time, and was about to turn and hurry away when the tiny speaker crackled into life.

"What is it?"

"Hello? I'm looking for Troye Liptak."

"Who is?"

"I'm a friend of his." I wasn't about to broadcast my name, with the police searching for me.

"What's this about?"

"It's personal. I need to speak to Troye. Urgently!"

"The gallery's closed. Come back tomorrow."

"No, wait. Please. Is Troye there? I really need to speak to him. Is he there?"

"You're wasting my time. Tell me who you are, or get lost."

"I'm Marc Bowman," I said, in desperation. "And I want—"

"Marc? Is that you? This intercom's crap. I didn't recognize your voice. Wait there. I'll be right down."

I heard a door slam somewhere inside the building, then heavy footsteps on creaky wooden stairs. Chains rattled, a lock ratcheted back, and finally the door swung open to reveal a plump bald guy in a stained T-shirt and ratty sweatpants.

"Thank you. I'm looking for . . . Troye, is that you?"

"Of course it's me. Who else did you expect to be in my apartment?"

"But your voice? Your accent's different. And your clothes. And your . . ."

"Hair? I wear a wig when I'm working. It's part of the costume. Like the suits. No big deal. But what you see now—this is the real me."

"Why?"

"I'm an art dealer, Marc. That means I need to look like one, if I want to eat. You think people from round here are going a trust a slob from Paulsboro, New Jersey, to help them invest their millions? Of course they're not. They want an exotic East European with a flamboyant taste in clothes. So that's what I give them."

"OK. I'm just . . . surprised, I guess."

"You can't take anything at face value in this world, Marc. You should know that by now. Anyway, what's up? Look at you. Is that blood on your coat? And your face? It's filthy. Did you get mugged or something?"

"It's a long story. And no, honestly, I'm not OK. I need help, Troye. Can I come in? Tell you about it?"

"I suppose you better. But it's Brian."

"What is?"

"My name. It's Brian. That's what my friends call me."

THE MAIN ROOM IN Brian's apartment was a giant rectangle, the full length of the gallery beneath and maybe three-quarters of the width. One end was set up as a small kitchen, and there was a broad arch in the far wall that I guessed led to his bedroom and bathroom. One of the remaining walls was taken up with floor-to-ceiling bookshelves, and the other was filled with a random jumble of paintings and drawings. The floor was covered with rugs—maybe a dozen, different sizes and patterns—which didn't quite meet in places, revealing patches of rough, unfinished floorboards. There was no TV or stereo, and not much furniture. Just a coffee table, a worn La-Z-Boy chair, and a couch that looked like a reasonable copy of a Robin Day design from the sixties.

"Make yourself comfortable." Brian gestured to the couch.

I lowered myself down, happy to rest my aching muscles.

"Are you hungry? Have you eaten? I have leftovers."

"Now you mention it, yes. I'm starving. Thirsty, too."

"Leave it to me." Brian crossed to the kitchen area and pulled a cardboard delivery box and a bottle of Evian out of the fridge. "Eat. Drink. Then tell me what the hell you've gotten yourself into."

BRIAN SAT IN THE CHAIR opposite me and between bites of cold pepperoni and spinach pizza—a strange combination, but it worked—I replayed everything that had happened since I left his gallery on Monday. Well, not quite everything. I didn't get into every last detail of the situation with Carolyn. I gave him the sanitized version that I'd fed to the police and Homeland Security. I figured that would be enough for him to get the gist of things.

"I don't believe you, Marc." He leaned forward and the impassive expression on his face finally cracked.

"It's true. Every word. Which part don't you believe?"

"I believe what you're telling me. I just don't believe you'd come here. To my *home*. What were you thinking, dragging me into this? This is your mess. It has nothing to do with me."

"I need help. I've got nowhere else to go."

"What if you were followed? I'm harboring a fugitive right now. Did you think of that? If I get arrested, do you know what that'll do to my business? And these other guys? With the bikes? Whoever they are? Sounds like they'd do a lot more than flush the gallery down the toilet. Probably flush me down there with it."

"You're right. I'm sorry. I shouldn't have involved you. But I didn't know what else to do."

Brian crossed to the window and peered out.

"OK." He stepped back after a moment and flopped into his chair. "Well, you're here now, and no one's kicked the door down. Yet. So, I'm thinking industrial espionage? Is that what this thing's about?"

I shrugged.

"I bet it is." He nodded encouragingly. "I bet there's a secret on those memory sticks, and that's what the motorcycle guys were after."

"Maybe. But I can't think what. There's only a bunch of run-of-the-mill data on the sticks."

"Not run-of-the-mill if there's a new kind of virus, too."

"New viruses appear all the time."

"Maybe. But you thought the virus was to spy on your work. What if you're wrong? What if AmeriTel's the target? Like I say, industrial espionage."

"If it was just the police after me, I'd buy that. Maybe. Or the FBI. But not Homeland Security. They don't get out of bed for stuff like that."

"If it was about a company's secrets, I was thinking there might be a few dollars to be made." Brian crossed to the couch and sat down next to me. "But sabotage of a government database? That's big-time. Maybe you should think about turning yourself in. Homeland Security, you can't outrun."

"I would, but who do I trust? Peever? Or McKenna? What if I pick the wrong one? I need to figure out who's on the level, first. And I need proof that I'm not involved, in case I get it wrong."

"How do you do that? What do you need?"

"I don't know. A bed for the night? I need time to think. I'm making this up as I go."

"No." Brian shook his head. "No way. You're not spending the night here. That's way too dangerous."

"Brian, please. I've got nowhere else to go."

"No. And don't ask me again. Don't make *me* the asshole."

I looked around the room, taking in all his possessions. I thought about the years they must have taken to collect. The memories they must represent. And suddenly I was hit by a wave of guilt.

"You're right." I stood up. "It was stupid of me. I'll go. And if I get picked up, your name will stay out of it. I promise."

"Where?"

"What?"

"Where will you go?"

"I don't know. But I'll figure something out."

"Have you got any money?"

"No."

"What about your cell phone?"

"The Homeland Security agents took it."

"Good. They can track your cell phone. You're better off without it. OK. Wait here."

He disappeared through the archway and I heard a couple of drawers and maybe a cupboard being opened and closed. When he came back he was holding four things, which he gave to me—an old flip-style cell phone, a charger, a black suit jacket, and a wad of cash.

"That's a pre-paid phone. It's safe to use. And here's two hundred dollars. That's all the money I have in the house."

"Thank you." It took me a moment to overcome the surprise.

"You can't keep wearing your own jacket. And you better lose the old guy's suitcase. Just don't dump them anywhere near here."

"Right. Yes. And, Brian? I'll pay you back. As soon as I can."

"No rush. Now, listen carefully. This is what we're going to do about getting a roof over your head for the night. First, you're going to wash your face. And then I'm going to give you an address. It's a house. It belongs to a friend of mine. He's in Europe. I'm keeping an eye on the place. You should be able to walk there in ten minutes, quarter of an hour, tops. Find it, go to the end of the yard, and you'll see a wooden summerhouse. It won't be locked. You can sleep in there. But only for tonight. I'll come by tomorrow to straighten up. And if you're still there—"

The intercom crackled. Neither of us breathed for a moment, then · Brian crept back to the window.

"A squad car." He turned to face me. "I'm sorry, Marc."

He'd been alone, when he was fetching the phone and the cash. For what? A couple of minutes? Long enough to call 911 . . .

"I didn't call them, Marc." It was as though he was reading my mind.

"I know." I picked up Mr. Schmidt's suit carrier, feeling guilty for the suspicion. "I'll go down there. Give myself up. And don't worry. I won't drop you in it."

"Don't be stupid. I can take care of myself. I'll go down. You—go through the archway. Second door on the right. It leads down to the gallery. Get out that way. I'm not going to screw myself, but I'll buy you as much time as I can."

I MADE IT HALFWAY ACROSS THE DESERTED GALLERY, THEN STOPPED. Running had almost got me caught. More than once. Maybe it was time to hide?

But hide where? I knew the gallery well, and nothing sprang to mind. There were no alcoves or storerooms, and all the sculptures in the place that night were too short. The only other option was the desk. But was that too obvious? It was a giant thing, antique, probably French, made from polished mahogany with gold inlays and grotesque Grecian statues supporting the four corners. It completely dominated one corner of the room. Brian couldn't have found a more extreme contrast for the brand-new iMac he'd placed on it if he'd tried.

An iMac? That set my thoughts running in a completely different direction.

I rushed to the desk, woke the computer, and searched for a connection to the gallery's security system. Twenty-nine seconds later I was inside the CCTV archive. I located the records for Monday. Identified the file for the parking-lot camera. Opened it. Skipped ahead to lunchtime. And found the image of me, striding back to my Jaguar.

Holding my breath, I isolated the video frames I needed—starting with me two paces from the car—and imported them into the Mac's home movie program. A few keystrokes later, I'd made the background darker to roughly approximate the parking lot at night. I turned the computer around so its screen was facing the door to the stairs. Crossed to the main exit. Pushed it open, triggering the alarm. Then dived under the desk, taking the Mac's wireless mouse with me.

The door crashed back on its hinges four seconds later, and I simultaneously clicked to start playing the doctored camera footage.

"Look!" A voice yelled above the racket. "He's outside."

Heavy footsteps sprinted across the floor, but I couldn't be sure the cops had really left. And I couldn't hear anything else above the screeching of the alarm, which was boring into my head, stopping me from thinking straight. Eventually I peeped out from behind the desk. I caught sight of movement. But it was only Brian, keying his code into the alarm console and shutting off the infernal noise.

"Marc, you devious bastard!" Brian spun around when he heard me emerge. "Amazing move, my friend! But the cops won't be fooled for long. They'll be back. You better hurry. Grab your things. You remember the address I gave you? Where the summerhouse is? Go there. Quickly. You'll be safe."

I retrieved the jacket and suit carrier, then Brian bundled me out through the door. He slammed it behind me and I was left silhouetted against the pale building. The hairs on my neck prickled in the chill night air. Somewhere to my left I heard a motorcycle engine. A deep growl like a Harley, not the trail bikes from earlier. But still, it broke my trance. I started to run, replaying Brian's directions in my head, when another sound reached me. A siren. I changed course and dived behind Brian's Rolls-Royce. Seconds later the parking lot was flooded with pulsing red and blue light. Then the sound and the colors abruptly died, the motor fell silent, two doors slammed, and a pair of heavy feet pounded away from me across the asphalt.

I peered out in time to see two officers disappearing around the side of the gallery, heading for the entrance to Brian's apartment. If I was going to escape, this was my chance. I counted to thirty, giving Brian time to come down and open the door. Then I broke cover.

For a moment I wished I'd taken the keys to the Rolls, but then thought better of it. A gold Rolls-Royce is hardly a discreet getaway vehicle. And stealing his car wouldn't have been fair to Brian, after all he'd done to help me.

Wait. What *had* Brian done to help me? The police had turned up at his apartment, and his first thought had been to deny calling them. Why? Then he'd sent me down to the gallery, which was pretty much a dead end. When I didn't get caught there, what was his top priority? Before kicking me out? To make sure I remembered the address of the summerhouse. The unoccupied, perfect-for-an-ambush summerhouse. And now the police had returned, just as he'd predicted they would.

Or just as he'd known they would?

The officers had been in Brian's apartment for too long. What were they talking about up there? Had he sold me out yet? Or were they still negotiating? Haggling over the price on my head? Changing tack, I headed for the north side of the gallery. I slipped Brian's jacket on over the top of mine. Swung the suit carrier up onto the first Dumpster. And sprang back as something launched itself at me from the darkness. A cat, all claws and teeth and fury, howling and hissing and slashing at my face. I swung the bag, using it like a shield, and pushed the animal away. Then I scrambled up onto the Dumpster, and from there onto the fire escape.

The door from Brian's apartment had a window, and through it I could see—nothing. He'd hung a curtain over it. And I couldn't hear anything, either. Whatever was going on at his little summit meeting, it remained a mystery. All I'd done was waste precious minutes that I could have used to put some distance between me and the police. Frustrated, I started back down the fire escape and was about to lower myself onto the Dumpster when I heard two car doors slam. An engine start. A siren spool up. Tires squeal.

Whatever Brian had told them, the cops had left in a hurry. There was no way I could risk the summerhouse now.

But where else could I go?

SLEEP CAME TO ME SLOWLY THAT NIGHT.
The metal rungs that formed the platform at the top of the fire escape were square, but they were set at an angle with their sharp edges pointing upward. They were painful to lie on so I unzipped the suit carrier and laid it out as a makeshift mattress, using the old guy's rolled-up dress pants as a pillow and his dinner jacket as a comforter. His shoes served no immediate purpose but I held them in reserve anyway, in case the cat came back for revenge.

The wind plucked at my clothes, chilling me, and carrying a constant barrage of sound. A persistent car alarm. Passing vehicles. A helicopter. A couple staggering home at three am, drunkenly squabbling. Stray dogs barking. The odd car stereo, cranked up to eleven. And the muffled bass notes of the music Brian kept blaring in his apartment to drown out his guilt.

BRIAN WAS STILL INSIDE when I awoke, shivering, in the early hours. But the guilt had relocated to my side of the wall. What was wrong with me? There was no reason to believe Brian had betrayed me. If anything, the opposite was true. He'd gone out on a limb to help me, and all I'd done was mistrust him. Despite taking his money. And his things. I'd even thought about stealing his car. So I resolved, there and then, that when the nightmare was over I'd make it up to him. And that wasn't an idle promise. Because at some point, between the noise and the discomfort and the fitful moments of sleep, I'd had a revelation. And from that, at last, I could make a plan.

The data I'd taken from AmeriTel wasn't—on its own—the key. What really mattered was *the virus*. Discovering it on my laptop was what had gotten everyone worked up into a frenzy. But there was also something critical about my home computer. Something serious enough for someone to steal it from under the detectives' noses. I couldn't see how everything was connected, before. But now the beginning of an explanation was coming—very slowly—into focus.

The laptop had been at AmeriTel's offices, hooked directly into their corporate network. My home computer hadn't been, but I'd loaded it with AmeriTel data to test my new algorithms. So, the common factor linking the two computers was AmeriTel. The company was the epicenter of whatever was wrecking my life. The virus *must* have come from there.

McKenna was on the right track. He'd been keeping AmeriTel—including Carolyn—under surveillance for a while. It didn't throw any light on Peever's real intentions, though. Or the identity of the guys who'd attacked us on the bikes. But that didn't matter. I could sidestep them. All I had to do was call Homeland Security directly and report a suspicious virus on AmeriTel's computers. Give them time to go and check. Then surrender to the police. Once I was proved innocent, someone else from Homeland Security could protect me. Finding out who all these other players were would be their problem. And they might even be able to catch whoever'd stolen my prototype, as a bonus.

THE BATTERY IN THE CHAUFFEUR'S phone died before its browser could open again, so I hit the Power key on the old Motorola Brian had lent me and waited impatiently for it to light up and find a signal. I called the operator, and she didn't miss a beat when I asked for Homeland Security. She even offered to connect me. Within seconds I was through to an automated service, which came as a relief—it's easier to lie to a machine—and I happily spun a tale about what I'd found when I was working for AmeriTel.

———

I FIGURED THAT TWO HOURS should be long enough for Homeland Security to take some action. Cautiously I made my way down to ground level, in case anyone spotted me and I had to run again. And then I settled back into the shadows to wait.

Normally hanging around for that length of time would drive me crazy, but that morning things felt different. I wasn't exactly happy—that implied something more active—but I was certainly content. Like when you've just taken a long, hot bath after a grueling session on the tennis court. Only after a couple of days of being the ball—and getting smashed all over the court by unseen opponents who were playing by their own private rules—I was finally back in charge of the game.

The first hour I spent resisting the urge to try Carolyn's number, still anxious about the consequences. And the second being bounced repeatedly into her voicemail. The only consolation was that she had no way to recognize the number I was using, which meant she wasn't ignoring me in particular.

Then, when I was finally ready to leave, another upside dawned on me. I didn't need to go off wandering the streets in search of the police. I had a cell phone and two detectives' cards.

The police could come to me.

*O*UR DESTINATION WAS TWENTY MINUTES' DRIVE AWAY, BUT NEIther Hayes nor Wagner said a single word to me the whole time we were on the move.

The station house was a square, single-story structure with brick walls, a flat roof, and bars on the windows. It reminded me of a doctor's office I'd visited once, when I was in college. I was helping Carolyn do community service in a housing project. Only this building was about fifty times bigger, and it wasn't swathed in razor wire.

Hayes dumped the car in a lot that was separated from the rest with thick red lines and she and Wagner led me to a side entrance. A pair of glass doors parted and the detectives ushered me into a small, square room. It was divided down the center by a chest-high wooden counter, and the air was heavy with the stink of sickly sweet disinfectant. An older, uniformed officer on the other side of the divider got to his feet as we approached. Hayes nodded to him, and he smiled back at her. The old cop made a show of looking me up and down—filling me with a strange sensation, as if he could somehow see right through my clothes—then he slapped a large Ziploc bag down on the countertop.

"Possessions," he said.

I looked at Hayes. She nodded, so I picked up the bag and filled it with my keys, Brian's cell phone and charger, and the money he'd lent me. I'd dropped the chauffeur's phone in one of the Dumpsters outside the gallery along with the old guy's suit carrier and clothes, not wanting to explain how I came to have them.

"Sign." The officer slid the bag to his side of the counter and handed me a worn wooden clipboard with a blank form attached to it. A cheap ballpoint pen dangled from it on a length of filthy twine.

"It's not filled in," I objected.

"Sign," he insisted.

Hayes nodded, and I figured it wasn't worth making a big deal out of. Aside from the keys, none of the stuff was too important. The phone wasn't mine. The cash could be replaced. And soon I'd be home with this living hell safely behind me. I smiled and scrawled my name across the bottom of the page. Although I did use the vague "deniable" version of my signature I'd developed years ago in my first job.

The officer took the clipboard back, grunted, then hit a button that released a door to our right. It opened onto a long corridor with more doors, evenly spaced along both sides. The detectives led me to the second from last on the left. Hayes opened it, and Wagner shoved me through. She pushed a lot harder than she needed to, and concentrated the force through one knuckle which gouged into my back, but when I turned to complain the door had already closed behind me.

The room was very simply laid out. There was a table in the center, and a chair on either side. All three were made of metal. And all three were bolted to the floor. A thin rubber strip ran around all four walls at waist height—probably a trigger for a panic alarm—and there was a CCTV camera in a metal cage in the corner above the door. The only other feature was a large mirror on one wall, but I'd watched enough cop shows to know that this would be made of one-way glass. So, in keeping with my new cooperative image, I sat down, clasped my hands on the table in front of me in my best Roger LeBrock pose, and tried hard to look innocent.

There wasn't a clock in the room, but I guess they kept me waiting for over an hour. My sense of well-being was ebbing rapidly and when I moved my arms and saw a line of words that had been crudely scratched into the tabletop, my spirits sank even faster:

your screwed theyll never let you go

It's a joke. It's not aimed at you, I was telling myself over and over, when the door opened and a woman walked into the room. She was very tall—over six feet, even in the flat shoes she was wearing—and very skinny, with shoulder-length auburn hair and a long, pointy nose. I couldn't help thinking that if you dyed her hair black and gave her a tall hat and cape, she'd sweep the board as a Halloween witch.

I stood up and held out my hand but she brushed straight past me, went to the spare chair, and sat down.

"My name's Agent Brooking. I'm sorry to keep you waiting, Marc, but I was on the phone. To my boss. He's not happy, because of you. And you know how these things go. Shit rolls downhill. Which means I'm not happy, either. So, now's a bad time for you to be playing games."

"I'm not playing games. I came here of my own free will. Because I want to help."

"When you come out with shit like that, remember Homeland Security still has agents in the hospital after your performance last night. Now, do you still say you're not playing games?"

"I do. People tried to kidnap me last night. I nearly ended up in the hospital myself."

"Yada yada yada. I won't ask again, Marc."

"I'm telling you. I'm not playing games."

The woman flashed a sour smile, then pulled Brian's Motorola out of her jacket pocket. She straightened a tag attached to its antenna, which showed its number. Then she placed a sheet of paper next to it—a call log—with an entry from that morning highlighted in yellow.

"You acknowledge this is your phone?"

I nodded.

"Do you really need me to do this?"

"Do what?"

She shrugged. Then she took out an iPhone, tapped the screen, and a sound file began to play. It was a recording of the call I'd made that morning. To Homeland Security. My tip-off about AmeriTel.

She let the recording run right through to the end. "No games, huh?"

I was stunned. My plan was unraveling before my eyes. It had never crossed my mind that they'd connect me with the phone call. All the confidence I'd built up earlier had deserted me and I suddenly felt stupid and out of my depth.

"Please. Let me explain. What happened was—"

"What happened was, on top of the six guys I've got on the disabled list till goodness knows when, because of you, I had another four tied up all morning on a wild-goose chase. Because of you, Bowman. So, stop bullshitting. And start explaining."

"The four guys this morning. They weren't on a wild-goose chase. Unless—you did send them to AmeriTel?"

"Oh, I did. Just like you wanted me to. I swallowed your story, hook, line, and sinker. Only, after going over AmeriTel with a fine-tooth comb, what do you think they found?"

"The virus. The one that was on my computer. AmeriTel's the only place it could have come from."

"Nope. They found nothing. No virus. Nada. Zip. Zero. Ameri-Tel's computers are as clean as the day they were installed."

"That's impossible. There's no way—"

"Forget this. We know the AmeriTel thing was just a diversion. You won that one. I concede. Now, let's talk about the virus. Did you create it?"

"No. Of course not!"

"Are you being pedantic with me, Mr. Bowman? Because I may not be a big computer expert like you, but I know enough to understand that a virus as complex as this one would be created by a team of people. What I'm asking is, are you a part of that team?"

"No. Absolutely not. I've never written any malicious code in my life. I'm a victim of this virus. I have no idea where it came from. If I didn't catch it from AmeriTel, I'm completely stumped."

"Oh, I doubt that. I doubt that very much. See, our programmers have been working around the clock, picking the virus apart. They've got a ways to go, granted. I'm not saying we know everything about it. But we know what it's designed to destroy. A particular combination of very specific machines. A combination that exists in only one place on earth. And unless the virus finds that exact combination, it lies dormant. Which makes it almost impossible to detect."

"Like Stuxnet?"

"Just like Stuxnet. Only this virus isn't aimed at Iranian nuclear centrifuges. Its target is the White House."

*T*WO WORDS WERE BOUNCING AROUND INSIDE MY HEAD. *Collateral Damage*.

They were words I'd only read before. In relation to hostage rescues in faraway, train wrecks of countries or drive-by shootings in the written-off, gang-ridden neighborhoods of distant inner cities. Dramatic events. Sometimes exciting. Usually tragic. But always completely divorced from my own life.

Until now.

Until I'd fallen down a rabbit hole and woken up, mute, in an alien universe. The virus on my computer was akin to Stuxnet? That was so far out of my league I could hardly comprehend it. Stuxnet was a bleeding-edge cyber weapon, used to cripple a foreign enemy's nuclear arsenal. Something from a world where a single misstep could mean all-out war. It could bring death and destruction on an unimaginable scale. Not the loss of a wife. A job. A new product. Another painting. What chance did I have, dealing with stakes like these?

Was *I* destined to become collateral damage myself?

It was a holding cell I'd been thrown in after the interrogation had come to an end, rather than a desert hideout. And they were accusations that were being fired at me, rather than bullets. But I was boxed in tight. I had McKenna on one side, sniffing around AmeriTel. Brooking on another, chasing down this insane plot. Then there was Peever—wherever his loyalties might lie—and the mystery guys on motorcycles completing the square. Carolyn had abandoned me in favor of her precious career—maybe even helping to jam me up in the first place—so she wasn't about to raise the alarm. No SEAL team was about to swoop down and rescue me. And how could I free myself, with the damn computer virus linking me to all of them like an unbreakable chain?

Worst of all, it was my own fault I was in that cell. I couldn't believe my plan had gone off the rails. What kind of idiot was I? I'd been certain the virus had come from AmeriTel. Nothing else made any sense. How could I have been so wrong?

I ran through the possibilities again, but nothing had changed. I was still convinced. It had to be AmeriTel. Unless—could Brooking have been lying to me? Could she have not sent the other agents there, after all? Or could they have missed it? If they were regular field agents, would they even know how to search for a virus? Particularly a new kind. One that everyone outside a specialized lab had missed. I was kicking myself for not questioning her more closely about that, but she'd thrown me for a loop with all her accusations.

I lay down on one of the benches that were bolted to the cell walls and tried to think. My performance in the face of Brooking's onslaught was spilled milk. There was no point crying over it. I'd just have to try to do better next time. That was my mantra with my work. Always make the next thing better than the last. Like my new project. It was going to— It was going to do nothing. Not for me, anyway. Not after the prototype had been stolen. My only copy had been deleted. And I was locked up, instead of sitting at my keyboard rebuilding it.

Wait. *Deleted.* Was that the answer? The prototype had been deleted from my computer by the time I came downstairs on Tuesday morning. Could the virus have been deleted from AmeriTel's system by the time the agents went there today?

If the virus was designed to attack the White House, there was no point in it being on AmeriTel's corporate network. But Peever had mentioned the ARGUS node that was in the same building. Maybe someone was planning to use that as a conduit? I didn't know how it was all connected—the topology was top-secret—but it was reasonable to assume that the President would want access to the most sophisticated intelligence system in the world. So if the ARGUS system was infected, could the President's own systems—at the White House, and wherever else he may be—also be infected?

Whoever was behind this must have known the virus had spread to my home computer. Which is why they'd had it stolen. They never wanted that particular computer to see the inside of a police lab. They couldn't risk someone finding any signs of infection. But my laptop had slipped through the net. It had already disappeared into the parcel carrier's system. It had accidentally become invisible in exactly the way I'd been accused of hiding it.

It made perfect sense.

I was off the bench and halfway to the bars at the front of the cell, ready to yell for Brooking, when my heart sank again. My theory wasn't enough to put me in the clear. It only accounted for what had been done. Not who had done it. She'd still believe I was involved.

I sat back down, and another sickening possibility hit me. Another reason for the agents not having found the virus at AmeriTel. Who's to say they actually looked for it? They might have ignored it on purpose. Or they might have found it, and covered it up. The dominoes of suspicion were tumbling in my head now, one after the other. Brooking could be behind everything. And Brooking could be working with Peever. They could be lining me up to take their fall.

No. Brooking and Peever couldn't be behind *everything*. They could be framing me for the virus. They could be pulling the strings at Ameri-Tel. But they couldn't be betraying my work to Karl Weimann. And they hadn't sold me out to boost their own careers.

Only one person had done those things.

Carolyn.

But what the hell kind of game was she playing? And who was she playing it with?

*T*HERE WERE NO WINDOWS IN THE CELL. THERE HADN'T BEEN ANY in the interview room, either. That meant I hadn't seen daylight since I stepped inside the building.

I didn't have a watch. Or a cell phone. And I couldn't see a clock, even if I went to the front of the cell and peered all the way down the corridor in both directions, craning my neck around so far it hurt.

I knew because I'd tried four times.

I understood, rationally, that I could only have been at the station house for a matter of hours. But emotionally, not knowing the time was killing me. There was too much I didn't know. All the unanswered questions were multiplying and combining and braiding themselves together like a rope around my chest. It was wrapping itself tighter and tighter around me, so hard I was struggling to breathe. I'd never been claustrophobic before, but all of a sudden I was desperate to leave that cell. I wanted a lawyer. I wanted answers from my wife. But more than anything, I wanted *out*. No amount of school or college or work experience or marriage can prepare you for getting locked up, on your own, for something you didn't do.

After twenty minutes I heard a sound in the distance. An alarm. I sat up, and for a moment I thought I could smell smoke. Then I was sure I could. *Smoke.* Which meant fire. In a building I was locked inside.

I grabbed the bars at the front of my cell and heaved against them with all my strength, but they wouldn't budge. I yelled for help, but the only answer that came was from a disembodied, automated recording:

> Attention. The fire alarm in this facility has been activated. This is not a drill. You are in no immediate danger. Go to the back of your cell and stand by for further instructions. You will soon be evacuated in accordance with police department emergency procedures. I repeat, you are in no immediate danger. *Atención . . .*

The message alternated between English and Spanish, and seemed to be on a perpetual loop. It was never reassuring—not even the first time I heard it—and before long it had become so annoying I was almost more eager to get away from it than I was to escape any flames.

Then, without warning, the announcement died mid-sentence and a uniformed officer appeared on the other side of the bars. A huge, stocky guy with the kind of overdeveloped chest muscles that prevented his arms hanging straight down at his sides.

"Turn around," he ordered. "Face the wall. Walk forward till your nose is touching the bricks. Good. Hands behind your head. Lace your fingers together. Good. Now, do not move until I tell you. Try anything cute, and I'll knock you out and leave you to burn. Are we clear?"

"Crystal." The smell of the smoke was getting stronger by the second, so I wasn't about to waste any time.

I heard the cell door open, then the officer cuffed my hands behind my back, spun me around, and drove me forward by jabbing something hard into my ribs. Then he steered me along the corridor, out through an emergency exit, and into the parking lot.

It was a relief to be outside, away from the cramped cell, but I didn't have much time to enjoy it. The air wasn't exactly fresh—exhaust fumes from dozens of vehicles were mixing with a plume of oily smoke that was rising from somewhere near the center of the building and blowing in our direction. And the whole area was a frenzy of activity. Scores of people—civilian aides as well as uniformed officers and plain-clothes detectives—were heading to their designated assembly zones, and the crews from half a dozen fire trucks were hurrying in the opposite direction, loaded down with hoses and other pieces of equipment.

The officer took me to the far side of the parking lot, away from the melee. I realized we were heading toward a cluster of four trucks. They were lined up a few feet apart, with their rear doors facing the building. The trucks' cabs looked standard, but the bodywork was tall, square, and utilitarian, like the kind the network engineers from AmeriTel use. Except that instead of a corporate logo painted on the side, these had DEPARTMENT OF CORRECTIONS PRISONER TRANSPORT stenciled in harsh, black letters.

The officer gestured to the truck at the end of the line.

"Where are you taking me?"

"Nowhere." The officer opened the rear door and shoved me toward the little step below it. "This is just to keep you out of harm's way till we get the all clear from the fire chief. Then you go back in the station house."

Inside the truck there was an empty space about three feet wide, then a wall made of metal mesh, which formed the mobile cell itself. The officer reached past me and pushed open a small door in its center, then jabbed me with his nightstick to encourage me to go through. He didn't release the handcuffs, but if he had, I bet I could have touched both sides of the vehicle without moving. I had the choice of a narrow metal bench on each side to sit on. There were no windows, and once the outer door was closed it looked like the only light I was going to get would have to find its way through a rectangle of opaque Plexiglas in the roof.

"I thought it was, *out of the frying pan, into the fire,*" I said. "Not the other way around. Look at this place. How long will I have to stay in here?"

"Till I get the green light on your regular cell."

"When will that be?"

"How should I know?" He stepped back and locked the mesh door. "Do I look like a firefighter to you?"

The outer door banged shut, and after standing in the semi-darkness for ten or fifteen seconds I sank down onto the right-hand bench, resolving to make the best of the situation. I was still wondering exactly how to do that when I heard a door slam ahead of me, in the truck's cab. Almost simultaneously the other cab door slammed, a little harder. Then the whole truck shook for a moment before settling back into an uneasy, coarse rumble. Someone had started the engine. I figured they must need it to power some kind of equipment. A heater would be nice. Or a light. But I was out of luck.

Instead, the truck started to move.

We reversed, turning in a wide, lazy arc, then lurched forward abruptly enough to tip me off my perch. The farther we got from the station house the faster we went, and I was beginning to feel seriously sorry for myself—pitching and rolling on the hard metal floor—when all of a sudden the truck swung hard to the right and braked to a halt. Nothing happened for a few moments, then my enclosure was flooded with light as the rear door swung open. The officer who'd led me to the truck appeared at the top of the step, leaned in to unlock the mesh door, and gestured for me to slide over to him.

"Turn around." He took a smaller key from a pouch on his belt. "Cuffs."

"Where are we?" I massaged my wrists. "Why did we leave the station house?"

"Ask the other guy." The officer squeezed past me and sat on the right-hand bench. "Go on. Get out."

I climbed down from the truck, struggling to believe what had just happened. And when I saw who was waiting for me at the base of the ladder, the situation didn't make any more sense.

It was Agent McKenna.

MCKENNA EASED THE TRUCK BACK OUT ONTO THE ROAD AND was surprisingly gentle with the gas until we were safely around the next bend.

"What's going on?" I asked, as we began to pick up a little speed. "Why did we leave the station house?"

"You were in danger. It wasn't safe for you there."

"Why not? What kind of danger?"

"I'll explain later. There's something I need to show you." McKenna winced as the truck's front wheel hit a huge pothole. "Thanks for getting me into that car last night, by the way. You've still got credit in the bank for that, no question. I'm just sorry we had to leave you behind. That wasn't part of the plan. Where did you go?"

"I found a place to crash." It struck me that I liked McKenna, in a strange kind of way. I wanted him to respect me, so I was in no hurry to confess how dismally my scheme to clear my name had worked out. "How's your head? If I'd hit the ground like you did, I'd still be out cold."

"It's fine. It looked worse than it was."

"Agent Brooking said you were still in the hospital."

"Agent Brooking has a habit of exaggerating." He winked at me. "Anything that woman tells you, take with a pinch of salt."

"And the accusations she throws around. Does the same go for them?"

"Definitely. First sign of trouble she starts slinging mud, and watches who it sticks to. Not scientific, but gets her results, I suppose. She's tossed a little in your direction?"

"The virus they found on my computer? She accused me of creating it. And using it to attack the White House."

McKenna let out a long, low whistle.

"Wow. She's really trying to lay the whole nine yards on you. Well, Marc, don't worry. We know you're not behind that virus, whatever it's supposed to do."

"Thanks. And the virus? It got onto my computer while I was working at AmeriTel, right? I can't figure out any other way it could have happened."

"Yes." He paused for a moment. "I'm sure it spread to your computer from there."

"Thank you." I felt my grip on reality grow a little tighter. And with that, I suddenly saw how another piece of the puzzle might fit into place. "The memory stick. The one that was stolen. That's why you pressed me on it, isn't it? You knew about the virus, even then. That's why you wanted the stick, or anything else that could have AmeriTel data on it."

"We knew about the virus," he admitted. "But we didn't know for sure it had spread. We needed to find out."

"Is that why someone broke into my house? To check if the virus was on my home computer?"

"I don't think so." McKenna reached out and adjusted his door mirror.

"But, maybe why the computer was stolen from the police?"

McKenna grunted, but I couldn't tell if he meant yes or no.

"How come you knew these things days ago, but Brooking and Peever were still in the dark?"

McKenna didn't respond right away, and for a moment I thought he'd clammed up for good. Then he raised his right hand, like he wanted to stop me from saying anything else.

"I shouldn't be doing this, Marc. You're a civilian. But you're up to your ass in this thing, and I think you've proved I can trust you. Just don't make me live to regret it."

"I won't. I promise."

"You better not. Because the picture I'm going to paint—it doesn't show the department in the best possible light."

"I understand. What you say in this truck stays in this truck."

"Good. Because the truth is, there's a helluva lot we just don't know. And part of that's my fault. Look at Peever. He's probably dirty. I should have twigged to that earlier. But Homeland Security's like any other agency, anywhere in the world. You're never quick to suspect your own."

"I get that. But what about Brooking?"

"She's clean, as far as I know. Only she was recently brought in, so she's not up to speed."

"And the police? The detectives, and the others?"

"In the clear, as far as I can tell." McKenna paused. We'd reached an intersection, and he couldn't turn left as he'd intended, due to some construction. "The problem is, they don't have high-enough security clearance. Fewer than a dozen people in the country do. That's why I couldn't let that officer stay within earshot when I pulled you out of the back."

"And the fire? At the station house? You started it."

"It was just a smoke generator. No flames. No damage done. Hits the spot every time. Want to get people running around like headless chickens? Make them think there's a fire nearby. Tap into their primal fear."

"And the motorcycle guys?"

"My guess, they're the muscle for whoever's behind all this. The attack—be it on ARGUS, the White House, or both—is going through AmeriTel. But we don't think it was dreamed up by anyone who works there. Their background checks all pan out. The AmeriTel guys are most likely just patsies."

"You know, you're the only one who doesn't try to bullshit me, or stonewall me, or frame me. And I appreciate that."

"You're a good—"

McKenna broke off mid-sentence as we swung through a tight turn and almost slammed into two cars that had just run into each other. Both were on our side of the road, blocking our way forward, and a man's body was sprawled in the other lane.

"Oh my God, they've had an accident!" I reached for my door handle. "We've got to help—"

"Leave it!" McKenna slammed the truck into reverse. "Get down. Ambush!"

The truck had moved back about three feet when McKenna stamped on the brake again. A man had raced across the road behind us. He was pulling a kind of chain. But instead of smooth round links, it was made of vicious three-inch spikes.

"A stinger." McKenna shifted into Drive and hit the gas again. "Can't risk it. The tires would shred."

He steered sharp left, accelerating hard, aiming directly for the body in the road. Our wheels were going to crush the man's head. I was about to shout a warning—how could McKenna not see what was happening?—when the guy raised himself up like a sprinter in the blocks and flung himself toward the curb. He was dragging something behind him. Another stinger. And he'd cut his move so fine there was no time for McKenna to react.

There were two bangs. Our tires had blown. McKenna fought the steering wheel, trying to keep going. For a moment I thought we might make it. But then the truck pulled left and shuddered to a halt. McKenna flashed a worried look in my direction, then pulled out his gun.

"Wait here." He opened his door. "Lock the truck after me. And stay down. Do not get out under any circumstances."

As he spoke, a third guy appeared from behind one of the wrecked cars. His face was hidden by a black balaclava, and he was holding something in one hand. A glass bottle. It was a quarter full with clear liquid and a rag was sticking out of the top. He had a lighter in his other hand, and with one swift movement he set fire to the rag, flung the bottle toward the truck, and ducked down out of sight. I heard the glass smash, and then a dull *whump* as the liquid went up in flames.

"Come on!" McKenna yelled, unnecessarily, because my door was already open. "The prison officer. In the back. We've got to get him out."

A pool of liquid was burning fiercely in my path. I started to loop around it, but someone grabbed my arm. It was the guy who'd thrown the bottle. He pulled me back, slammed me against one of the cars, and pressed a heavy brown envelope into my hand.

"RUN!" he said, then let go of me.

I stayed still.

"What are you waiting for?" he snarled. "Go."

"Who are you?"

"Your guardian angel. Now, go."

I hesitated, tempted to rip the mask from his face.

"RUN!" he snarled again. Only this time he pulled a gun.

FOR THE SECOND TIME IN TWENTY-FOUR HOURS I FOUND MYSELF running blindly through an unfamiliar neighborhood. Only this time, I knew exactly where I wanted to go.

I just had no idea how to get there.

The net was tightening around me so I forced myself to keep moving for another fifteen minutes, then paused to take stock of my situation. A giant oak at the side of the road gave me some cover, and as I leaned against its gnarled trunk, wheezing, I realized I was still clutching the envelope the guy in the balaclava had given me.

I tore it open and tipped its contents onto the ground. There was a cell phone, and a wad of ten-dollar bills. A couple of dozen of them. It was spookily similar to what Brian had given me at his apartment, the day before. Was he involved, somehow? Or was this a kind of standard urban survival kit, to be handed out to IT consultants on the run? I didn't waste too much time thinking about it, though. Because I knew right away I wasn't just looking at *things*. I was looking at a way to untie the noose from around my neck and turn it into a lifeline. Maybe the only lifeline I had left.

I powered up the phone, dialed a number for a pizza restaurant, and gave the address I could see painted on a shiny red mailbox on the other side of the street. Then I settled down to wait, dreading the howl of a siren or the pulsing of red and blue lights.

Twenty minutes later I picked up the sound of an engine. But not a throaty V8 like the police use. More like a couple of bees in a beer can. Moments later a delivery guy wobbled into view on a decrepit moped.

He pulled up at the side of the street, opposite me. Took off his helmet, and hung it on the handlebars. Then retrieved a pizza from the insulated box behind the saddle and set off up the drive on foot.

I ran to the bike and strapped on the helmet. I took half the money from the mystery guy's envelope and left it on the ground, weighed down with a stone. Then I fired up the tiny engine and launched myself onto the road.

I hadn't ridden a moped for ten years, when Carolyn and I spent a week together in Rhodes. I'd been happy tooling around the island, back then, recharging my batteries at the beaches and the bars. Her plans had been more ambitious. She'd been obsessed with taking a ferry to Turkey, to see the remains of some ancient theater. The clash of agendas hadn't made for a peaceful vacation. But it had taught me to move fast on two wheels.

I made it as far as my street without a problem, but then I spotted two cars parked near the entrance to my driveway. Both were dark blue, unmarked Fords. I drew level with the first one, and its engine roared into life. I managed another ten feet before it started to move. It was coming after me, with its twin glued to its tail. I eased back on the throttle, deflated. There was no way I could outrun them. But the cars swept past me, still accelerating, until they were around the corner and out of sight.

My heart was racing as I looped around, coasted to the side of the road, and killed the engine. Then I started to wheel the bike down my drive, trying to balance my urge to get out of sight with the need to move quietly across the gravel.

I reached my door, and realized there was another problem. I didn't have a key. It was still at the police headquarters. But I'd come too far to give up. The house had plenty of windows. I could break one. Climb inside. Get what I needed. And disappear back into the night.

The question was, which window? Do smaller ones make less noise when they shatter? Or would it make more sense to break one in the kitchen, to be closer to my objective? I was weighing my options when it occurred to me that if glass had to be broken, there was a better option close at hand.

I picked up a small, pointy stone and crossed to the trunk of my

Jaguar. I smashed the lens covering the license-plate lamp. Removed the bulb. Used the clasp on the helmet strap to bridge the terminals, which shorted out the light. And with it, the central locking. Just as the auto club guy had done last summer, after Carolyn had locked the keys in the trunk in her haste to drag me to *The Tempest* in Central Park. And that guy'd had a whole van full of tools at his disposal . . .

My garage remote is built into the Jaguar's sun visor so I reached in and hit the button. The door began to clank its way up, agonizingly slowly. I waited until it was half open then ducked underneath, crossed to the kitchen door, and let myself inside. I lifted up the loose section of countertop, held my breath, and slid my fingers into the gap. Sure enough, the memory stick was still there. I pulled it out, dropped the slab back in place, and turned to leave.

Only I couldn't. Because my path was blocked.

A man was standing in the doorway.

*P*RETEND TO WITHDRAW, AND BRING YOUR QUARRY RUNNING OUT into the open. A ruse that's been in use since Genghis Khan's time. Probably longer. And I fell for it. I felt like a twenty-four-carat fool.

"Officer, this isn't how it looks. Or should that be *Agent*?"

A hint of a smile spread across the guy's face.

"No agents here, Marc." He shook his head. "And the police? They were the guys who just left."

"You know my name?"

"I know all about you."

"How—"

"Doesn't matter how. I know."

"No. I was going to ask, how did you get rid of the police?"

"It's amazing what a well-placed anonymous tip can do."

Not when I tried making one, I thought, which did nothing to lift my spirits.

"OK," I said. "What do you want?"

"The memory stick. That's all. Put it down, and back away slowly."

I didn't know what to do. The guy looked like he meant business, but I needed that memory stick. Without it, I'd never get the police and Homeland Security off my back. I felt my fingers tighten, pressing it into my palm.

"Put it down." The guy shifted his weight very slightly so that his jacket gaped open, revealing the handle of a pistol. "Drop it on the countertop. All I want is the memory stick. Then I'll leave."

A sudden shiver rippled down my spine, triggered by something in the tone of the guy's voice. I'd heard it before. Earlier that day. And then it clicked. This was the guy who'd thrown the Molotov cocktail. The one who'd given me the money and the phone, and told me to run. Only when I'd met him earlier, his face had been hidden. Now it wasn't. I could see him clearly. I'd be able to describe him to a sketch artist without any problem at all. And I couldn't imagine a single circumstance where he'd leave me alive to do that.

"You'll let me go, if I give it to you?"

"Absolutely. The stick is all I want."

"OK. You can have it. No problem. But can I keep the other one?"

"What other one?" He took a step into the room.

"Well, I had three. I brought them home from my old job, after I got fired. One got stolen—I had a break-in—and the police are doing nothing about getting it back. You're going to take this one. Can I keep the third one? I'm being cooperative, here. And the data on that third stick would really help me with my research."

"You stole that data." He took another step toward me. "So, no. You can't keep any of it. You can't start trying to do deals for it. You can't use it in your research. What you can do is give it to me. And then forget you ever met me."

"OK, OK." I held my left hand up as if in surrender and used my right to slip the stick into the back pocket of my jeans. "You can't blame me for asking. Nothing ventured, nothing gained, right? I'll get it for you right away. You're welcome to it. And after that, if anyone asks, no one was here tonight. Not you. Not me. Not anyone else. OK?"

"Get it, then. What are you waiting for?"

"Give me two minutes." I tried to steer a path around him to the door. "I'll be right back with it."

"Are you looking to take a beating?" He stepped across, blocking my way. "Where is it?"

My mind was in overdrive. If I couldn't run, I'd have to hide. Or barricade myself in, somewhere. But where? Ours was a regular suburban home. It hadn't been designed with defense against home invaders in mind. There certainly wasn't anywhere suitable on the first floor. What about upstairs? The attic? That was the farthest away. But no. It wouldn't work. The retractable ladder was broken. It shot uncontrollably down through the trapdoor when you opened it, and always took five or ten tries to fold it back up. So where else? Our bedroom, maybe? The door had a lock, and if I could get in fast enough I could drag the dresser in front of it for extra security. That should be enough to hold the guy at bay for a few minutes, at least.

"It's in the safe. It'll only take a moment to grab it. Why don't you—"

"Bullshit. I already checked. The safe was the first place I looked, Monday night. There's only passports and papers in there."

"The safe in the bedroom?"

"In the home office."

The bastard had been in my study while I'd been upstairs, drunk and asleep. And that creeped me out more than the current situation with him standing in front of me, armed and full of threats.

"That's the old safe. The last owners installed it. The really valuable stuff I keep upstairs, in the new one. It's much better."

"In the master bedroom?" He sounded suspicious. "Where? I didn't see one."

He'd been in my bedroom, that night? What if Carolyn had been there? I felt a surge of anger start to replace my fear.

"It's very well hidden. Impossible to find if you don't know it's there. That's why it cost such a fortune."

The guy didn't look convinced, so I pressed on before he could ask any more questions.

"Come on. I'll show you."

He let me walk down the hallway in front of him, but I paused at the bottom of the staircase, foolish enough to try one more thing.

"There's no need for both of us to troop up there. Hang out here, if you want. I'll grab it and be right back down. The bedroom's on the second floor. Where am I going to go?"

"Shut up and move." The guy planted a hand between my shoulder blades and shoved hard. I went down, face-first, into the stairs. The edge of a tread hit me just below the bridge of my nose. I heard a crunch and felt a sharp, stabbing pain. Two, three, four red dots appeared on the carpet, looking like burn holes in the light-colored pile, and when I lifted my head I could feel the blood running down onto my chin.

I scrambled up the first few stairs on all fours, like a child. My upper front teeth felt like they were falling out. My heart was slamming against my ribs like a hammer, and that made me think—dresser or no dresser, I wasn't going to be able to keep this guy on the right side of my bedroom door for long, given the strength he'd just shown. And the temper. I'd need help. But who could I call? McKenna? Was he still alive? The last time I'd seen him he was trying to rescue a man in a burning truck from three armed attackers. The odds of him having survived weren't good. That only left the police. They'd arrest me. Throw the book at me for breaking out of jail. Resisting arrest. All kinds of things. Or hand me over to Brooking, who'd add whatever had happened to McKenna to her list of accusations. But it was a risk I'd have to take. Jail—or Guantanamo Bay—was better than the cemetery, even if it was unjustified.

The guy stayed tight behind me on the stairs. But when we reached the top he dropped back, offering me a brief glimpse of an alternative way out. He was bigger and stronger, but I was lighter and—I hoped—faster. So I feinted right, the opposite direction from the bedroom, then twisted back around and made a desperate leap for the stairs. If I could get to the hallway before him it would give me half a chance. To run back to the kitchen. Or dive out through the front door. I didn't care which. All that mattered was getting away.

The factor I hadn't bargained for was the length of the guy's arms. What he lacked in speed, he made up for in reach. He just stretched out, grabbed me by the collar, and hauled me back up to the landing. Then he flung me forward, slamming me into the wall. I spun around and collapsed onto the floor. The blood from my nose was gushing again, running down the back of my throat, choking me, so I rolled onto my front, struggled to my knees, and half spat, half puked the warm sticky mess onto the carpet.

Carolyn's going to kill me, I thought absurdly.

Before I could move he was on top of me again. He seized my belt as well as my collar and launched me forward, even harder. Only this time he didn't throw me straight. I veered sideways, away from the wall, and crashed against the spindly wooden uprights that support the bannister rail. Several gave way under my weight, leaving nothing between me and a nine-foot drop to the solid floor below. I scrabbled and flailed my arms, desperate to arrest my momentum, but couldn't find anything to hang on to. My eyes clamped shut and I braced for the long fall. But it didn't come. I stayed where I was. Poised on the brink. Then I was conscious of strong fingers clamped around my right elbow.

I'd been saved by the same long arm that had nearly killed me.

The guy helped me to my feet and I moved slowly as we made our way along the landing, trying to shake off the residual dizziness. He urged me forward, but I dragged my feet even more. Then, when we were ten feet from my bedroom door, I broke away. I dived into the room, slammed the door back into place, and forced my trembling fingers to work the lock.

Step one was complete. I was bleeding and bruised, but I'd done it. A burst of triumph exploded within me as I grabbed the dresser and started to pull, eager to finish the job. It moved easily at first. Then it slowed. And after eight inches, it stopped dead.

Strands of the carpet's long pile had wrapped themselves around its legs, snagging them like silky ropes. Cursing, I crouched down to free them. The edge of the door slammed into my arm. A whole section of the frame cartwheeled into the room, coming to rest at the foot of the bed. And then the guy appeared, lashing out with his foot and leaving me flat on my back, surrounded by splintered wood.

I'D HATED PLAYING CHESS WHEN I WAS AT SCHOOL.
Not because I couldn't understand the rules. Not because I was terrible at it. In fact, I usually won. But because of one kid. The only one who could ever beat me. And even then, it wasn't the losing that got to me. It was the expression on this kid's face. An expression that said, *Is that the best you've got? Really?*

I saw that same expression on the guy's face as he stood in my bedroom doorway, looking down at me sprawled on the floor.

"Are you a moron?" He stepped toward me. "Or do you just like pain?"

"Wait!" I scrabbled away and pushed myself up until I was sitting with my back against the bed. "You don't understand. I'm getting you the memory stick. I just didn't want you to see where the safe was. That's all. I'm sorry. It was stupid of me."

"There's no safe. And no other memory stick."

"There is. I swear. The safe's right here."

"OK. Show me. But no more stupid stunts."

"Of course. May I get up?"

The guy nodded.

I hauled myself back to my feet and shuffled toward the bathroom door. A picture was hanging on the wall next to it. A half life-size print of Lichtenstein's *VAROOM!* from the days after I'd graduated from posters but couldn't yet afford the real thing. I reached out, pretending to swing the frame away from the wall. Checked the guy's reflection in the glass, to make sure he wasn't moving. Then lifted the picture off its hook and flung it at his head like a giant square Frisbee.

I didn't wait to see if I'd hit my target. I just charged through the bathroom door, locked it behind me, and looked around for a weapon. I don't know what I expected to find, but as I scanned the towels and toothbrushes and shaving stuff I felt like I might as well have been in the cuddly animal aisle at a toy store. Then the door crashed open behind me so I snatched up a bottle of Carolyn's shampoo—plastic, unfortunately—pivoted, and threw it as hard as I could at the guy's head.

He leaned to the side and it sailed harmlessly past him.

"Tell me something." He took out his gun and used it to gesture toward a point on the wall to the side of my head. "What's with all these cartoons? You've got them everywhere. With all the money you've got, couldn't you have bought any real art?"

"Real art?" I ignored the echo of Carolyn's sentiments, reached out, and took down the picture he'd just pointed to. "Let me enlighten you. This was painted by Roy Lichtenstein in 1964. Each one of the dots was drawn by hand. If it were real, not a copy, it would be worth a few million dollars. And if you look closely, right here at—"

I jabbed at the guy's throat with the corner of the frame, but he saw it coming. He slapped me on the forearm with his left hand, knocking the picture out of my grip. It smashed into the wall above the bath and fragments of wood and glass rained down into the tub. Then he whipped his arm back the opposite way, slapping me on the side of the face and sending me staggering into the corner of the room.

"Listen!" The blood stung my tongue, making me lisp. "I'll give you the memory stick. There's only one, but I guess you've figured that out by now. And one of the paintings? The cartoons? It's real. It's worth a fortune. I'll show you which one. You can have it. You can take it, if you leave me alone."

"One of these kid's drawings is worth something? Which one?"

"I'll show you."

"Tell me."

I didn't reply, shaking my head, trying to clear my vision and wondering what on earth I could try on him next.

"Having trouble with your memory?"

He reached out and grabbed my collar and belt. Then he launched me sideways into the little set of shelves where Carolyn kept the clean towels and her spare potions. The wooden framework shattered and I half fell, half rolled onto the floor, surrounded by a scattering of dainty bottles and jars.

"Stand up!" The guy seemed eleven feet tall, looming above me.

I felt around in the debris for anything I could use to fend him off, and my fingers closed around a plastic bottle. A liquid—more of a thick green slime—was oozing out of a crack in its side. I waited until he was only inches away. Then I slammed the bottle down on the floor between us, covering a row of tiles with shiny, slippery gel.

The guy stepped over the puddle, grabbed me by the collar, lifted me to my feet, and punched me in the stomach.

"The valuable painting. Remembered where it is yet?"

I would have answered if I could have breathed, but as I struggled to suck in air he lost patience and shoved me backward into the bathtub. He planted one of his feet on my throat. Then he worked the lever that closed the drain.

"Last chance!" He was reaching for the faucet.

I couldn't believe he was going to drown me over a painting, but I changed my mind the instant the first drops of cold water hit my face. I started thrashing around, desperate to lift my head to safety, but his foot was pinning me down. My arms and legs were banging against the sides of the tub, and I could feel broken pieces of picture frame digging into my back. My right hand pulled back from something sharp and the sudden pain drove a desperate thought into my head. I reached out, forcing my fingers to seek whatever had just hurt them. It was a piece of glass. Triangular. Narrow. Maybe eight inches long and two across at the wider end. I scrabbled to get a grip. Then I raised it up and slashed furiously at the guy's leg.

I'd aimed high, and judging by the pitch of his scream and the volume of blood that sprayed in all directions, I must have hit something important. He released the faucet and staggered back, howling. I didn't see what happened next. All I heard was a hollow thud, then silence. I sat up cautiously, still gasping for breath, and peeped over the edge. The guy was sprawled out on his back, one leg—the one I hadn't stabbed—tucked awkwardly beneath him, his arms pointing straight out, and a crimson halo of blood crowning his head.

I had no medical training. I didn't physically examine him. But there was no doubt in my mind. He was dead. He had the same subtly relaxed contortion I'd seen once before, in the body of a guy who'd thrown himself on some electrified train tracks.

There was only one difference. The other time, the cause of death was suicide.

This time, the cause of death was me.

*I*T HAD NO LOCKS OR BARS, BUT FOR THE NEXT HALF HOUR THE bathtub held me as securely as any jail cell could have done.

In the end it was the relentless dripping of the water that forced me out. I'd turned my head to stop the drops from hitting my face, but the sound—one splash every second, like clockwork—was driving me crazy. So I stretched up to turn off the faucet, and whether it was the movement, or the sudden silence, the spell was broken. I climbed over the side and, stiff from the beating and the cold, I hobbled away from the bathroom.

I'd gotten almost to the front door when one of my senses finally returned. I couldn't go outside in those clothes. They were sprayed with blood, soaked in water, and covered with fragments of glass.

I returned to our bedroom and pulled on clean clothes, not really concentrating, just grabbing whatever was closest to the front of my closet and transferring my few remaining possessions. But before I could leave again a strange force drew me back to the bathroom door, like I was a mawkish spectator at the scene of a grisly car wreck.

I looked in at the body, steeled for a wave of revulsion, but it never came. The guy's remains no longer looked like a *he*. More like a thing. And then a practical, dispassionate voice started to whisper inside my brain. *Things can be useful, Marc. Turn over a rock, and you never know what you might find.*

I didn't take the dead guy's gun. That would be like inviting the police to shoot me, if I did get caught. I did take his wallet, though. There was no ID, but he wouldn't be needing the cash anymore. And his credit cards would be safer to use than mine, if I needed access to more funds.

Rifling through his jacket was one thing—I could lift it up, away from his body—but his jeans were another proposition altogether. Sliding your hand into another man's pocket seemed way too intimate. Inappropriate, even. More so when you're the one who just killed him. In fact, I nearly walked away without doing it. I would have, if it weren't for one more insistent thought at the front of my mind. I needed transport. Especially now that a man was dead. The stakes had skyrocketed. I couldn't risk using my Jaguar, even though it was sitting invitingly in the driveway. And this guy must have had wheels, to follow me here.

My hand hovered above his hip for a moment, then shot forward to grab his keys. He had two sets, clipped together. One was from a rental car company, with a logo I'd never seen before. The other bunch was bigger. And very familiar.

Because it belonged to Carolyn.

ALL THE FIGHT HAD GONE OUT OF ME, WHICH LEFT ONLY ONE option. Flight.

The last thing I did before running out of the house was grab my passport from the downstairs safe. South America. Europe. Australia. I didn't care. I just knew I had to get far, far away.

IF THERE'D BEEN ENOUGH gas in the dead guy's car to take me all the way to JFK, maybe I'd have gone through with it and tried to get on a plane. To put the maximum distance between me and his corpse and Carolyn and whoever else she was hooked up with. But when a little red light started flashing on the dashboard, that brought me back to my senses. Not all the way, but enough to persuade me to pause. So when I neared the next intersection and saw signs for accommodation, I pulled off the highway. I found the smallest and drabbest of the motels that were clustered around the sprawling cloverleaf. And I let the dead guy's credit card stand me a night's room and board.

I had no desire to eat or watch TV or even to get undressed. I just threw myself down on the bed. On top of the covers. The light was off. The curtains were open. My mind was still blank. But sleep refused to wash over me, so I lay still and stared up at the ceiling. It was stained. Maybe from a water leak. The line of vaguely round marks looked like the instrument panel in the dead guy's car. They reminded me of my first product. My life had seemed on such a promising track, back when I was developing that. How on earth had it led me from there to here?

Despite all the miles I'd driven that night, I felt like I was only going backward. I couldn't see the way ahead at all. And that made me think of something Roger LeBrock had said, a hundred years ago, back on Monday morning. He'd justified his decision to fire me by claiming I focused only on the past. That I had no eye for the future. I could have punched him for it, at the time. But now I was wondering if he had a point. Because my entire career was based on understanding what people did. Not who they were. Like myself. Was I a criminal? A thief? A fugitive? A murderer? I had no idea what the truth was anymore.

MY BODY HADN'T MOVED by the time my eyes opened the next morning—sleep having crept up on me at some stage—but my brain had been busy. It was telling me that things were nowhere near as hopeless as they'd seemed in the wee small hours. Because I had a key advantage. The memory stick. It was still safely tucked away in my pocket. And assuming the virus was on it—and it had survived the ordeal in the bathtub—that meant my lifeline was still within reach. The drawback was, I'd need help making sense of the secrets it held.

Asking for that kind of help wouldn't be easy. And wouldn't come cheap. I had to call Information to get the number I needed, because it wasn't a friend's. What would have been the point? And it wasn't a colleague's, because I was pretty sure they wouldn't have the stomach for what I had in mind. Greed can only take you so far. Instead, I asked the operator to connect me with a guy who'd be motivated by something else. The chance to step out of my shadow, once and for all.

The number I asked for was Karl Weimann's. I'd used him before, to torpedo Carolyn's career change. It seemed poetic to use him again now. And if Carolyn got caught in the crossfire, so be it. All was fair, after I'd almost been killed in our own bathroom.

"Karl?" He took an eternity to pick up. "Marc Bowman. Got a minute to talk?"

"A minute for you, Marc. Then I have to run."

"I'll keep it brief. The deal is, I'm working on something new. It's big."

"The Supernova?"

It was interesting he should ask that. The Supernova was the idea I'd had on the back burner when I started at AmeriTel. The one I'd been talking to Carolyn about, right around the time the photo of her and Weimann must have been taken.

"No." I forced myself to stay on track. "Something else. The Nova was going to be big. But the new thing—it doesn't even have a name yet—it's going to be massive."

"Sounds interesting. But why are you telling me?"

"Because I'm offering you a slice."

"How big of a slice?"

"Say, twenty-five percent?"

"What would I have to do?"

"Meet me. We'll talk about it."

"OK." He paused. "Where and when?"

"Today. My hotel. The Buckingham. In Harrison, just off the 684. Let's say, noon?"

"No can do. Too short notice."

"Well, it has to be today. It's a limited-time offer. Other people are interested. This thing's going to be huge, and you'll kick yourself if you snooze and lose."

"OK." He paused for longer. "You've got me. I'll be there. What room number?"

"I haven't checked in yet. I'll text you as soon as I do."

"I'll be watching my phone. Ciao, *partner*."

*C*AVEAT EMPTOR.

Buyer, beware. The oldest rule in the book when it comes to business. And however you chose to read my proposition—whether Weimann was buying a slice of my product, or I was buying a piece of his expertise—I was going into the deal with my eyes open.

I called the Buckingham and reserved two rooms in the dead guy's name, then I left the motel. I hadn't formally checked out, but since I was wearing the sum total of my possessions, and I had no wish to run the gauntlet at reception again—dopey as the clerk had seemed the night before—I didn't waste the time.

I recalled passing a giant Target store on my crazy drive from home, so after a brief stop at a gas station—one with a pay-at-the-pump option—I set off to find it again.

I parked close to the entrance and headed for the electronics aisle. First into the cart was a pair of Sony laptops. I didn't need the bells and whistles, but when you're shopping with a dead guy's credit card, why hold back? My next pick was a handful of memory sticks—the same brand I'd been using at AmeriTel. Then a few changes of clothes, in a variety of colors. Three baseball caps. A pair of reading glasses—the weakest they had. And finally a suitcase, to carry everything in.

THE HOTEL WASN'T QUITE where I thought it was, but after five minutes of rising anxiety I tracked it down. I found an out-of-the-way space to leave the car, put on the glasses and one of the hats, and made my way to reception. The clerk looked surprised when I asked for the rooms I'd booked to be at least four floors apart, but when I mentioned teenaged kids and stopping en route to an anniversary getaway, he grinned and said no more.

The higher room was on the twelfth floor, so I texted its number to Weimann and took an elevator to the seventh. That's where my second room was, all the way at the end of the corridor. Once inside I unpacked the new laptops, got them running—not hard, when you work with computers for a living—and set up a video link between them using the hotel's free wireless. Then I picked up the nearer one, slipped one of the new memory sticks into my pocket, and headed to the stairs.

The room on the twelfth floor had exactly the same layout as the one I'd just left. A pair of twin beds against one wall, with gaudily patterned covers and giant heaps of unnecessary pillows. A wardrobe, dresser, and desk against the other wall, in some kind of pale, fake wood. A doorway to a small bathroom. An uncomfortable-looking couch beneath the window. All perfectly functional, but nothing you'd miss—or even remember—five minutes after you left. Typical of a place designed as a stop along the way to somewhere else, not a destination in its own right. Appropriate in more ways than one, I thought, as I positioned the laptop on the corner of the desk and made sure its built-in camera had a good view of the entrance. Then I sat the memory stick on the other corner of the desk and left, careful not to let the door close all the way and lock itself behind me.

Back in my room on the seventh, I set the camera to privacy mode and checked the screen of the second laptop. The view was perfect. When Weimann arrived, I'd see him without him ever knowing I was watching. I'd see how he reacted to finding the memory stick. I'd see if he wasn't alone. I'd see if he'd sent anyone else in his place. And I was five floors closer to the exit. If I wasn't one hundred percent certain everything was the way it should be, I'd be out of the hotel and back on the highway before anyone even knew I'd been there.

All I had to do now was wait.

———

I'M NOT USUALLY ONE for changing horses mid-race, but after ten hour-long minutes it dawned on me that I was missing an opportunity. I'd left the fresh memory stick displayed prominently for a reason. It was a tell. If Weimann came because he wanted to work with me, it wouldn't mean anything to him. He'd ignore it. But if he came because he was already working with the crooks Carolyn was mixed up with, getting his hands on my memory stick would be his goal. He'd pounce on it. As would anyone else he sent. And if that did happen, wouldn't it be better for me if they were satisfied with what they took? The only guy whose face I'd seen was dead. What good would it do them to waste time trying to find me once they'd recovered their prize?

I took a deep breath and plugged the original memory stick and another new one into the laptop and set the contents to copy between them. I figured the laptop would get infected in the process, but I wasn't too worried. The one I'd used at AmeriTel had still worked fine, even once the virus had taken hold.

The file transfer took four minutes. That left eleven minutes before Weimann was due to arrive. Not much time to run to the other room, switch sticks, and get back to safety. I was wondering if I should just content myself with the original plan when my phone received a text.

Traffic brutal. ETA now 12:15. Sorry! KW.

I took that as a sign, said a silent prayer, and set off down the corridor with the freshly filled memory stick in my hand.

Friday. Lunchtime.

*T*HE DOOR SWUNG OPEN, FIVE FLOORS ABOVE ME, AND A FIGURE appeared on my computer screen. Tall. Skinny. Slightly stooped. Shorter hair. But definitely Weimann.

And he was on his own.

He walked forward hesitantly, looking around, puzzled to find no sign of me. I could see his mouth moving, as if he was calling out, but no sound made it through to my computer. He shrugged. Then stepped over toward the desk. Stopped. And picked up the memory stick.

He turned it over a couple of times, peering closely at it, near enough to the computer's camera for me to make out the lines of curiosity creasing his face. Then he tossed it down, turned his back, pulled out his phone, and started typing.

A couple of seconds later, my phone beeped.

I'm here. Where are you?

Just stepped out for a sec, I texted back. On my way back now. Please wait!

WEIMANN WAS SITTING ON THE BED when I arrived a few minutes later. He was wearing jeans and a black, pin-striped jacket over a purple paisley shirt, like one Carolyn had bought me once. The ensemble didn't suit him at all.

"What the hell, Marc?" he said, before I could even offer him my hand. "I cancel a long-standing appointment and drive two hours to meet you, and you're not even here?"

"Karl, I'm sorry. There was something I had to check on. It was important, believe me, or I'd have been here when you arrived. Anyway, we're both here now. This is going to be the start of a beautiful—and extremely lucrative—friendship, so let's not argue. Would you like a drink?"

"No, thanks."

"Lunch, then? I could order room service."

"I didn't come here to eat. Just tell me what you're proposing, Marc. Twenty-five percent of what?"

"OK. Here we go, then. Excuse the pitch. It's a bit rough. I've not told anyone about this before, but you're going to be blown away."

AS IT TURNED OUT, *blown away* wasn't the best way to describe his reaction. Judging by his expression, anyway, and the sardonic grunt he greeted my description with. I couldn't believe that deep down he'd failed to see the potential, though. Weimann was too smart. And too greedy.

"And my part would be, what?" he asked, when I'd finished.

"Bringing this piggy to market'll involve all the usual steps. You've done it a dozen times yourself. You know what they are. I have people lined up for the specialist stuff. But in this case, there's one extra thing that needs a little attention. Something unusual. I don't have the time or the resources, so that's where you come in."

"OK. Explain?"

"This is between us, OK? Because I don't want the unwashed masses talking about it. What's happened is—and I know this sounds bizarre, but I'm not making it up—I've been accused of creating a virus. It's like one of those bogus lawsuits people bring for the nuisance value. I can't move forward with the real work till that's dealt with, and I don't want any delay. I want you to take care of it. Find out who did create the virus. Where it came from. How it spread. As much detail as possible. That's up your alley, right? Everyone says you're the best at cyber security, and all that stuff."

"Oh. OK. So, you do all the interesting work—and later on take all the credit—while I sweep up the shit that someone's dumped at your door?"

"I wouldn't put it like that. It's important work, and we'll share the kudos—and the profit—just like I offered on the phone."

"No." He got to his feet. "No deal. I'm not interested. Clean your own house. Because honestly, Marc, screw you. Who do you think you are? Your days of lording it over everyone else are coming to an end."

I HAD NO IDEA WHAT MY NEXT MOVE WAS GOING TO BE.

None. Not even a hint of a Plan B. All I could imagine at that moment was escape. Scenes from South America flooded my mind, but they were culled from TV shows rather than experience. I had no idea which city would be best. Which country, even. And now that I was thinking straight, I knew flying was out of the question, anyway. With Homeland Security on my case—and the police, and whoever else— I'd never make it through airport security.

What about driving? How far away was Mexico? Or Canada? My desperation was getting the better of me when I heard my phone begin to ring, still in my pocket. I was in no mood to answer it, but the noise wouldn't stop. Whoever was calling wouldn't give up, either. Eventually I pulled the phone out, ready to silence it, but when I saw whose number it was, I paused. Then hit Answer.

"Marc?" It was Weimann. "Thanks for picking up, buddy. Can we talk?"

"About what?"

"I want to apologize for how we left things. I was way out of line." I didn't respond.

"The truth is, Marc, I've been hanging on to your coattails for so long, there is a little resentment in me. I didn't listen. I didn't give you a chance. But now I can see I made a mistake. I'm calling to find out if I can fix it. I appreciate the gesture you were making. And if your offer is still on the table, I'd love to talk about it."

I still didn't respond, but not because of any negotiating stance I was taking. Because I didn't have the mental capacity to form any coherent sentences right then. I was too astonished.

"Marc? You've gone quiet. Is that a *no*? Because I understand I screwed up. But, please. Don't pile another mistake on top of mine. That won't make things right."

"I know." I finally found my voice. "And it's not a *no*. I just lost signal for a moment."

"Great. Your offer stands?"

"It does. Are you in?"

"I am. With a couple of tweaks."

"Such as?"

"The virus thing. I don't want to get boxed into it. I'll take care of it first, of course. But then I've got some ideas for the real project I'd like you to consider."

"I'm always open to ideas, Karl. Of course I'll consider yours. But I'm not promising to run with them. It depends what they are."

"Good enough. They'll sell themselves. Next thing? When you pitch to major clients, I want to be right there with you."

"You can be in the room. But I decide what we present. And how."

"OK. You're the boss. Which leaves one last detail."

"Which is?"

"Money. I want fifty percent."

"I'm hanging up now."

"No, wait. Forty."

"The offer's twenty-five."

"Twenty-five's not enough."

"Forty's too much."

"Thirty-five?"

"Twenty-eight."

"Thirty?"

"Done. You buy the champagne."

"My house, an hour?"

"I can't. I'm still at the hotel."

"Leave now. You'll make it."

"You said you were two hours away."

"I was. But I wasn't at home then."

———

I TOSSED MY HASTILY packed suitcase in the trunk of the car, then paused. Could I trust Weimann? What if his change of heart was the result of another phone conversation? One with the AmeriTel guys. What if they'd told him to lure me to his place so they could finish what their crony had started back at mine?

I didn't like it, but there was only one way to find out.

Friday. Afternoon.

*I*F YOU SCALED DOWN A MAP OF WHERE I LIVE TO EIGHTY PER-
cent, you'd end up with a decent facsimile of Weimann's neighborhood. The lots were smaller, the trees were shorter, but the areas were
definitely similar.

I found Weimann's house and turned in off the street, afraid there'd
be police cars in the driveway. Or agents'. Or murderers'. But the car I
did see surprised me. It was a Jaguar. Parked outside Weimann's front
door. The same model as mine. And the same color. Racing green.

I rang the bell, jumping with every rustle from every bush.

"Nice car," I said, when Weimann finally appeared.

"Thanks." He turned to lead me through to his kitchen. "I wanted
the supercharged one, but Renée balked at the cost. She made me go
the pre-owned route, too. Women, eh? What can you do?"

I didn't reply. I was having too much trouble with the irony.

"Can I get you a coffee?" he asked.

"No, thanks." I glanced around the room. The units and appliances
were good quality, although it must have been a few years since they'd
left the factory. The countertop was solid granite, but there was a hazy
film all across the surface. A pile of empty pizza boxes was blocking the
draining board, and there were half a dozen dirty mugs in the sink. "I
already had too much, at the hotel."

He fixed a cup for himself and then directed me farther down the
hallway—skirting around a heap of muddy sneakers and a half-
dismantled golf cart—and into a room that was part office, part den. A

few framed certificates and photographs dotted the walls, and a collection of six prints was lined up neatly in two columns above the larger of his two desks. The image was the same in all of them—an Apple computer monitor, ancient, from the mid-eighties—and each one had been overlaid with a different bold color.

"I like the Warhol effect," I said.

"Thanks. It's fun. It's not an original Lichtenstein, though."

No shit, I thought, shifting a box of magazines from the least cluttered IKEA armchair in the center of the room and sitting myself down.

"All right," he said. "How do you want to play this? Shall we get started?"

"Why wait?" I pulled the newly replicated memory stick out of my pocket. "Only, be careful with this. It'll infect anything it comes in contact with."

"No problem." He took the stick, crossed to his smaller desk, and lifted the lid on a laptop computer. "This is an old machine. I dug it out as soon as I got home. It doesn't have Ethernet hooked up, and the Wi-Fi's switched off. We can keep it completely quarantined until we know for sure what we're dealing with."

WEIMANN WORKED WITH THE STICK and the laptop for thirty minutes, then spun his chair around to face me.

"You're making me earn my money with this one, Marc. I've tried everything. Every virus detector on the market, plus a couple that aren't, and all the other tricks I know to make a naughty little program show its face. Nothing worked. If you hadn't told me otherwise, I'd have sworn the stick's clean."

"Clean's the last thing it is. Whatever's on there is new, and it's clever. And we need to find out about it, or I could end up in jail."

"Don't worry. It won't come to that. I know a guy who can help."

"Oh? Who?"

"Best you don't know too much. We hooked up years ago. I can vouch for him. He owes me a couple of favors. OK, now, I've copied all the data onto the hard drive, just in case we need it, and I'll run the stick over to him now. He'll have something for us in a day or two, I would hope."

"Where is he?"

"Not too far away."

"I'll come with you."

"Better not. If he sees anyone he doesn't recognize, he'll bolt. You know how edgy these cyber nuts are. And he won't be able to help us if he goes underground. Look, I won't be gone long. In the meantime, make yourself at home."

"What if Renée gets back and finds me here? Won't she think that's weird?"

"Renée left me, Marc." He paused for a moment. "Seventeen months ago. I thought you knew. If anyone comes back and finds you, it won't be her."

"Oh. I'm sorry, Karl. I didn't know. What happened?"

"Remember that theater company she joined? Well, she ended up screwing the director. I found out. Confronted her. And she chose that long-haired ponce over me."

"That's awful. I'm truly sorry."

"Water under the bridge." He shrugged. "Occupational hazard. We may rake in the dough, but it's hard to compete with glamour, right? And power."

I was about to disagree, then I thought about my situation with Carolyn. And the photo of her and Weimann.

"Karl, did you know that Carolyn had wanted to join that company, but Renée took her spot? Right back when it was getting off the ground?"

"Of course. Everyone knew. But you didn't want to lose her fat paycheck from AmeriTel. So you fixed it for Renée to get the job instead of her."

"I'm sorry. I never would have done it, if I'd known what would happen with her and this asshole director."

"Bygones." He shrugged again. "Anyway, I'd have done the same thing, in your shoes."

"One more thing, Karl. Did you tell Carolyn about it? What I did?"

"No. But, Marc? I didn't have to. She's not stupid. She's known all along."

TIME HAS NEVER SAT easily on my hands. Being cooped up alone in a stranger's house was no exception and before long, like a pianist in a room with a Steinway, I gravitated to Weimann's laptop. I was desperate to find out what was happening in the outside world. Had the body been found in my house? Did the police have any leads? How hard were they looking for me? But the computer wasn't online. I couldn't risk hooking it up, because of the virus. So I moved on to the next best distraction. The AmeriTel data.

I found the files Weimann had copied from the memory stick easily enough. But that wasn't all. He had a prototype of a product I'd abandoned mid-way through its development. The *Dreadnaught*. No one should have it but me. My first reaction was anger. But my second was more worrying. Weimann had a stolen version of an older program. The thieves who broke into my house had stolen my newest one. What if there was a connection?

For every suspicion I quashed, another sprang into my head. It was like mental whack-a-mole, so to distract myself I fired up the *Dreadnaught* and used it to run some simple reports on the AmeriTel data. Nothing too profound—there wasn't time—but the type of simple toe-in-the-water routines I usually did at the start of a consultation.

Some clients are easy pickings. They have lots of closets, with lots of skeletons waiting to burst out. With others, I have to work a little harder to sniff out the juicy stuff. AmeriTel's data put them in the second category. But well-hidden secrets are no less tasty than the low-hanging fruit. Often, it's the reverse. And with my former employer, that certainly turned out to be true.

It took time to dig it out, dust it off, and make sense of what I was seeing. But there was one tiny, innocuous entry amongst the tens of millions that—put in context—turned my understanding of recent events completely on its head.

WEIMANN GOT HOME NINETY MINUTES LATER AND CAME straight to his study with a bottle of Moët & Chandon in his hand.

"The other side of my bargain." He held up the champagne. "No virus in this baby."

"Did you meet your contact?" I didn't feel like celebrating with a guy who'd been stealing from me, even if he was my new *partner*. And my head was still spinning from what I'd found in the AmeriTel data.

"I did. I told him we're in a hurry, and he promised to get right to work. I'm checking in with him tomorrow morning for an update."

"Quicker than you thought. That's good. What's the guy going to do? Call? Email?"

"Hell, no. He only does face-to-face."

"I'm sorry you have to go schlepping around again, then. Where are you guys meeting?"

"At the train station, in Valhalla. He feels safe there. Lots of people moving around. Lots of ways in and out. Lots of places to hang out where you don't look suspicious."

"What time?"

"You still can't come, Marc. He'd run if he saw you."

"Is my leprosy that obvious?"

He didn't answer, and I realized he hadn't come within ten feet of me since he'd walked back into the room.

"Are you having second thoughts, Karl? Because you don't sound like the guy who was here earlier. Did you have a change of heart when you were out?"

He moved across to the window, still keeping his distance.

"I have a question, Marc. The car you came in. Is it yours?"

"No. It's a rental."

"What's wrong with your Jag?"

"Nothing's wrong with it. It's at home. Why?"

"So why drive that piece of crap outside?"

"I was delivering something for a friend. It wouldn't fit in the Jag's trunk. You know how shallow they are."

"What were you delivering?"

"Why does that matter?"

"And the hotel, Marc. Why have me meet you there? Why not at your house?"

"Why does it matter where we met?"

Weimann plonked the champagne bottle down on the windowsill and looked out into the yard. He didn't move for two minutes. Then he turned and came across to me, holding out his BlackBerry.

"Here. Read this."

The phone's browser was open to a news page. The story Weimann had found was about me. It told how I'd escaped from jail. How I was wanted for murder. And how my wife, Carolyn Clark—note their use of her maiden name, to distance her from me—was missing in suspicious circumstances.

I dropped the BlackBerry and jumped to my feet, but Weimann was blocking the way to the door. And he was holding the champagne bottle, again.

"Marc—Is it true?"

"No. Not all of it. Some of it might be."

"Then I'm sorry. I'm calling the police. I can't get mixed up in this."

"You're already mixed up in it, Karl. The virus. The memory stick. Your contact. You did deliver it to him?"

"I did." There was regret in his voice. "I didn't see the news report till I was on my way back."

"OK, then. Now, listen. I know you're spooked. I am, too, after seeing that stuff in black and white. But, please. Don't do anything rash. Because there's a lot of weird stuff going on. I don't understand all of it, but I absolutely haven't done anything wrong. So how about this? Hear me out. And if you still don't believe me, call the police then. But at least give me a chance to explain."

Weimann paced up and down in front of the window, taking short rapid steps, changing direction a little sooner each time until he ground to a halt, facing me.

"OK, Marc. You get one shot. If you don't convince me, I'm making the call. But stay in the chair. And keep your hands where I can see them."

I WAS PRETTY HONEST, about most things. I admitted taking the data from AmeriTel. I told Weimann about the break-in. That McKenna was convinced of my innocence, and had been the one who'd released me from jail after Brooking had accused me of creating the virus. I was vague about Peever, because I still didn't understand how he fit into all this. I was sketchier still when it came to Carolyn's situation, because I didn't want to contradict anything Weimann might already know. I skirted around Troye/Brian's involvement, for his own sake. And I skipped the dead guy in my bathroom altogether, for mine.

"Wow," Weimann said, when I paused for air. "My head's spinning."

"Try living through it. And there's more. I discovered something else while you were out. Which reminds me—my *Dreadnaught* prototype? Hello?"

Weimann's face was blank for a moment, then I saw the penny drop.

"A little clunky. Not up to your usual standard. I can see why you canned it."

"How did you get hold of it? It never even went to my beta testers."

"Handed to me on a plate." He waved his hand dismissively. "Anyway, does that matter, now? Keep going."

"The Homeland Security woman—" I stalled for a moment, wondering how anyone other than Carolyn could have passed him that plate. "Agent Brooking? She thought I'd created the virus to attack the

White House. But can I show you something? It's on the screen. On your laptop. I couldn't print it because of the quarantine."

"Stay where you are. I'll take a look."

Weimann was at the desk for ten seconds, then he returned to his spot by the window.

"A record of an email trail?" he asked.

"Correct. But did you see how it had been bounced around? It came from one place, got redirected half a dozen times, went to a Hotmail account, and then got forwarded to AmeriTel?"

"I saw."

"And what does that tell you?"

"That there are two people involved. One smart. One stupid."

"Exactly. The smart one used all the right moves to hide the fact he'd sent an email to a throwaway account. And the stupid one ruined it by sending it on to his work address."

"He probably didn't know that when it was forwarded all its history came with it. If you know where to look. The schmuck."

"And not just any schmuck. I know the guy. Michael Millan. AmeriTel's CFO."

"Wow. Not very smart, for a CFO. I wonder who was emailing him?"

"I think I know that, too. Did you see the time stamp?"

"No. Is it important?"

"Very. The email hit the Hotmail account at eleven twenty-three pm, last Saturday night. Millan forwarded it at five twenty-three the next morning. Sunday."

"So what?"

"So, on Sunday, the board of AmeriTel met to discuss the bid they were about to submit for the government bandwidth auction. The revised bid. They were expected to get creamed. But they didn't. Out of the blue they upped the amount they were offering, and they won huge. We're talking hundreds of millions of dollars."

"You think they had a tip? They had an insider thing going?"

"I think that's safe to assume."

"Which means this Millan guy's bent. Maybe the whole AmeriTel board is."

"It means a lot more than that. Where do you think the tip came from?"

"I don't know. Who'd be able to feed them that kind of information? Someone in Washington?"

"Someone in the White House."

"Are you sure?" Weimann put the champagne bottle down.

"I was around that office every day for weeks. People were talking about the auction the whole time. It sounded like a three-ring circus, and the White House was at the center."

"I have the tools. I could track those IP addresses."

"Do it."

"It would be dynamite, Marc. It would put AmeriTel out of business. People would go to prison. And it would prove the White House has a leak."

"More than that. It would prove the White House has a virus. Think about that. If the White House was shut down by terrorists, there'd be chaos. The government would grind to a halt. Wall Street would melt down. No one would get paid. There'd be no food on the shelves. Riots. Looting. People would die."

"And there'd be repercussions. Civil liberties would take another hit. Maybe even another war would get started."

"Right. But narrow it down. From where I'm standing, it means the virus I'm accused of creating actually started at the White House, and spread to AmeriTel. Not the other way round. It means Homeland Security's been looking in the wrong place."

IT ONLY TOOK WEIMANN sixteen minutes to confirm the original email had come from the White House, but when he turned back to me I could see he had something else on his mind.

"We got carried away." He looked disappointed. "This doesn't prove the virus was already at the White House. It doesn't look good, insider-trading-wise, given the attempt to hide the message and the timing and whatever, but the virus? That part doesn't hold water."

"So what's your theory? A virus, custom-made for the White

House turns up at a company that just received an email from the White House, and it's all just a coincidence?"

"It could be. Yes. The one thing doesn't prove the other."

"Of course it does."

"It doesn't prove squat, Marc. We've got nothing."

*N*ATURE, OR NURTURE? THOSE WERE THE TWO OPTIONS I'D always heard about for explaining people's behavior. And I'd always thought they covered the whole spectrum pretty well. Until that afternoon. That's when I realized there's a far more significant factor.

Whether it's your ass that's in the sling.

WEIMANN WAS PACING AGAIN.

"We should call the police. Or Homeland Security. What do you think, Marc? Homeland Security?"

"We should call no one. Not till we figure this out the rest of the way. I think I'm close, though. Here's what I have. Someone at Ameri-Tel realized I was capturing their data, and could find the record of the White House email coming in. They didn't want any ticking time bombs, so first thing Monday, before I could set foot in a room with a computer in it, they canned me. Problem solved. Or that's what they thought."

"Because they found out you had a copy of the data."

"Right. Which is why they sent Carolyn to ask for it back. Then the burglars to steal it, when she walked out. Then the thugs."

"Right."

"Only, sending out burglars and thugs is pretty hard-core for telecoms guys."

"These were no ordinary telecoms guys, Marc. They were guys with billions to win, and everything to lose. And consider this. If they

were bribing or blackmailing a White House insider to spill government secrets, they'd already crossed a pretty major line. Once you've
crossed a line like that, where do you stop?"

"I don't know. I guess—it's just that I worked with these guys. I've
known Roger LeBrock for years."

"Maybe you don't know LeBrock as well as you thought. But bad
as it looks for him and the company, there's still no proof this virus
came from the White House. Information—yes. Virus—no."

"It must have come with the email."

"Then why wasn't AmeriTel's corporate network infected?"

"It would have been. But by the time Homeland Security went to
check, it had been cleaned."

"How? Who by? When? You can't do that kind of thing remotely.
And even if you could, you'd still need someone on-site to look for any
machines that were offline for maintenance or whatever."

"Like my laptop."

"That's completely circumstantial. We have no proof. So how about
this? Go to the FBI, instead. I know a guy who works there. Cooper
Demonbruen. He took a college course I was teaching. I could feed
him the corruption angle. Let him run with that. Homeland Security
is already chasing down the virus, after all. And if we come up with
anything else, we'll pass it on when we're sure it's for real."

"No."

"You want to go to Homeland first?" He started pacing again. "I
just don't think—"

"I mean, we're not going to anyone. Not yet. I need insurance first.
Something that proves I'm clean. I've seen how Homeland works. It's
a machine. It only cares about its own priorities, and any little guys
who get in the way—i.e., me—get rolled over and crushed. The FBI's
probably the same. That's why I asked for your help with the virus in
the first place."

"The virus—of course. Why don't we hold fire for twenty-four
hours? See what my guy comes up with?"

"We should see what's he got. But I'm not sitting on my hands for
another day. Not when there's another trail to follow."

"What other trail?"

"Roger LeBrock." I stood up and checked I had my keys. "I'm going to see what he can tell me about his White House buddy."

"Why should LeBrock tell you anything?"

"That ticking time bomb? I'm going to drop it down his shorts. And, Karl? One last question before I go. How come you weren't surprised just then, when I let slip that Carolyn had walked out on me?"

WEIMANN'S EXPRESSION OF GUILT taunted me throughout the hour's drive to LeBrock's house. But when I arrived, I found myself face-to-face with a far bigger distraction.

The car at the end of LeBrock's driveway wasn't his.

It was Carolyn's.

I'D THOUGHT CAROLYN WAS THE BEDROCK MY LIFE WAS GROUNDED on. Instead, she was quicksand. How could I have misjudged her so badly? Or had I brought everything on myself, by sabotaging her career all those years ago?

In the absence of answers, my mind filled with clichés. Fish, and sea. Time, and healing. Pastures, and green. And then something else. An echo from a management course I'd been on, years ago. About assumptions, and the danger of making them. I got out of the car and headed toward the entrance to LeBrock's driveway. Our marriage was on the line. I owed it to Carolyn not to jump to conclusions. And I had business to discuss with LeBrock, either way.

His house was hard to sneak up on, as it was made entirely of metal pillars and glass, like a high-tech cross between a pyramid and a Swiss chalet. It was four stories high, and each one grew successively shallower to allow every upstairs room to have a balcony. The roof was steeply pitched with a gap in the center, and the two sections appeared to be hovering magically above the walls. It was the kind of place I'd only ever seen as a backdrop for fashion shoots or high-end car advertisements, so it was a surprise to find that someone might actually live here. Especially someone I knew.

And now, my wife?

I drew level with the rear of LeBrock's black Mercedes, and stopped. There was nothing else between me and the house to hide behind, and every window in the place seemed to be blazing with light. That killed any hope of a stealthy approach, so I had to make do with a direct assault on the front door. I broke cover and strode straight along the path leading to it, but still couldn't resist looking into the rooms I passed on the way.

There was a kitchen, full of stainless-steel appliances and counters that were like trolleys on wheels. A den with a horseshoe of leather couches facing a giant TV on a metal stand, like an oversize easel. And a huge living room.

Normally, I'd have been looking at the furniture and scoping out any art on the walls—if there'd been any walls—but that day, all I could focus on were the people. LeBrock, slumped in an Eames lounge chair, like mine but in the standard walnut and black. And Carolyn, perched on the matching ottoman at his feet. As I watched she leaned forward and took LeBrock's hand in both of hers. I couldn't see her face, but it was clear from LeBrock's expression they were staring into each other's eyes. Any moment now she was going to lean forward, and then they'd kiss. I knew it. Because she used to make that exact same move on me.

I hammered on the glass, watched them spring apart, then continued to the front door. It took an eternity for LeBrock to show his face. And when he did appear, he just stood in front of me, pale and silent. I was looking at the man who'd fired me. Bribed government officials. Made a fortune cheating in the bandwidth auction. Sent thugs to burglarize my home. And had links to a computer virus that threatened the security of the nation. There were serious questions I should have asked him. But after what I'd just seen, none of that mattered.

I drove my fist into LeBrock's face. Hard. Spikes of pain shot through my knuckles and into my wrist. LeBrock staggered back, arms flailing. He slumped down on one knee. I stepped in, ready to finish him off. And heard a car engine fire up. Behind me.

It was Carolyn's.

She was running out on LeBrock. Just like she'd done to me.

This time, I went after her. I left LeBrock on the floor in his hallway and ran to my car. I raced down every street in the neighborhood. I backtracked, every time the trail went cold. Checked people's driveways. Their yards. Chased every shadow that looked remotely like

Carolyn's BMW. But after forty minutes, I had to admit defeat. I had no idea what her destination could be.

Her head start had only been a few seconds, but she'd made them count.

CAROLYN WAS GONE, but there was one last connection still in play. Weimann hadn't blinked when I let slip that she'd left me. Which meant he already knew. Which meant he'd been in touch with her. Recently. Whether it was just to buy my secrets from her, or whether there was anything more R-rated about it, they'd been in touch since Monday.

As I drove back to his house, my thoughts about Weimann were steadily replaced by a flurry of doubts. How much could I trust him? How long had he been stealing my work? Had *he* been sleeping with Carolyn, too? Or just paying her to spy for him? Had it been a mistake to ask for his help with the virus? Why wouldn't he let me meet his contact? And what about his threats to call the police on me? I'd been able to talk him out of it earlier, face-to-face, but what about while I was gone? Would I get back to his house and walk straight into a room full of detectives?

My nerves weren't helped by the police cruiser that raced up behind me, a mile or so from Weimann's street. It gave me a burst of its siren and a flash from its light bar, convincing me I was about to be arrested again. But a second later it pulled around me and sped away. Then a second cruiser appeared, with an ambulance laboring to keep up in its wake.

My conscious brain kept insisting it was a coincidence, the three of them all going the same way as me. But my heart rate accelerated, anyway, and I could feel the muscles around my stomach clamping down tight. I leaned a little harder on the gas, anxious to prove my paranoia wrong, but as I rounded the next bend that became much more difficult. A plume of thick, black smoke was rising from the heart of Weimann's subdivision. And a moment later, denying my suspicions became impossible.

Two fire trucks were parked on the street outside Weimann's house.

Thick hoses snaked down his driveway, past the blackened skeleton of his Jaguar and on toward the burning shell of the building. And to extinguish any last shred of hope, I saw the paramedics loading a gurney into the back of the ambulance that had passed me, minutes before.

A gurney with a body bag strapped to it.

*I*N THE MOMENTS AFTER I PASSED WEIMANN'S HOUSE I FELT PROUD of myself for mastering the panic and continuing to drive, slowly and evenly, not drawing attention to myself, not giving the watching cops the slightest clue that a wanted man had just slipped through their fingers. I told myself it was a sign of growth. Of change. Of increasing competence and self-reliance. And then I turned the rearview mirror all the way to the side to make sure I didn't catch sight of my face.

Because if I was honest, I wasn't sure exactly what I'd become. But I had a feeling the truth would be far less flattering than the self-deception.

THE TV WAS STILL flickering in the corner of my room on the seventh floor of the Buckingham when the sun finally rose. I'd spent most of the night pacing, hoping for something to show up on the local news that would break the endless circle of questions in my head. Could the fire have been an accident? Or had Weimann been murdered? Who'd want to kill him? Why? Had anyone told Renée, now that they were separated? How had she taken it? Where were the police?

And how long until the blame came crashing down on me?

In the end, though, there was only one thing I could be sure about. I wouldn't find any answers—or make sure Weimann hadn't died in vain—if I was in jail. I needed proof of my innocence. I had to follow my one remaining lead.

———

I KNEW THE RENDEZVOUS with Weimann's virus expert was set for Valhalla station, sometime in the morning. I found my way there easily enough and parked without any trouble. But when I put on my baseball cap and glasses it hit me how thin my disguise was. The whole area was crawling with people. How many of them had seen my face on the news? Had there been more stories, since I left the hotel? I wished I could get online to check. Or call someone and ask. But I had nowhere to go. And no one to turn to. Weimann's contact was the last iron I had in the fire. If I couldn't find him, I'd be on the run for the rest of my life.

No one recognized me as I hurried toward the station concourse, but the first thing I saw when I stepped inside was my own face. It was front and center on all four papers on the newsstand. My plan to hole up somewhere and watch the passersby, hoping to latch onto the fellow IT-geekiness of the virus guy suddenly seemed like madness.

"Hey!" The voice was behind me. "Stop!"

I dived around the back of the coffee cart, whipped off my hat and glasses, and shoved them behind its oversize ornate wheel, desperate to change my appearance. Then I crept to the giant barrel of ferns next to it and peered into the crowd, frantically trying to spot my pursuer.

I could see maybe fifty people, but only one likely candidate. And he wasn't pursuing me. The guy had been calling to his teenage son. The kid had forgotten his lunch box. The dad had brought it for him. And I'd jumped like a scalded cat. It was a wake-up call. I had to accept the inevitable.

I retrieved my hat and glasses and waited for my moment to slip out from behind the cart. Then I slunk back to my car, feeling the gaze of everyone I passed boring into me like they all knew who I was, and were only delaying turning me in to draw straws for the honor of making the call.

IF I'D HAD A COIN with me when I slid back into the car, I'd have tossed it. Heads, stay in the parking lot and hope for a miracle. Tails, run for cover and try to come up with a plan that had a prayer of succeeding. But as things turned out, the choice was taken out of my hands.

"Marc Bowman!" A man opened the passenger door and jumped in beside me. "I was expecting you, now your buddy Weimann's dead."

I was half out of my seat, my heart accelerating so fast I could hear my blood bouncing off the inside of my eardrums, before I registered who it was.

"Sweet heaven above, Agent McKenna. I thought I was getting arrested! Or lynched!"

"Nothing that dramatic. I'm just waiting for a friend."

"Wait. There's no way. You're the virus guy?"

"Of course not. I'm here to meet him. Just like you."

"I don't understand. How do you know him? I don't even know his name."

"His name's not important. He probably can't even remember it, he uses so many aliases. But he's the top of his field. A morally confused field, granted, but that's how the world works, these days. Most of the time we turn a blind eye. And in return, if he finds anything of interest to us, he drops a dime."

"He told you about the virus?"

"He told me someone—Weimann—gave him a memory stick with the virus on it, along with a bunch of AmeriTel data. Which leaves me puzzled. How did your friend Weimann get his hands on such a thing when he didn't work at AmeriTel? But you did. And you specifically told me you didn't have any of their data."

I didn't answer. This was exactly what I'd hoped to avoid when I found the memory stick in the box with the fresh tequila bottle, but it was too late now to go back and undo all the mistakes I'd made.

"Never mind." McKenna glanced over his shoulder. "We'll talk about that later. In the meantime, start the car. I'll give you directions. This is no time for you to be seen in public."

MCKENNA DIRECTED ME BACK to the highway, and from there toward a hotel his team was using as an HQ while they were working the case.

He told me it would take the best part of an hour to get there, then leaned against the side window and stared at me, unblinking, and in silence.

"What?" I caved after a couple of minutes. "Could you stop that, please? You're making me uncomfortable."

"OK. I'll stop. The moment your comfort becomes important to me."

"Are you pissed at me?"

"You lied to me, Marc. About the memory stick. And the prison van thing? I saved your ass for what, the second time? The third? And you ran out on me. You made me look like an idiot. Things like that don't help build careers. This is a temporary thing for you. An adventure you'll brag about to your grandkids. But it's my life and my livelihood you've put on the line."

"It's no adventure. It's a nightmare. I was terrified. The guy cornered me, and told me to run, and—"

"You went back to your house?"

I nodded.

"You'd hidden the memory stick there? The one you denied having?"

"I wasn't lying. I didn't know I had it when I told you that. I found it later. Then I put it somewhere safe."

"Where?"

"In my kitchen. Under a section of countertop."

"OK." McKenna frowned. "We tossed the place twice, and never got a sniff. Did you have the countertop built that way specially?"

"No. It was an accident." I pulled out to pass a dawdling minivan. "The kind of thing that happens when you mix Carolyn, alcohol, and heavy pieces of domestic equipment."

"I see. So you recovered the stick and . . . the guy . . . what happened? He jumped you?"

I nodded, and a shiver ran through me. It wasn't an episode I had any desire to revisit.

"One thing puzzles me, Marc. You went to all that trouble to hang on to the memory stick. Why turn around and give it to your friend?"

"Weimann? He wasn't really my friend. But I needed help. And he was the only one I could think of."

"You couldn't think of me?"

"I didn't know if you were still alive."

McKenna nodded, as if conceding the point.

"The papers say *you* killed Weimann, Marc."

I felt my chest tighten, and I involuntarily eased off the gas.

"Did you?"

"God, no."

"Who torched his place?"

"I don't know. I wish I did."

"What were you two working on?"

"We started with the virus. That was a dead end, so I dipped into the AmeriTel data. And I found something crucial. Mike Millan? Their finance chief? Someone sent him an email, late last Saturday night. Right before their board decided to revise their bandwidth bid."

"You think this Millan guy received a tip? An illegal one?"

"Definitely. The email was sent to his Hotmail account, and Millan forwarded it to his work address. That was a huge mistake, because it made it visible. To me, anyway. So they fired me before I could do anything with the data."

"Can you prove that?"

"Absolutely."

"OK. I'll get you set up with the fraud guys, and they can take it from there."

"I'll give them whatever they need. But there's more going on here than just fraud. I know where the email came from."

"Where?"

"The White House." I braced for a reaction, but I didn't get one. "Its origin was pretty well disguised, but we tracked it."

"You're talking about high-level corruption? The AmeriTel boys had a tip from the top?"

"Yes, but that's not the point." I swerved to avoid the squashed remains of a skunk. "What I think is this: The virus was already at the White House, and it spread to AmeriTel via the crooked email. Brooking's theory is backwards. If I'm right, and you're the one to straighten her out, that's got to be worth something to you, right? You could be the one who stops an attack on the White House. You could get a commendation? A medal?"

"Oh, Marc." A grin spread across McKenna's face. "That's priceless. But make me a promise? When this is all done, go back to your computers. James Bond, you're not."

"What?" I didn't get the joke.

"When we found out the virus was targeted at the White House, where do you think was the first place we looked?"

"The White House?"

"Right. And yes, the virus *was* already there. Sent *from* AmeriTel. That's why three state functions got moved this week. And next week's are all canceled, too."

"Sounds like chicken and egg to me, with the virus."

"You could be right, I guess. But it would be a hell of a coincidence. We think AmeriTel's ARGUS node was the insertion point. It's not likely the virus would loop back around to the same place it started, because of a separate fraud thing."

"You're sure the fraud thing's separate?"

"I am." McKenna took out his phone and started to type. "But you know what? We haven't specifically checked. It would be wrong to rule it out. I'm getting my guys onto it right away. And because it's you, Marc, if you are right, I'm not going to take any of the credit. I'm going to let you take everything that's coming to you."

FROM A DISTANCE, THE ROTUNDA INN LOOKED LIKE A BROKEN cartwheel with only three spokes remaining. Then, from the parking lot, like a Mercedes logo with no outer circle. But either way, Reception was in the hub at its center. It had sliding glass doors that faced the parking lot—curved to match the building's contours—and a transparent dome covering the check-in area. From there, the residential wings radiated outward, and each was painted a different primary color.

Ours was red.

"Wait here a second." McKenna knocked on a door halfway down the corridor. "There's something I have to check on. Then I'll get the key for your room."

The door opened, and I recognized the woman who'd been driving the sports car when I'd been rescued from Peever's people on, when, Wednesday? It felt like years ago. McKenna disappeared inside, leaving me to wrestle a sudden urge to run again, and when he emerged a couple of minutes later he was holding a little cardboard wallet.

"You're in 112, down the hall. The place is a little primitive, I'm afraid. It was probably cool when it was built, but now all it's got going is a weird shape, the most basic cable package known to man, and rates low enough to make Uncle Sam's nightly allowance look generous."

"I don't care, as long as no one's shooting at me. But what if someone sees me and calls 911? I don't want the cops smashing down my door."

"Don't worry. The staff here know we're federal agents. They know not to interfere. And the local P.D. knows to liaise with us before mounting any kind of operation. You're safe here. Just don't set foot outside without me or one of my people, OK?"

"What about my things? I left my suitcase in the car. Can I at least go get it?"

"No. But give me your keys and I'll have it brought to you."

MCKENNA DELIVERED MY CASE HIMSELF, five minutes later.

"Mind if I come in?"

"Be my guest. I'd offer you a seat, if I had one."

"Thanks. But I won't stay long. I just have a quick question. One of the loose ends we're tying up. It's about your friend Weimann. Did he give you the memory stick back, before he . . . before the . . ."

"Before the fire? No. He didn't have it. He gave it to the virus guy, remember?"

"He didn't, actually. The virus guy told me Weimann made him copy it, then he took it away with him."

"Are you sure?"

"The guy had no reason to lie. So if you don't have it, that leaves a wrinkle. Odds are it got destroyed in the . . . house, but I'd prefer to know for sure."

McKenna's words had prompted another explanation: I'd been on my way to talk to Weimann last night because I knew he'd been in touch with Carolyn. I'd made assumptions as to why. But what if I was wrong? What if Weimann hadn't been getting something from her? What if it was the other way round? Carolyn had been desperate to get her hands on the memory stick from minute one. Could she have found out he had it? And made a deal?

Suddenly the theory took on a much darker shade. One of the thugs Carolyn was hooked up with had been to our house. He'd tried to kill me because I had one of the sticks. Last night Weimann had taken a stick, and now he was dead. Killed at *his* house.

A 9mm. A box of matches. What's the difference?

Carolyn's thugs already knew where I lived. And Weimann would have been easy to follow after he'd rendezvoused with her. Cars like ours stand out a mile.

That was the clincher. The matching Jaguars.

The murderer thought Weimann was me.

"Are you OK, Marc? You look like you're going to puke."

"No. I'm not sick. But something just hit me. Weimann's death? It was my fault."

I walked him through the logic, slowly, step by step.

"Don't blame yourself about your friend," he said, when I was finished. "But your wife? With the memory stick? That could be a problem."

MCKENNA LEFT ME AGAIN, hinting at vague but urgent aspects of the case that required his attention, but frankly at that point I was happier with the four featureless walls as company. I'd been coming to terms with the end of my marriage for a while now. But Carolyn running around in the shadows, making sure her AmeriTel buddies got what they wanted? While my heart was still breaking over her? That felt like a whole new level of betrayal.

It had wounded me. But it had cost Karl Weimann—*her friend*—his life.

I turned on the local news in the hope of updates, muted the sound, and tried Carolyn's number. I wanted to see what she had to say about Weimann's death, and the role she'd played in it. But not surprisingly, all I got was her voicemail.

MCKENNA SHOWED HIS FACE AGAIN an hour later. I was still on my feet, looking out the window. My room had a great view. Of the parking lot. I'd just noticed how my car was sitting all alone at one side while the others were clustered together in the center. Like a nerd at a nightclub, I thought.

Another unwelcome reminder of life with Carolyn.

"How are you feeling?" McKenna was carrying an aluminum briefcase which, since there was no desk or table big enough to hold it, he set down on the bed.

"I just want to get out of here and put this fiasco behind me."

"I thought you might feel that way. That's why I brought this." He indicated the briefcase. "Because aside from dealing with Peever and keeping the police off your back, there's paperwork we need to take care of. My fault, I'm afraid. Some of the things I told you along the way, I shouldn't have. We have to put the genie back in the bottle. Which, in twenty-first century America means there's a form to sign. We could put it to bed right now, so you can get out of here a little quicker? Or, if you'd rather wait till you can run it by a lawyer, I'd understand."

"Let me see?"

McKenna flipped open the case and produced a black leather conference folder with a Homeland Security logo stamped into the cover. Then he took out two pieces of paper and handed them to me. They were heavy gauge, thick, slightly off-white, watermarked with a government seal, and covered in fine print.

"I've tried to read government forms before. Is this one more understandable than most?"

"Hell, no." McKenna grinned. "Do you think we want you to understand what you're signing? Where would the open-ended liability be in that?"

"And suppose I do call my lawyer. He reads it, and asks for changes. What are the chances of the government agreeing to them?"

"Somewhere between zero and zero. But don't worry. There's a lot of bullshit in there, but it's really pretty simple. It says that everything I've already told you, and anything I tell you in the future, is classified under the Patriot Act. Think of it as being like attorney/client privilege. You cannot reveal, imply, hint at—basically do much more than dream about—anything I've said or you've learned while you're with me. If you do, two things will happen: Innocent people will die. And someone like me will crash through your door and take you to prison for the rest of your life. Clear enough?"

"I guess."

"What do you think? Sign now? Or sign when your attorney gets here? Because realistically, those are your only two options."

"I'll sign now."

McKenna passed me a pen and I scrawled my name in the space at the bottom of both pages.

"Good decision." He took the form and pen back, dropped them into the briefcase, then scrambled the combination lock. "It means I can go ahead and offer you a choice other than sitting around in this miserable hutch for a couple of days. It has to do with your wife. And the memory stick she has. Because we could be looking at a very serious situation here, Marc. I know it seems surreal, all this chasing around after something so tiny. But the consequences of not retrieving it are huge. And now you've signed that piece of paper, I can tell you why. Remember I confirmed the virus had reached the White House?"

I nodded.

"OK. This is what it does. It seeks out the climate control system. But not of the aboveground White House. Not the part you see on TV. It homes in on the equipment in the bunker, beneath it."

"There *is* a bunker? I thought it was urban legend."

"No. It's real. It gets used all the time, because protocol calls for the President and his staff to get evacuated down there whenever there's an environmental alert. And if ever there was a system with a hair trigger, it's the White House environmental system."

"The virus gives false environmental alarms? No. That wouldn't make sense. It suppresses the alarms, so the President doesn't take shelter when he should?"

"No, and no. It waits, dormant and undetected, until the environmental alarm causes an evacuation on its own. It doesn't matter if it's a real alarm, or a false one. What matters is the President goes down to the bunker. Because what happens when the doors lock behind him is the clever part. First, the climate control system does the opposite of what it's supposed to. It switches off the oxygen supply and the CO_2 scrubbers, and vents whatever clean air's left to the outside world. And while that's happening, the management system sends a stream of false data to the local monitoring station—and the remote sites in Nebraska and Washington state—which makes the operators think everything's peachy."

"The President would suffocate?"

"He would. And so would all his staff. His family, too, if they were around when the alarm was triggered. A hundred-plus people, depending on when it happens. All killed by the system that's designed to protect them."

"Like sticking a Polaroid in front of a CCTV camera. No one would know anything was wrong. Until it was too late."

"Exactly. And think of the damage it would do. The President, plus the cream of the political and administrative crop, all wiped out in one fell swoop. Not the worst terrorist attack in terms of numbers. But by impact? Off the charts. It would take the nation decades to recover."

I'd met the President once. Years ago. When he was still a Senator. I hadn't much liked him. I certainly hadn't voted for him. Since then he'd been nothing more to me than a smiling face on the front of countless newspapers. But the thought of that same guy—whose hand I'd shaken, who'd looked me right in the eye—lying dead on the floor of his bunker? His body contorted, lips blue, tongue bulging out of his mouth? It struck me: Stalin was right. One death can be a tragedy. And despite the warmth of the room, I felt a patch of goose bumps spread between my shoulder blades.

"Who's behind this?"

"Iran. Syria. Yemen. One of a dozen radical Islamic groups not tied to any specific state. America's not short of enemies."

"OK, wait. Back up. You stopped the massacre from happening. Why the panic over one missing memory stick?"

"We stopped the initial attack, yes. But we have to prevent future ones, as well. The virus is heuristic—it's self-learning. It's always adapting and evolving, which is why every known iteration has to be studied. And more than that, it's a question of containment. As a piece of programming—the way it can conceal itself, replicate, target specific systems—it's incredibly sophisticated. We can't risk anyone else getting hold of it. Imagine it in Air Force One, or a nuclear power plant. Actually, don't. Just help us get that copy back from your wife."

"How? What do you want me to do?"

"Call her. Sweet-talk her. Convince her to give it back to us. You can't share the reasons, but you can see how important it is she cooperates. And if she claims not to have it, there's no one else who knows her well enough to tell if she's lying."

I thought about his request, but I knew there was no chance of her answering me. It was like getting ready to ask for our first date. Except that back then, I only feared she hated me. Now I knew she did.

"OK. But I should text, not call. Because if you want Carolyn to cooperate, using me as the messenger may not be the way to go."

"I disagree." McKenna shook his head. "I know about the spat you guys are having, but think about it. If you're right and she somehow reached out to Weimann last night, she *could* have thought it was the quickest way to get the stick back for her cronies. That's one explanation. But equally, she could have done it to take the heat off you. Which shows she still cares about you. And will listen to you."

I felt a brief flicker of hope, hearing his words. But it was soon snuffed out by other thoughts. Like how she cared more about worming her way into LeBrock's affections—and his bed—than standing by her husband.

"Come on, Marc. Try. And if she doesn't respond to you, we'll take the next shot. But it'll go a lot easier on her if we don't have to."

"All right. I will. How do you want me to handle it?"

"First, confirm she has the stick. Then, set up a drop. There's a drive-through ATM in Pound Ridge. Tell her to approach it at three pm, today. Wait in line if other customers are there. Then put the stick on top of the machine, and drive away."

"I'll do my best."

"Ask if she made copies. If she did, we'll need those, too. And the computer she copied them on."

"Understood."

"Thank you, Marc. I know this has been a rough ride, and I appreciate you sticking with the program."

I nodded, then picked up my phone and starting keying in what I hoped would be a suitable message. But I didn't tell McKenna my real motive for helping him. I wasn't doing it out of patriotic duty. Or gratitude. Or to spare Carolyn from whatever alternative approach he'd been hinting at.

After everything she'd done, I just wanted to have a hand in bringing her down.

THE ATM MCKENNA HAD PICKED FOR THE AMBUSH WAS A HUN-
dred yards outside the original part of Pound Ridge.

There was only one entrance, flanked by a pair of huge stone eagles.
Beyond that the lane forked, leading to two separate machines. An
iron-and-glass roof covered a generous area, extending way out in all
four directions. The pitch was exaggeratedly steep, and it came down
very low at the sides. And bizarrely, that made it reminiscent of a bird
feeder Carolyn had bought for our backyard when we first moved in
together.

McKenna told me to park the car near the exit to a yard where
someone had spread out all kinds of broken-down, rusty agricultural
artifacts. I guessed they were for sale. In the town where I grew up,
they'd have been called junk. Here, I bet they were called art. With
price tags to match, no doubt. The white van had arrived before us,
and was already sitting at the edge of the ATM forecourt.

"Where are the others?" I asked, after McKenna stopped me from
switching off the engine.

"Patience. All will be revealed."

"Did we have to get here so early?" I looked at my watch. It was
only 2:07 pm. Still the better part of an hour to wait.

"We did. If you want to intercept your target, you have to be there
first. That's common sense. I just hope your wife uses common sense,
too, Marc. I hope she shows up. And brings the memory stick. And
that it's the right one."

"What if she doesn't show up? What if something stops her? If she gets in an accident?"

"Let's not borrow trouble. In the meantime, stay focused. You're still her husband. If she's not driving her own car, you've got the best chance of spotting her."

I MUST HAVE CHANGED my mind four hundred times over the next forty minutes, endlessly cycling through increasingly crazy and desperate reasons for wanting Carolyn to appear on time, then hoping she wouldn't come at all. All the contradictory mental flick-flacks were exhausting, so by the time I saw a car approaching the ATM—a white Camry—at just after quarter-till, I doubt there was any trace of emotion left in my voice.

"It's not her."

The Camry's driver took her time at the machine, and was still there when a red Volvo pulled into the other lane.

"Not her."

The Camry was replaced by a dark blue Chevy Volt.

"No."

A silver Grand Cherokee nosed in behind the Volvo.

"Not her."

The Volvo pulled away, the Cherokee moved up, and a black Chrysler 200 took the place of the Chevy.

"Not her."

The Cherokee gave way to a blue Dodge minivan.

"No."

The Chrysler swapped with a red Volvo.

"Not her."

The minivan rolled forward, and was followed up by a Camry. In white.

"Wait a minute!"

McKenna winked at me.

The same six cars—driven, I now understood, by McKenna's agents—kept up their slow-motion ballet for the next twelve minutes.

They never appeared in the same order. And they never left either ATM lane vacant, even when a stray civilian got in on the act.

The effect was mesmerizing. Before long I was making little bets with myself. Which car would be next? Which direction would it approach from? Which lane would it take? The process was strangely addictive, so it was almost an anti-climax when, at three minutes to three, I finally caught sight of Carolyn's car.

"There she is. A little early."

"Silver BMW." McKenna spoke calmly into a handheld radio. "License plate alpha mike golf, one two zero one. Incoming, from the south. Places, everyone. You know what to do."

CAROLYN'S CAR WASN'T MOVING FAST, and when it signaled, turned, and pulled smoothly up to wait behind the minivan, you'd have thought she was just an ordinary shopper needing some cash before getting the last of her groceries.

The driver in the Dodge finished her withdrawal and moved forward, heading for the exit. It was a perfectly innocuous maneuver. But she hadn't noticed the Chevy was also leaving, and was set to reach the point where the lanes merged again at exactly the same moment. The Chevy's horn blared. Its driver hit the brakes. The Dodge swerved, and took half a second longer to stop.

I couldn't tell if the cars had actually collided. They were too far away. But if they hadn't, it would be a miracle.

I glanced across at McKenna, but as usual his expression gave nothing away.

For ten drawn-out seconds no one moved. The mismatched vehicles remained locked in a kind of David-and-Goliath standoff on the far side of the ATMs. Then the Chevy pulled back six feet, the driver giving himself room to trace an exaggerated semi-circle around the front of the minivan before straightening and heading out through the exit.

The Dodge driver showed a little more caution after that, and when she finally moved on, Carolyn was left with the whole ATM area to herself. Her car rolled forward and the driver's door opened. I caught a glimpse of blond hair escaping from a baseball cap as her arm reached out and she placed a black nylon computer case at the foot of the nearer machine.

She'd been told to leave the bag on top of the ATM, but still. Carolyn was done for. The net would close around her any second . . .

But the net didn't close. Carolyn just shut her door and drove back toward the street, slowly and calmly. No revving of her engine. No screeching of her tires. And no agents to surround her, and lead her away in handcuffs to face the fate she so richly deserved.

Outraged, I reached for the gearshift. But before I could move it out of Park, McKenna stretched across and turned off the ignition.

"Calm yourself. There's no rush. Let's see what she left us. If we're not happy, then we'll go after her."

"How? She's getting away. We don't know where she's going!"

"Except that we do, Marc. Now. Because nothing that just happened here was an accident. And it wasn't a one-way exchange."

Saturday. Mid-afternoon.

*T*HE NYLON BAG CAROLYN HAD LEFT AT THE ATM WAS ONE OF A limited edition of corporate gifts that AmeriTel had produced, six months before I'd joined the company. I'd heard people talk about them. But I'd never seen one before, because Roger LeBrock guarded them like the crown jewels, releasing them only to his most favored cronies.

It always fascinated me how the richest people were the ones who pinched their pennies the hardest. That's what I focused on, anyway. It was better than speculating about how Carolyn had become one of the lucky recipients.

MCKENNA'S ROOM AT THE HOTEL was the same size as mine, but he'd somehow shoehorned a small table into the space at the foot of the bed. He placed Carolyn's bag down and—having already checked it with airport-style security wands and explosive detectors before moving it from the ATM—he went ahead and opened the zips.

Inside there was a laptop computer—a high-end Toshiba I'd never seen Carolyn use before—its power supply, two memory sticks, and a handwritten note:

No copies of the data were made. The computer was used only to check the contents.

"Your wife's handwriting?" McKenna asked.

I nodded.

"Let's see if she's telling the truth."

NORMALLY, WATCHING AN AMATEUR try to find his way around a keyboard is excruciating, but I have to give McKenna his due. He fired up Carolyn's computer, connected the memory sticks, used a DVD to load the Homeland Security virus suite, and started up the software without making any serious missteps. Then he left the diagnostic routines running in the background while he checked the computer's recent activity.

"Looks like she was on the level," he said. "All the data files for two twenty-four-hour periods have been deleted from both the sticks. But nothing's been copied. And assuming it's the AmeriTel data on the sticks, the virus check will be a formality."

Seven minutes later we had our confirmation. The White House virus was present, as expected. McKenna read the results from the screen then nodded, closed down the machine, and pulled the memory sticks from their sockets.

"Do they look familiar?" He held the sticks out for me to see.

"I couldn't swear to it. Probably. They're the right brand. I'm guessing one got stolen from my house. The other, Weimann must have given to Carolyn."

"Good enough for now. Forensics might be able to tell us more. But we have enough to wind things up here."

"Wait. You can't stop now. What about the deleted records? That's obviously an attempt to hide the information leaked to AmeriTel before the auction."

"I'm sure it is. And we know all about it now, thanks to you. We'll put people on it. Specialists. Heads will roll, believe me. But that's a separate investigation. It doesn't relate to containing the virus. It's tangential."

"What about Carolyn?"

"What about her? She gave us what we need."

"What if there are more copies of the virus? Or more infected machines? Shouldn't you bring her in? Question her, at least?"

"No, Marc. As far as your wife's involvement is concerned, I'm satisfied. The outstanding contaminated items have been recovered. We've done a thorough job."

It struck me that he didn't know the stick Weimann had given Carolyn was itself a copy, and that I still had my original in my pocket. But the way the conversation was heading, I didn't feel it was time to show all my cards.

"I still say you're making a mistake, letting Carolyn walk away."

"Is this really concern for the case I'm hearing, Marc? Or the desire to punish your wife? Because it seems to me you need a marriage counselor right now more than you need a field agent."

"So my wife walks. And what about me? If your investigation's winding up, can I go, too?"

"Of course not. Your situation's nowhere near the same as your wife's. You have paper out on you for murder. She has dubious taste in friends and poor impulse control, if you're to be believed. But listen. Keep this in perspective. We're on your side. We're handling the police. The charges will go away. Trust me. Now get some rest. And remember: Don't set foot outside unless I clear it first."

THE WOMAN SOUNDED BORED WHEN I CALLED HER, TWO MINUTES after McKenna had led me back to my room. "Reception. How can I help?"

"This is Mr. Bowman. Room 112. I can smell smoke. From the corridor."

"Sir?" The woman's voice was alive now. "OK. This is what I need you to do. Go to your door. *Do not* open it, but touch the handle and tell me how it feels."

I counted to five, but didn't bother to move. "Hot! Too hot to hold."

The hotel fire alarm began to wail.

"Sir, I need you to stay where you are. And stay calm. The fire department is on its way. In the meantime, please take a towel from your bathroom. Wet it in the tub. Then lay it along the bottom edge of the door. OK? That'll stop the smoke getting in."

I thanked her, then turned my attention to the agent who'd been posted in the corridor. He banged on my door and yelled for me to stay put until he found out what was going on. I agreed. But I was lying to him, too.

McKenna should have known it wasn't just the White House virus that was heuristic. I could learn from my experiences, too . . .

I CROSSED TO MY WINDOW, eased it up a couple of feet, and waited for the first of the guests to reach the parking lot. *Get people running around like headless chickens,* McKenna had said. *Make them think there's a fire nearby. Tap into their primal fear.* It was good advice. So I slipped through the space I'd created, lowered myself to the ground, and dodged from group to group until I was close enough to make a break for my car.

THE LAST VILLAGE BEFORE LeBrock's was picture-postcard perfect. I raced through at double the speed limit and could still take in the ice-cream parlors and artisanal produce stores, the vegetarian restaurants and the antiques emporia. And then, half a mile past the last pastel-painted building, I saw something less inviting. A line of police cars. Four of them, zigzagged across the road like fangs in a giant's mouth, light bars blazing, blocking my way.

I couldn't stop. And if I plowed into them, I'd be killed. I was certain. There was a stand of pines to my right. They'd be just as lethal, at the speed I was going. So I had to go left. There was a space to the side of the last squad car. Just a sliver. Not paved. But my only option.

My wheels left the blacktop and suddenly I was sideways. Then backwards. I locked eyes with a furious policeman as I slid past the roadblock, then he disappeared in the cloud of dust and debris thrown up by my tires.

I was sideways again. Facing the other way.

Then straight. I wrestled the steering wheel, battling to keep it that way. I was winning! Until the nose of the car dropped away and I lurched forward, the seatbelt biting into my shoulder and my chin slamming down into my chest.

Trees and bushes rushed toward me. I was off the road altogether. Plunging down a steep bank. Speeding up. My head was bouncing off the seatback and the window, rattling my teeth, blurring my vision. The brakes didn't work. I lost my grip on the steering wheel. A branch tore my side mirror off. Something hit the windshield, blurring it into a million opaque stars. Then the shaking died away. The car leveled out. I found the brake pedal. Hit it again with all my weight.

The car was slowing.
Definitely slowing.
It was back under control.
I was safe!
Then the airbags blew.

Saturday. Late afternoon.

I SAW A MOVIE IN SCIENCE CLASS ONCE THAT SHOWED WHAT happens when you stir up an ants' nest.

That's what it was like when I slammed my aching shoulder against the car door for the fifth time, finally freeing it from the twisted frame. At first all I could make out was chaos. Twenty or thirty people milling around, apparently at random. But then distinct groups started to emerge, each with its own purpose. The braver ones, coming toward me to investigate, or to see if they could help. The wiser ones, looking for cover until they were sure what was happening. Parents, gathering up their kids, anxious to shelter them. And the bewildered, wandering this way and that without a clue where to go.

I struggled out onto my feet and saw a long, low building thirty yards away beyond half a dozen rows of parking spaces. It was a supermarket. I would have plowed straight into it, if my car hadn't hit an old-model Lincoln Continental and stopped dead. Stretching back the other way, toward the slope, I'd left a trail of mud, rubber, and foliage. It was like an arrow, pointing to the police who'd been trying to stop me. I remembered the look in the one officer's eyes. They'd already be coming after me. But from which direction? Down the slope? Around, on the street? Or both?

THE SHOPPERS DRIFTED BACK toward the supermarket as their interest in my sudden arrival waned, so I went with them. The crush dissipated once we were inside, and smaller groups split away and started wandering between the checkouts and into the store itself. I had no idea how the place was organized, but I instinctively headed away from the entrance. The problem was, as supermarkets go, this one was tiny. There were only twelve aisles, lined up in parallel rows, and beyond them a frozen section and deli counter. I don't know what kinds of hiding places I'd imagined I'd find, but Macy's on 34th Street, this place wasn't.

An uproar erupted at the front of the store. The police had arrived. Half a dozen officers were trying to instill order, and it would only be minutes—seconds, maybe—before they swept me up and figured out who I was.

I dived behind the deli counter and pressed myself into the cold tiles on the floor. After a couple of seconds I looked up, and saw how stupid I'd been. Apart from the lower eighteen inches, which housed the refrigerator mechanism, the deli counter was made of glass. I might as well have been hiding behind a few boxes of cornflakes. I glanced round, desperate for something more substantial, and my eyes settled on the base of a door. It was standing open half an inch. Just enough to get my fingers around, push it open a little wider, and wriggle through to the other side.

I'd expected to find myself in a storeroom with shelves or piles of packages to crawl behind, but I saw the place was actually an industrial-scale kitchen. Which made sense, when I thought about it. It would be where they prepared the food for the deli. Long stainless-steel counters held various machines—slicers, mixers, a couple of microwaves, electric can-openers, and a few things I didn't recognize. There were three large ovens. A separate stovetop covered with giant pans. Two massive fridges. A pantry area that was partially walled off on the left-hand side. And a fire door, which I guessed would lead out to the back of the building.

It was decision time. Run? Or hide?

If I opened the door an alarm would sound, giving away my position. And there could be more officers outside, who'd spot me even if I was wrong about the alarm. But if I stayed, anyone who looked into the room would see me. Unless I could shift a few things around? Maybe create a little nook behind one of the fridges?

It was too late. I heard footsteps coming my way. At least two sets. Moving fast, but not running. Could I barricade myself in? I'd tried to close the door but it refused to fit in its frame properly, leaving the same half-inch gap I'd spotted before I took refuge in here. If I could slide something heavy in front of it, that might buy me the time I needed to slip out through the back. I took a step toward one of the steel trolleys, but memories of my last attempt at blocking a door slowed me down. I changed course, heading for the fire escape. And then a voice stopped me in my tracks altogether. Not because of how close it was. Or what it said. But because I'd heard it before.

"In there?" Agent Peever said.

"Right," a woman answered. "A couple of minutes ago. Slithering along the floor, like he thought no one would see him."

"How come you saw him?"

"I was working the deli counter. Supposed to be, anyway. Sneaked out to see what the fuss was about, and was trying to get back before my boss saw I was gone."

"OK. Was he on his own, the guy you saw? Or was anyone with him?"

"I don't know. I only saw him, but—"

"So he *could* have a hostage with him? You can't rule that out?"

"Not for certain, no."

"What about weapons? Was he armed?"

"Not that I could see."

"Where does the door lead to?" It was a different woman. Her voice was also familiar. It took me a second to pin it down. Then it clicked. It was Agent Brooking. Peever's boss.

"The deli prep room," the store employee said.

"Any knives in there?" Peever asked.

"Knives? Of course. Drawers full of them."

"Any other ways out?" Brooking asked. "Doors? Windows?"

"One door. It leads out to the Dumpsters."

"Don't worry," Peever said. "There are uniforms on every exit. If he sticks his nose out, it'll get blown off."

"Let's hope it doesn't come to that." Brooking actually sounded sincere.

"Um, do you need me anymore?" the store employee asked. "Because if there's going to be any shooting . . ."

"No," Peever said. "We don't. You can go. And thank you. You've been very helpful."

"OK." Brooking waited for a light set of footsteps to recede into the distance. "Options?"

"Do nothing, for now," Peever suggested. "Wait for the hostage negotiator."

"How do you figure?"

"Bowman's trapped. He can't get away, this time. But we're knee-deep in civilians. We can't account for them all. One could be in there with him. He has access to weapons. Why take the risk? What if we try to force something, and it goes wrong? Think how it would look."

"What's the ETA on the negotiator?"

"An hour, worst case."

"OK. I can spend an hour to avoid a PR nightmare. But you two stay here. And if Bowman makes any kind of contact, I'm the first to know. Understood?"

"Understood."

Another set of footsteps retreated from the door.

"Do nothing?" It was a man's voice. One I didn't recognize. "Wait for the negotiator? What the hell?"

"I know, I know." Peever sounded irritated. "That crap nearly choked me. But I had to get rid of Brooking, somehow. What if she was still here when McKenna shows up? And insists on trying to take him in? Tries to give him his rights? Have you read the procedures for a situation like this?"

"You think McKenna'll show?"

"He did last time we got our hands on his little buddy. It's worth a shot. It'd be a lot easier putting this business to bed with both of them out of the way. And we could do that with a lot less paperwork if we don't have Brooking breathing down our necks."

"Amen to that."

"You stay here and watch the door. I'll go spread the word that the goat's tied to the stake. Back in five."

From a sanctuary to a cell. And now to a coffin. For a moment I could have sworn the walls were closing in on me. Shrinking the space. Transforming the room into a tile-lined casket. But I pushed the image away. I only had time to think about one thing. How to get out. I had five minutes. Less, if Peever was faster than he'd thought.

The store employee had mentioned drawers full of knives. There was only one guard on my door, and surprise would be on my side. Maybe if I could . . . Wait. Who was I kidding? The guard was a trained Homeland Security agent. And he'd have a gun. There could be ten of me and a hundred knives, and it would make no difference. No. If I was going to survive, brawn wasn't the answer. I scanned the room, looking for something that could be. My eyes settled on the pair of microwaves. An episode from my past came rushing back to me. And I set off toward the fridges, moving as quietly as I could manage. Because now I knew what was going to save me.

I rummaged through the first fridge. I was thorough. But I didn't find what I needed. And had no luck in the second fridge, either. Was this the universe's way of telling me my time was up? Peever had just said as much. And then I remembered something a friend had told Carolyn in response to her gleeful account of my mishap with the egg.

I grabbed a container of dressing from the second shelf—it was the only thing I could see with a screw-down lid—and dumped the contents on the floor. I poured in a cup of milk and made sure the lid was fastened extra tight. Then I ran across to the nearer microwave, shoved the bottle inside, selected full power, and jabbed the ten-minute button three or four times.

The next thing I needed was cover. I figured the wall that partly separated the pantry area might work, but as I hurried toward it I spotted a white apron and hat. They'd been dropped on a sack of potatoes, so I altered course to grab them.

For the next ninety seconds I did nothing but slip off my shoes and put on the hat and apron. Then I took a deep breath and called to the guy Peever had left outside the door.

"Hey! Homeland Security? Are you there?"

The guy didn't respond.

"I know you can hear me. And you should know this. I do have a hostage. Peever was right. I've got a gun, too. And I'm going to blow her away unless you back off and let me leave."

"Mr. Bowman?" The agent took a couple of steps closer. "I understand what you're saying. And I don't want you to do anything hasty. Can you tell me your hostage's name?"

I didn't reply.

"Can I speak with her? To confirm she's OK?"

"The gun barrel's in her mouth, so, no. She can't speak to anyone right now."

"OK. No problem. Remember, don't do anything hasty. And listen. We have a negotiator on his way. He's the best we have, and he'll be here very soon. He can help you get what you want. Let's just relax, stay calm, and wait for our guy to arrive, OK?"

"Screw your negotiator. I'm coming out. Now. And if I see you, I'll spray this woman's brains all over the ceiling."

"Let's not overreact here, Marc. You want to leave? I get that. Hell, I want to leave, too. But are you thinking this through? If you come out of the kitchen, what's next? How will you get out of the building? We need time to let the other law-enforcement guys know what's going on, so they don't shoot you by mistake. Or your hostage. That would be an irony, right? And what then? Maybe you need a car? A driver? Some cash? If you just hold on a little longer, our guy can help you with all this stuff. He can coordinate everything. What do you say? Don't you think that would be a better way to go?"

The guy was annoyingly good. Even though I was bluffing and I knew he was lying through his teeth, I still felt a crazy desire to agree with him. My mouth was open and words had twice begun to form on my tongue when the pressure in the bottle of milk became critical. The lid could withstand it no longer and the container was ripped apart, tearing the front off the microwave and sending it cartwheeling across the kitchen in a jet of superheated steam.

Parts of the oven were still in mid-air when the door to the room crashed back on its hinges and the Homeland Security agent rushed in, his gun sweeping jerkily around as he struggled to make sense of the noise and the damage. He stopped after half a dozen paces, but that was far enough.

It meant I was behind him.

And after that, I was just another scared-looking employee in a rush to get somewhere safe.

Saturday. Early evening.

THE PARKING LOT WAS SWARMING WITH POLICE OFFICERS.
There were detectives, too. Peever and Brooking would be prowling nearby. And overhead I could hear at least two helicopters. Getting away on foot was a definite non-starter. My car was out of the question, too. It was a wreck. Panic was beginning to blossom inside me, then I spotted something I'd missed before. Around the side of the building, near the loading bays, there was a line of delivery trucks. Five in total, left stranded by the afternoon's events.

The first truck was from a liquor distributor. It was locked. As was the second, from a fish wholesaler. But the third—from a local bakery—was not. I rolled the door to its cargo area up just high enough to climb inside. I kept it open for a few extra moments, memorizing the layout of the interior. Then I shut myself in and navigated through the darkness to a space between two racks of shelves.

The van sat motionless for what felt like days, but when it finally got under way I was quickly wishing for stillness again. It was even louder and more uncomfortable than the back of the prison truck had been, and once again I had no idea how long I was going to be trapped inside. The only advantage it had was not being locked, so when we did finally come to rest I was able to get out without having to wait to be released.

I rolled up the door, ready to run if anyone saw me, and found we were at the back of a roadside restaurant. Someone was yelling at the driver for being late. *Another toxic side effect of mixing with Marc Bowman,* I thought.

Although this guy was still alive, at least.

I made my way deeper into the shadows and pulled out my phone. I asked Information to connect me with a cab company, but hung up before the first ring. I'd ridden my luck too often already. And besides, a safer alternative was right there, staring me in the face.

The van driver was still out of sight, returning the other unseen guy's ire in spades. His keys were still in the ignition. So, with a silent apology and a muttered prayer that the argument wouldn't end any time soon, I slid in behind the wheel.

THE NIGHT BEFORE, I'd been appalled to see Carolyn's car in the driveway outside LeBrock's home.

This time, I was devastated to find it wasn't there.

LeBrock opened his front door before I was halfway up the path. His feet were bare. His hair was uncombed. A bruise mottled the skin beneath his left eye. And his paisley dressing gown hung open over a pair of crumpled pajamas. He looked twice as old as the guy who'd fired me on Monday.

"You better leave." His voice was hoarse. "I'll call the police this time."

"I'm not looking for trouble, Roger. I just want to see Carolyn."

"She's not here."

Something Weimann had said started to ring in my ears. *We may rake in the dough, but it's hard to compete with power.* And it struck me, gazing up at his glass and steel palace—LeBrock had both power *and* money. What chance did I have?

"How long's it been going on? Between you?"

"Marc, you idiot! Carolyn and I aren't having an affair."

"I saw you together. Yesterday. Here. In your living room."

LeBrock made no attempt to deny it, and after a few seconds he stepped back and headed toward the rear of the house. I followed, and found him in a kind of study area—a horseshoe of pale wooden bookcases surrounding a glass desk with a task chair on one side and a pair of cream leather armchairs on the other.

"Carolyn was here, sure." LeBrock fell back into one of the armchairs and gestured for me to take the other. "She was offering a little consolation. As a friend."

"What do you need consolation for?" I stayed on my feet. "After the auction? You won huge. You proved everyone wrong, including me. And now you're going to need another place this size, just to hold all the cash you must have made."

"I did win. That's true. But at what cost?"

"Are you feeling guilty about something, Roger?"

"Don't play with me. You know I didn't win fair."

"You had a tip."

"I had the mother of all tips. That's why we needed those memory sticks back. Oh, Marc, if only you'd given them to Carolyn . . ."

"Was it the email record you wanted back? Or the virus, too?"

"What the hell are you talking about?"

"Doesn't matter. But what about the tip? It came from someone very high up. No offense, Roger, but you don't have that kind of juice."

"None taken. And you're right. I don't." He rubbed his eyes.

"So who does?"

"Look, AmeriTel was in deep trouble. You know that, Marc. You saw the numbers. What you didn't see was how desperate I was. And how stupid. I started putting feelers out. Looking for ways to bring in short-term cash, under the table, to keep us afloat. Then, when I was struggling with the repayments, the guys I borrowed from came up with an amazing offer. A way I could get off the hook without paying them anything. Save the company. And pocket tens of millions at the same time."

"Sounds too good to be true."

"It was. But by then, I had no choice."

"What did you have to do?"

"Essentially, nothing. Just keep going as if business was usual. Wait for the tip to come through. And revise our auction bid accordingly."

If the guys LeBrock had hooked up with understood finance, my guess was they'd have spent the last couple of years buying shares in other telecom companies. The ones that were supposed to win. Then they'd have sold those shares high. Bought AmeriTel's low, because it was struggling. And when the auction results came out, they'd have hit the mother of all jackpots.

"How many shareholders got burned, Roger? In other companies? How many people lost their jobs?"

He shrugged.

"And you handed someone a dynamite piece of blackmail material."

"I handed them more than that, Marc. They own the company now."

"Couldn't you have gotten out before the auction?"

"I tried to get out. But the price was too steep."

"How much did they want?"

"It wasn't *how much*. It was *what*. I told them I wanted to part ways. Then their top guy came to see me. He's relatively normal-looking. He seems civilized. I think I know how to deal with him. Until he takes out a little leather folder, like they put menus in at restaurants. He tells me to open it. And inside, it looked a bit like a menu, too. There were two lists. The first was punishments. *Killed in car accident. Right arm amputated. Left knee blown out. Run down by bus.* Things like that. The second list was names. Mostly AmeriTel employees, but my sister, too. And my mother. He told me if I ever suggested backing out of our deal again, he'd come back and make me pick one from each list. One name. One punishment. Who got what would be on me."

"Just scare tactics, surely. What if you refused to pick? How could they make you?"

"That's what I thought. I told him I wouldn't play. And do you know what he did? He picked up my cell phone, hit Redial, and took the first two digits that came up. It was a Nashville number, so one and six. One was *car accident*. Six was *Melanie Walker*."

"Wait a minute. Melanie Walker was the name of that finance manager who drove her car into a tree, the first week I was at AmeriTel. She died. But her death was an accident."

LeBrock shook his head.

"It was no accident, Marc. The guy ringed Melanie's name and her fate on those pages. He dated them. Initialed them. I still have them at the office, in my safe. And he told me that if I refused to pick another time—or if I went to the police—he'd use the phone to select three victims. My next choice would be pick one, or have three picked for me. And I couldn't live with that either way."

"I don't blame you. I couldn't, either. And I don't blame you for sharing the burden. But did it have to be Carolyn? Was there no one else you could turn to?"

"It wasn't deliberate. I didn't mean to involve her. But she found the folder. The safe's lock jammed. The contents were in a drawer while a guy was fixing it. Anyway, she saw what was written in there—including the stuff about Melanie—and she freaked out. She was going to call the police, so I had to tell her the truth. And, Marc? There's one other thing."

"What?"

"Carolyn's was one of the names on the list."

I slumped into the armchair opposite him, and neither of us spoke for several minutes. I thought back to my first week at the company. Imagined myself getting home, and not finding Carolyn. Assuming she was working late. Hearing tires on the gravel outside, but not seeing her car. Seeing the police instead.

"I feel sick," I said.

"Me, too."

"I can't believe she didn't tell me."

"Don't blame yourself. I convinced her not to. The more people who knew, the more dangerous it was. For Carolyn, and for the others."

"No wonder she was totally stressed."

"Right. And when you wouldn't give her the memory sticks, she just snapped."

"If only I'd known. I'd have given them to her in a heartbeat. I'd never have taken them. You should have told me, Roger."

"I know that. Now."

"My house getting burglarized? The thugs who chased me? Threw firebombs at me? Tried to kill me? Was that all down to you, too?"

"No. The guy who's in charge? He gave me one shot to get the data back. Carolyn volunteered. She was certain you'd cooperate, if she was the one who asked. When you refused, it was taken out of our hands."

"And Karl Weimann? The fire? That was them?"

LeBrock nodded. "Karl and Carolyn were friends. And they had this running joke. He was always pretending to pester her about selling him your secrets, but of course, he had them already. It was just an excuse to talk to her. Or take her to lunch."

"How could he have them already?"

"Your online security. It's a farce. Everyone in the industry knows. You might as well have handed your secrets to him on a plate, he told me. Anyway, the other day he called Carolyn out of the blue. Apparently you'd summoned him to a meeting and offered him a job. Karl wanted to know, if hell was freezing over, why had nobody else told him?"

"We did meet. I did make the offer, but he turned me down. At first. Then he changed his mind."

"Yes. After he talked to Carolyn. She saw the chance to get hold of the second memory stick and return it. She thought those guys would leave you alone, then."

"So Weimann's change of heart was because of Carolyn? She *was* trying to help me?"

"That's right."

I think LeBrock continued to speak for a while longer. I vaguely remember seeing his mouth moving. His hands gesticulating. But I mainly remember realizing that everything I'd believed had been wrong. Carolyn hadn't betrayed me. She'd stayed loyal to me. And even in her darkest hour, when she was in mortal danger, *she'd* been trying to save *me*.

LeBrock had opened AmeriTel's doors to these maniacs. But Carolyn only worked there because of me. I hadn't just wrecked her acting career. I'd almost gotten her killed.

"Did you hear me?" LeBrock was looming over me. "The fire? It convinced Carolyn she couldn't trust Homeland Security, and—"

"Is Carolyn OK?"

"She was half an hour ago."

"Thank God. But where does that leave us? Her? Me? You? The guys who were threatening you?"

"Come with me. Let me show you something."

I levered myself out of the chair and followed LeBrock around the side of the staircase. The space under it was enclosed, and the wall had been painted to look like a Mondrian, with the metal beams taking the place of the black lines between the fields of color. LeBrock pressed the edge of the largest white panel and stood back, allowing it to open and reveal a little closet with two shelves. The lower one was bare, but on the upper one there were twin piles of money—serious, life-changing piles—and a pair of U.S. passports.

"Forty million dollars," he said.

"In thousand-dollar bills? I didn't know they still existed."

"They do. But they're rare. Collectors' items, basically. Shows the kind of people I'm dealing with."

"And the passports?"

"Take a look. See what you think."

"Isobel Draper." I flipped through the pages. "And Daniel Abbot. But there are no pictures. Who are they?"

"They were going to be Carolyn and me. My guy's adding her picture on Monday."

"You said there was nothing between you. Now you're running away together under false names with a ton of cash?"

"Going away. With new names. But not together. Not like that. The money's nothing. A drop in the ocean, compared to what I made in the auction. And anyway, I'm not going, now. What would be the point?"

"Staying alive? Hang around here, and those guys will come knocking again. You know they will."

"I could run from them, Marc. Sure. But from a ghost? Two ghosts now? How would I do that? So, no. I'm going to stay. I've doubled my life insurance. Installed security cameras. Built a safe room—the best money can buy. And if there's a price to pay on top of that, so be it. I've had enough."

"Good for you, Roger. Very noble. But what about Carolyn? You can't condemn her, too."

"I'm not. Weimann's death was the last straw. It convinced her to run. She's saying some goodbyes, right now. Then she's meeting me here tomorrow. To get her picture taken. She's leaving on Monday, when the passport's done. With her half of the money. All the money, if she wants it."

I opened Isobel Draper's passport again and imagined how it would look with Carolyn's photograph in the empty space.

"Was I on Carolyn's list of goodbyes, Roger?"

"I don't know. She didn't say. But she'll be here tomorrow, at noon. For maybe half an hour. If you haven't heard from her, come over. Tell her goodbye yourself."

LEBROCK HAD SWORN I COULD DEPEND ON HIS DRIVER, AND I prayed he was right as I asked the guy to stop the car half a mile from the Rotunda Inn and wait while I stepped out to use the phone.

The first number I dialed was McKenna's.

"Marc?" He picked up immediately. "Is that you?"

"It is. Are you at the hotel?"

"Which hotel?"

"The weird round one."

"No. Why? Are you?"

"No. How soon could you be there?"

"Say, ninety minutes?"

"That'll work. I want to meet. I have something for you. Another memory stick. One final copy. My wife had it. I'm hoping that'll balance the books, after I skipped out on you."

"OK." He paused. "Have you still got your key card? For the room?"

"Yes."

"Good. The reservation's paid for through tomorrow. If you're there before me, just let yourself in and wait."

"Hold on. I have a condition. I need a promise from you, first."

"What?"

"That you'll come alone. Just you. No tricks. Otherwise the deal's off. I'll disappear and you'll never see me or the memory stick again. Deal?"

"Deal."

"I need your absolute guarantee, Agent McKenna. I'm dead serious."

"You have it, Marc. See you in ninety."

MY NEXT CALL WAS to Peever, and I offered him the same terms. I'd hand over the last remaining memory stick, but only if he met me alone at the Rotunda in ninety minutes. He agreed, too, with no hesitation. And finally I called *News 12*. I told the duty editor I was a limo dispatcher, and I'd just overheard my boss on the phone. He'd taken a top-secret job to meet a pair of mystery celebrities from England at Valhalla train station, sometime in the next two hours. He'd mentioned the Secret Service. A rendezvous with a private plane at Westchester airport. An official car that had broken down. And two names.

Catherine. And George.

Finally I dropped the phone in a little cardboard box I'd taken from the bakery van before leaving LeBrock's. I gave it to his driver with instructions to deliver it to the guy running the coffee cart at Valhalla station, or to leave it behind the rear wheel if no one was there. And then I set off toward the hotel on foot.

I MADE IT TO my old room undetected, and was surprised to see my suitcase sitting on the floor. I'd forgotten that's where I'd left it. My two laptop computers were still inside so I pulled them out, set them at the foot of the bed, turned on the TV, and found the *News 12* channel. It was in the middle of a documentary about how Westchester residents had campaigned to save a local arboretum, but after ten minutes the picture changed. The show was replaced by a special news report.

An outside broadcast.

I recognized the exterior of Valhalla station, behind the reporter's head.

I leaned in closer to the screen, scanning for every detail, but there was no one of interest to be seen. The commentary was banal, and I realized the station was reluctant to make any bold promises on the strength of my call. The guy I'd spoken to mustn't have swallowed my story the way I'd hoped. My heart sank. How long would the report continue? What if they lost interest, and switched back to their regular programs? Or worse, if the sight of the cameras frightened off my prey?

Had I made a fatal miscalculation here?

The reporter filled the airwaves with drivel for another five minutes, then the camera pulled in close for the wrap. And without meaning to, the director did me a huge favor. Because along with his star's face, the view through the station entrance was also magnified. Just enough for me to make out a pair of familiar figures, lurking nonchalantly near the unmanned coffee cart and pretending to be deep in conversation.

Peever. And the other agent I'd seen at the supermarket.

Liars.

Which just left McKenna to worry about.

I COULDN'T BEAR THE RETURN TO REALITY, SO I SWITCHED OFF the TV and lay down to wait.

My head was immediately filled with thoughts of Carolyn. All the things I wanted to say to her. All the ways I could try to apologize. I dreamed up and discarded dozens of possibilities, and when McKenna knocked on my door thirty minutes later I was still no closer to settling on anything even remotely adequate.

McKenna's hair was wet, even though it wasn't raining, and one of the buttons had fallen off his jacket since I'd last seen him. He nodded to me, then sat on the bed next to the laptops and leaned back until half his face disappeared in the shadow thrown by the room's single, low-wattage bulb.

"Talk to me." He picked at a loose thread from the bedspread. "Where have you been?"

"I went to find my wife. I was mad at her. I was mad at you, too, if I'm honest. But I found out some stuff that changed things. See, she was being blackmailed. Her, and Roger LeBrock. AmeriTel's CEO. I convinced her that giving in to these guys was the wrong thing to do. And that if she cooperated with you instead, you'd protect her. She had one more copy of the stick. She'd kept it as insurance. She handed it to me to pass on to you. As a gesture of good faith."

A blank expression came over McKenna's face as if he were running my words through a mental lie detector.

"OK. I'll buy that. If you can produce the stick."

"I've got it right here. And you can take those computers, too. Carolyn used one—she didn't remember which, they both look the same—to make the final copy, so it's probably infected. But I do have one condition."

"*Another* condition?" He pulled at the thread harder, breaking it loose. "What?"

"I promised Carolyn you'd protect her. I need you to do that."

"Consider it done."

"No. Really. I mean it. These guys who are blackmailing her? They're seriously dangerous. Sick. Evil. And their organization has tentacles everywhere. So those fraud experts you mentioned? I want them on the case. I want this to be their top priority. I want you to hand it to their best guy, personally. I don't just want an email getting sent, and then getting lost in some administrator's in-box for months."

"I'd want nothing less, if it was my wife." He rolled the thread into a tiny ball and flicked it away. "Get Carolyn to write it down. Make it as specific as possible. I'll see it doesn't get ignored. I give you my word. And tell her not to worry. Dealing with guys like that is what we do for a living."

"Good enough. And I have something else for you. Do you remember that guy, Agent Peever, you warned me about?"

"Of course. What about him?"

"On the way to find Carolyn, I had a little problem. You probably heard about it. You were probably behind it. Anyway, for a while I was hiding out in a supermarket. Peever was there. I overheard him saying it would be easier to put the AmeriTel case to bed if you were out of the way. Permanently. He was talking about avoiding paperwork. It sounded pretty sinister."

"Thanks for looking out for me." He got to his feet and scooped up the two laptops. "But don't worry about Peever. He won't be a problem for much longer. Now, is there anything else?"

I shook my head.

"Then if I could just have the stick, we can say our goodbyes." He held out his hand.

I stood, too, dug the stick out of my pocket, and handed it to him. He held it up at eye level for a moment, as if the virus it contained was biological rather than electronic and the light would reveal lethal microbes swimming around inside. Then he nodded and turned toward the door. But he stopped again as soon as he touched the handle.

"Actually, I have a favor to ask." He turned back to face me. "But please, feel free to say no. This is a genuine, bona fide, no-strings-attached request. Me to you, Marc. Your answer won't affect how well your wife's problem gets handled, or anything else."

"What is it?"

"Here's the situation. My team—not Peever's—is within touching distance of putting the whole AmeriTel investigation to bed. There's only one more task to complete. With good luck and a fair wind, we'll be done with it before breakfast, tomorrow. But this thing? It's a little specialized. And it's something that's right down your alley. So it occurred to me, maybe you'd help us?"

"I don't know. What would I have to do?"

"Not much. The job's pretty simple. We have a thing—I can't remember the name of it—but it's a little electronic gizmo. You'd know it if you saw it. Anyway, we need to plug it into the ARGUS node. Wait for a light to go green. And unplug it again."

"Why?"

"We've confirmed the node as the insertion point of the virus. But we don't know who the guy on the ground was. This gadget will collect the information we need to cross reference with the list of legitimate users and narrow down our pool of suspects. And because it's a computer system and you're a computer guy, and it's in AmeriTel's office and you used to work there, I'd be stupid not to ask."

"This has to happen in the morning?"

"It doesn't have to. But Sunday morning is generally the quietest time to be at an office. I don't want to be tripping over people while we're there. Why? Is there a reason not to do it then?"

"No. As long as I can be on the road by eleven. I'm meeting Carolyn. We still have a few fences to mend."

"Eleven? No problem." McKenna nodded to me. "I have a good feeling about this, Marc. Sleep well. I'll pick you up at five."

———

I GUESS THERE WAS STILL a part of me that was prepared to help a guy do the right thing. And another part that believed in quid pro quo. McKenna had gone out on a limb for me enough times. But the biggest part was the one that was gambling on Carolyn's reaction, when she heard how connected I'd become to the guys who'd be keeping her safe.

If she agreed to stay.

I'D JUST FINISHED SHAVING WHEN MCKENNA KNOCKED ON MY door at a couple of minutes shy of five am. He was wearing a plain gray coverall, stiff, with sharp creases in the arms and legs.

"Here." He handed me another one, still in its packet. "Slip this on. We're being mainframe installation contractors today. Should be right down your alley."

I took the coverall and grunted, which was all the communication I could muster at that hour of the morning.

"I doubted it would fit." He watched me struggle to fasten the buttons. "They only come in army sizes. Too big, or too small. Still, it's more convincing than jeans."

MCKENNA REACHED THE PARKING LOT first and nodded toward his white van.

"You're riding shotgun, next to me."

Two more agents were in the back. The woman from the Mercedes, whose nails were now violet, and a guy from one of the other cars. His hair was cropped a touch too neatly for his coveralls, and his shave was a little too smooth, reminding me of the undercover cops who used to show up at the bars near my old college campus. I smiled, and nodded a greeting as I belted myself in. Then McKenna fired up the engine and pulled away, taking the entrance lane because it was closer than the exit.

No one spoke until AmeriTel's roof was visible in the distance, then a question popped into my head.

"How are we going to get inside? And move around? There are security doors between every work zone, and you need special swipe cards to get through. You weren't relying on mine, were you? I don't have it with me. I had to turn it in, when I was fired. It wasn't authorized for the ARGUS node room. And anyway, it'll be deactivated by now."

McKenna pulled four plain white plastic cards from his pocket and fanned them out for us to each take one, then slid his own away again. "They don't have fancy logos. But don't let that fool you. They'll get us through any door in the place. Guaranteed."

"Where did you get them from? A sales guy tried to copy his once—so he could sneak his girlfriend in on weekends—but he was told it was impossible."

"Marc, do we look like sales guys?" McKenna turned in through AmeriTel's gates. "You really don't know who you're dealing with, do you?"

We looped around the back of the building, and I saw the exuberant pink Cadillac exiled in its usual spot.

"Look." I pointed to it. "That's good news. The security guard who drives it? I know him. He'll be asleep right now. In Reception. If we go in the side, through the engineers' entrance, he'll never see us."

"Good to know." McKenna nodded. "Anything else?"

"Yes. Park over there. The space that's straight in front of us now. It was my usual place. It'll bring us luck."

McKenna gave me a sideways look, but he did what I asked and then turned to the agents behind us. The woman was sipping a coffee she'd produced from somewhere, and the guy was polishing a pair of mirrored Aviators.

"Everything looks quiet, so I want you two to stay here for now. Keep your eyes and ears open. Marc and I will go in. Marc? Are you ready?"

I nodded, then we got out and hurried toward the side entrance. It made sense to me to be in the open for as little time as possible, but McKenna took my arm and slowed me down.

"Do you always walk this fast, Marc? Relax. You're just doing your job. It's boring. You'd rather be home, in bed, but you can't be. So you're at least going to milk the overtime. Get the idea? We can't control whether anyone sees us. But if they do, we want them to think, *Oh, look at those IT guys. They're here again.* Not, *Wow, look at those really suspicious uptight guys who are obviously pretending to be IT contractors. I better call 911.*"

I listened, and I tried to do what he told me. Moving slowly was like torture, but we did reach the entrance without incident. The access card he'd given me worked fine, and it was a relief to hear the door click back into place behind me. From there it was plain sailing—across the engineers' area, up a flight of stairs, and along a corridor all the way to an innocuous-looking, unmarked wooden door at the far end of the building.

"Is this it?" McKenna asked.

I nodded.

"OK, then." He swiped his card. "In we go. I was expecting something a little more impressive for the money, is all."

McKenna was already disappointed with the outside of the node room so there was little scope for his face to fall further when he saw the inside. It was really a closet rather than a room—six feet by six feet, pale green paint, scuff marks on the walls near the door frame—and there was no furniture or fittings other than a pair of standard equipment cabinets and a heavy-duty air-conditioning vent in the ceiling.

McKenna pulled the door closed and produced a black box about the size of a cigarette packet from his pocket. It had a USB plug protruding from one side, and a label with two lines of printed characters stuck to the underneath. I'd never seen anything like it before.

"I know we have to plug this in. But where? Does it even matter?"

"In there." I pointed to the right-hand cabinet. The glass in the door was frosted, but if you looked closely you could see the space above the middle shelf was much taller than the others. A monitor and keyboard sat there, and a USB port was visible in the piece of equipment below it. "See? That's the interface."

"Well spotted." McKenna pulled the handle on the cabinet door. It didn't move.

"What now?" He looked at me. "Can we break in?"

"Probably. But we might not have to. Give me a second."

I reached up to the top of the cabinet, slid my fingers across to the side, and sure enough I felt them brush against something small and loose. I took it down and showed McKenna.

"A key? You're kidding me. This place is supposed to be secure."

"It doesn't surprise me." I shrugged. "You wouldn't believe what you come across in secure buildings. I had a government contract once where I had to wait six months to get clearance for one particular site. I turned up, and walked straight in. No lock on the door at all. But when I went to the kitchen to get a coffee, the fridge was locked up tighter than Fort Knox. It's just how people are."

"Ridiculous." He worked the lock and opened the cabinet.

"Go ahead." I passed him the box.

Very gingerly he lined up the plug and socket and pushed. It slid easily into place. And nothing happened.

"What now? Is it broken? Or did I do it wrong?"

"Neither. I think I know what the problem is. With systems like this the USB ports look normal, but you often have to activate them before you can use them. It's a security thing, to stop unauthorized people plugging stuff in. That'll be what that writing is, on the bottom of the device. The user name and password. Let me see?"

McKenna disconnected the box and passed it to me. I switched on the monitor, keyed in the details, and within a few seconds I was logged on. The procedure was the same as with any of the dozens—hundreds?—of systems I interrogated every year. But this was no ordinary network. This was ARGUS. The electronic equivalent of the all-seeing, hundred-eyed giant. It constantly monitors every detail of every kind of communication between every citizen in this country and beyond. And it had given me administrator-level access. The IT geek in me was drooling at the possibilities, but McKenna was watching. So, reluctantly, I had to restrict myself to the couple of minutes' searching it took me to find the option to enable the USB port.

"OK." I handed the box back. "Try it now."

McKenna plugged the box back in. This time, a little light on its top surface glowed red.

"Marc, you're a genius. All we've got to do now is wait for the green light. Literally."

———

IT WASN'T UNTIL MCKENNA'S words had died away that the full weirdness of the situation hit me. Locked in that small space with nothing to distract me and only the red light to stare at—on a piece of IT equipment I'd never heard of, attached to a top-secret government database I should never have had access to—I was close to walking away and telling McKenna to unplug the thing himself. Another thirty seconds, and I might have done that. But then the light changed to green. It took a few more keystrokes to close the USB port down, and we were finally free to get out of there.

McKenna tucked the box safely into his coverall pocket and gestured for me to lead the way as we reversed our path from earlier. The upper floor was still deserted, and my thoughts had run ahead of me by the time we reached the door to the engineers' area. The prospect of seeing Carolyn was foremost in my mind so I swiped the access card and pushed the door open without thinking to peep through the observation window first. I took a step inside. And saw the security guard. He was on the other side of the room, stretching up to touch a shiny metal fob against a small circular pad on the wall. Instinctively I started to turn, but McKenna had read my mind and he took a firm hold of my arm.

"No," he breathed into my ear. "He'll see, and that'd be way more suspicious. If word spreads, the inside man will disappear. We'll never catch him. You'll have to bluff this out."

I was about to object when the guard saw us and waddled across in our direction.

"Pete!" I tried not to make it obvious I was squinting at his name badge. "How's it going? Weekends again? You and me—we always draw the short straw."

"I'm good, thanks, Mr. Bowman. And I have no problem with weekends. Less work. More pay. What's not to like? I'm pulling a double today."

"You've got a point, Pete. More pay's never a bad thing. But look, I've got to dash. These guys I'm with have got another job to get to."

I DON'T THINK I breathed again until we reached the parking lot, and I was just turning to ask McKenna if he thought we'd pulled it off when I caught movement out of the corner of my eye. It was the other two agents, walking down the path toward us.

"I beeped them." McKenna responded to the question on my face. "In case we had any trouble with that security guy."

"You doubted my bluffing skills?" I was still buzzing a little from the encounter.

"Maybe. At first. But not any longer. You're a natural."

I watched as his guys strolled closer, wondering if that's how McKenna and I had appeared in our matching outfits, when I noticed the others' coveralls weren't quite the same as ours. They looked older and scruffier, like they'd been worn before. And there was a logo on their chests, while ours were plain.

And then I knew.

Look at those IT guys. They're here again.

I'd seen that logo before. On Monday, when I was leaving the building after being fired. Two unfamiliar contractors had been walking in, carrying a degausser. I'd assumed they'd been summoned to clean up my old machines. But could McKenna have picked the exact same uniforms for our cover, today? There was no way I'd buy that as a coincidence. Which meant it must have been McKenna's guys on Monday, sneaking in to remove the virus.

Which meant McKenna was working for whoever had created it.

And then another one-two combination landed. Carolyn's protection was in McKenna's hands. And McKenna knew she'd found out about the virus.

Both because of me.

I'd trusted him with one, and told him the other.

A WEEK EARLIER, I WOULDN'T HAVE KNOWN WHAT IT WAS. I still couldn't tell you the brand. Or model. Or what caliber of bullet it fired. But by then, I at least recognized a gun barrel when one was jammed against my neck.

My fingertips froze, an inch from the van's scuffed plastic door lever. McKenna completed the turn through AmeriTel's fancy gate, then hit the gas. I drew my hand back onto my lap. My chance to jump out and run back to the safety of the building had gone.

No one spoke for the rest of the journey, but inside my head I was cursing myself. These guys weren't Homeland Security agents. *Peever's* guys were. And it wasn't like I'd been kidnapped and locked in a hidden basement. Peever had been in my home. I had his phone number. I'd been two feet away from him yesterday, hiding in the kitchen at the supermarket. But instead of throwing myself on his mercy, I'd run from him. And then set that stupid test. So what if he'd tracked the cell phone to Valhalla train station? All that proved was he had Homeland Security's resources behind him. As an agent—and only an agent— would. My reasoning had been completely back to front.

I was an idiot.

Or was I? McKenna had been polite. Helpful. He'd kept rescuing me. Sharing information. Making me feel valued. That's how he'd dug the trap. But I hadn't walked into it on my own. Peever had tripped me, with his macho bullshit. He never missed a chance to push me around, or put me down, or try to throw me in prison for something I hadn't done. He was an asshole. And if he'd kept his word and met me at the hotel, the mess would be swept up by now and Carolyn would be safe.

I'D ASSUMED WE'D HEAD BACK to the hotel, but it soon became obvious we were making for my house. My stomach turned over at the thought of the body I'd left in my bathroom, the last time I was there. I was still feeling queasy when we turned into my street and I saw my driveway was now sealed off with a lone, drooping strand of police tape.

"Come on, Marc." McKenna pulled over to the curb and opened his door. "Time to get out."

I climbed slowly down onto the sidewalk and was surprised when the van pulled away and continued down the street.

"Where are they going?"

"They have other things to do." McKenna lifted the police tape and gestured for me to duck underneath. "It's just the two of us now."

I followed him down my driveway and saw that my Jaguar was still there, with remnants of gray powder around the door handles, the trunk, and over most of the interior. The fragments of broken license plate light were gone. And beyond the car, more police tape had been stuck across my front door, zigzagging its way from bottom to top.

"Have you got your keys?" McKenna asked.

"Only Carolyn's." I dug into my pocket and handed them over. "We'll have to go around the back."

MCKENNA UNLOCKED THE DOOR, pushed it open, and ushered me into my kitchen.

"The hiding place." He stayed by the doorway. "Where you put the memory stick. Show me, please."

"Here." I stopped next to the loose section of counter. "This piece lifts up. The stick was underneath."

"Show me."

I pried the moveable part up about twelve inches, hinging the rear edge of the slab against the wall, and McKenna took a step forward so he could see the space underneath.

"Perfect." He handed me the black box we'd used in the node room at AmeriTel. "Take this. Put it in. Then lower the countertop, but don't let it go down all the way. Make sure it stays wedged up a little. I want anyone searching the room to see it. Don't make it too obvious, though. I don't want a neon sign pointing to it."

I did what McKenna asked, then turned to face him.

"Thank you, Marc. Nicely done. Now please join me in the study."

"Why?"

"We have some writing to do."

I'D SAT AT MY DESK a thousand times, but always to use my computer. Not a pen and paper. And never with a gun trained on me.

"You know what?" I threw the pen down and turned to face McKenna. "I'm not doing this. If you're going to shoot me, go ahead. I won't make it easier for you. And it won't work, anyway. No one will believe I'd ever kill myself."

"Marc, you're wasting time. Pick up the pen. I can dictate, if—"

McKenna's phone beeped. He glanced at the incoming message, and a flash of annoyance crossed his face.

"What's up?" I felt a flutter of hope. "Change of plan?"

"No. Just a delay with my ride out of here."

"So we have some time? Long enough for me to see Carolyn? And say goodbye, properly? If you could let me have, maybe, a couple of hours—"

"Don't insult me. And don't ask for more time. You've had more, already. When I broke you out of jail? That's when this was supposed to happen. And even then, it was your fault. I tried to help you. I gave you chance after chance to cooperate. But your greed wouldn't let you, Marc. All this—your house, your car, your paintings, your marriage—it wasn't enough for you. So you lied. You meddled. You pushed your luck so far my people lost patience with you."

"Why not kill me yesterday, then?" I was desperate to keep him talking. "Why wait, to make it look like I planted the virus?"

"Because when Homeland Security checks ARGUS, they'll find a ton of evidence—a *ton,* more than you could ever outrun, even if we let you live—linking you to half a dozen Syrians. Sleepers. They'll be neutralized. And the United States will go on the offensive against the people they think tried to kill the President. You're the last link in the chain. Now, write."

I turned away from him, but left the pen where it was. The harder I tried to think, the slower my mind seemed to work. My last hope was fading away. Then I looked up at my Lichtenstein, and the spark of a new idea took hold.

"One last question." I spun around in my chair. "Just out of curiosity. You know how your guys searched the house but missed the memory stick hidden under the countertop? I was wondering. Did they find the other one? Upstairs?"

"What other one?"

"The one I hid in the attic. In case the one in the kitchen was found."

"What crap are you trying to pull here, Marc? You told me your wife handed over the last one."

"I had some insurance, too." I shrugged. "And now I'm curious. I thought I'd found a secure spot, but you can never be sure."

"In the attic?"

"Your guys aren't back yet. We've got time. I could show you . . ."

CRUSTY DROPLETS OF DRIED BLOOD were still visible near the bottom of the stairs, reminding me not to be too clever this time. I stepped over them, and led McKenna up to the second floor. And as soon as we turned toward my bedroom, I made sure I stayed between him and the wall.

"There it is." I pointed to the trapdoor in the ceiling. "Do you want to do the honors, or shall I?"

"I'll do it." He reached up, grabbed the cord, and pulled. The catch released. The door dropped down and the ladder shot out of the darkness, metal shrieking against metal. McKenna leapt out of its path. And I launched myself off the wall, slamming against his shoulder and sending him spinning into the banister rail.

The same banister rail I'd been thrown against myself, on Thursday. It had been three-quarters wrecked then, so it was no match for McKenna's weight and momentum. Pieces of wood broke free and scattered in all directions, and for a moment McKenna's body seemed to pause, frozen at an impossible angle.

I could have reached out and saved him, if my arms had been longer.

And he hadn't just tried to kill me.

Sunday. Late morning.

*I*T LOOKED LIKE JACKSON POLLOCK HAD BEEN TO WORK ON MY hall floor.

I went to the linen closet and pulled out all the sheets and blankets I could find. I kept one back, and threw the others down until they'd formed a cover over the worst of the bloody mess. Then I ran down the stairs and along to my study. I grabbed the spare keys to my Jaguar. Fished an old cell phone out of a drawer. Took my Lichtenstein off the wall. Wrapped it in the sheet. Made doubly sure the canvas was well protected. Moved to the kitchen to recover McKenna's black box from under the countertop. And then left my home for the last time.

WHEN CAROLYN'S DESPERATE FOR something to happen a particular way, she visualizes the outcome she wants. A new contract. A raise. The Mets to beat the Yankees. I'd never been convinced, personally. But that morning I needed all the help I could get. So, as I reeled in the miles between my house and LeBrock's—and the hands on the clock crept ever closer to noon—I conjured an image into my head. His driveway. With Carolyn's car on it. Just like it had been on Friday night.

Her method worked. A hundred yards from LeBrock's drive I caught a glimpse of silver paint through the trees. Two glimpses. Carolyn's BMW, and another car. An Aston Martin. The photographer's? My heart jumped. I leaned harder on the gas, and seconds later I was out of the Jaguar and hurrying along his front path.

For the second straight day, LeBrock opened his door before I got there. But this time he was fully dressed—in black jeans, boots, and a faux biker's jacket, which looked ridiculous on a man his age—and he wasn't coming to greet me. He actually flinched when he saw me, which scotched a fleeting hope that Carolyn had sent him out to give us a little privacy.

"Going away somewhere, Roger?" I nodded at the gray polycarbonate suitcase he was wheeling behind him.

"No."

"Then why do you need luggage? And what about Carolyn? Is she here?"

"Change of plan, Marc. Sorry. Carolyn couldn't make it, after all."

"No? Then why's her car on your drive?"

"She asked me to sell it for her. Dropped it here earlier, and took a car service to the airport."

"But she's having the fake passport photo done at noon. That's in, what? Ten minutes? She can't have left already. She wouldn't travel under her own name. So spill. What's really happening?"

"Nothing. I had the photo guy come early. She didn't want to wait till tomorrow to fly out, is all."

The lower lid of his left eye started to tremble.

"What's in the case, Roger?"

"Nothing. Sorry, Marc. I have to go."

I grabbed the handle, ripped it from his grip, and held him off long enough to ease back the zipper.

The case was stuffed full of neatly-wrapped bills.

"The forty million? You're running off with my wife, after all? You lying bastard."

"No." He lunged for the case, but I shoved him away. "There's no we, here. Just me. Carolyn's not coming."

"You stiffed her, too? You piece of shit."

"I didn't. This isn't my idea."

"Then whose is it? Carolyn's? She asked to be left behind, vulnerable and penniless?"

LeBrock didn't reply.

"This makes no sense, Roger. Look, neither of us is blameless. I'm not looking to pin anything on you. I just want to understand what's happening."

"OK. But not here. Come away from the door."

LEBROCK PERCHED ON THE HOOD of his Mercedes, and his head dropped.

"Carolyn is in the house," he admitted. "In the basement. But you can't see her."

"Why not? Is she OK?"

"She is. At the moment."

"Stop this cryptic bullshit. Tell me what's happening."

LeBrock took a small leather folder from his jacket pocket and handed it to me. Inside, a piece of paper was attached to each cover. On the left, two names: *Roger LeBrock* and *Carolyn Clark Bowman*. On the right, three words: *Death by suffocation*.

"Note there are only two names," he said. "And one outcome."

"This is from the guy you were telling me about?"

"He gave it to me this morning. Showed up in my bedroom and handed it to me like a room-service breakfast menu."

"And you chose to save yourself, leaving Carolyn to die? How could you do that?"

LeBrock didn't answer.

"Oh." I raised the suitcase. "Maybe this made the choice a little easier. Did the guy know the cash was in the house?"

"Of course he did." LeBrock looked up at me, his back stiffening. "He brought me the case to carry it in! Don't you get how this guy works? It's not just psychopathic with him. It's psychological. Think about it. If I walk away with the money, how can I enjoy it? Knowing what I did to get it?"

"And yet you're doing it anyway."

"Easy for you to sit on your high horse and judge! You think you'd have done the noble thing? Because let me tell you—you wouldn't."

"I would."

"Yeah? Like when you shot down Carolyn's chance to leave Ameri-Tel? So you could live off her fat paycheck? Like a damn pimp?"

"That was different."

"Prove it." LeBrock dived across the hood and this time he managed to claw the case away from me. Then he zipped it open the rest of the way and started to hurl handfuls of wrapped-up bills at me. Dozens of them. He didn't stop till they were heaped and scattered at my feet like bricks at a construction site. "There. That's five million, at least. Go inside and offer your life in your wife's place. Or scoop up the cash and drive away."

"Wait. What about other options? How many guys are in there with her?"

"One."

"Only one? There's two of us. Why don't we go inside and bring her out? And tell this guy to fuck himself at the same time?"

"We can't. You don't understand. Carolyn's tied up in my safe room. The guy's cut off the air supply. Right now, the door's open, which means she's still OK. But he's holding a dead-man's switch. Can you believe I paid extra for that? Anyway, all he has to do is let go, and the door closes. Automatically. And once it's closed, there's no way to open it from the outside. Literally, no way. The thing's impregnable. And totally airtight."

"OK. Then we call the police. They have negotiators. And hostage rescue teams. They deal with this kind of thing all the time. That's got to give her a better chance than walking away and leaving her. Unless you think the guy's bluffing?"

"The one thing this guy doesn't do is bluff. Ask Melanie Walker's husband."

"Then I'm calling 911." I pulled out my phone.

"No point. There's not enough time. Because regardless of the dead-man's switch, the guy's closing the door at noon. The only question was who'd be inside. Carolyn, or me? Now it's Carolyn, or you."

"Noon?" I looked at the phone. "That's six minutes away!"

"Then you better make your choice." LeBrock picked up the case and climbed into the Mercedes. "Let's see how strong those morals are now, buddy."

I looked across at the door to the house.

Then started to grab up the money.

*L*EBROCK'S BASEMENT WAS LIKE A PRIVATE OUTPOST OF THE Container Store.

The stairs opened into the center of a broad, brightly lit space. In one direction all I could see were rows of shelves, perfectly fitted to the height and length of the walls, and filled to capacity with color-coded boxes and baskets and buckets. But on the other side of the staircase there was just a single object. A giant cuboid. Fifteen-feet wide. Twenty long. Ten high. Plain, gloss white surfaces.

The safe room?

I kicked myself for not asking LeBrock to explain how it worked. Where the controls were. Or even to tell me the name of the bastard who was holding my wife hostage.

"Hello?" I hurried around the far side of the smooth, white perimeter. "Whoever you are? I need to talk to you."

"Marc?" Carolyn's voice was shrill with stress. "Is Roger with you?"

I ran faster, turned the corner, and found the door to the safe room. A six-inch-thick slab of steel, which looked like it had been stolen from a bank vault. It was set on rollers, top and bottom. And it was still open. I breathed again. But I couldn't see much more because my way was blocked. A man was sitting on a Barcelona chair in front of the doorway, his immaculate black suit merging against the leather so that his head and the front panel of his shirt seemed to be floating in space. His hair was parted in a neat, anonymous style, but his skin was waxy and his face immobile, like he was made out of parts from a mannequin. Even his eyes moved only once, homing in on mine and holding me in an unblinking stare.

His left hand was resting on his lap but his right was out of sight, tucked away in his trouser pocket.

"Is Carolyn Bowman in there? I just heard her. Is she all right?"

"Where's Roger?" Carolyn yelled. "Is he coming back?"

"Be my guest." The guy smiled. "See for yourself."

I peered around the door frame. Carolyn was dressed in an outfit I hadn't seen before. A casual gray dress with a matching cashmere cardigan and low-heeled sandals. They'd have made good travel clothes. Except that she was standing on tiptoe, hands above her head, chained to a ventilation duct.

"Marc?" Her face was white with panic. "Has Roger gone? Has he left me here?"

"Five million dollars." I tore my gaze away from Carolyn and stepped back toward the guy in the suit. "Five million. Maybe a little more. I didn't have time to count it. But it's yours, if you let my wife go. Every cent."

"It's no good, Marc," Carolyn yelled. "You don't understand. You have to find Roger!"

"The five million?" The guy stood up. "Do you have it here?"

Had LeBrock been lying? Had he even tried to save Carolyn?

"I can get it in two minutes."

"Good. Then you can have the same deal as LeBrock. I close this door. You walk away, and take the money with you."

"No!" Carolyn's chains clattered as she tried to rip them free of the duct. "Marc, you fool! You've messed everything—"

"Quiet!" the guy interrupted. "Or, Marc, you take your wife's place, and *she* walks away with the money. Only, I wonder how much she'd enjoy the rest of *her* life, knowing the price you paid for her freedom?"

Carolyn stopped moving and the chains fell silent. I wanted to throw myself on the guy, knock him down, and beat his head against the shiny concrete floor. But then I remembered the switch LeBrock had mentioned. The guy's hand was still in his pocket. Could I take the chance?

"Those are your choices," he went on. "Only you've got less money on the table than LeBrock had, so I'm giving you less time to decide. You mentioned two minutes. Let's go with that."

"No. Listen—"

"Did LeBrock fill you in on the details? In case you're thinking of anything stupid."

"Yes, but—"

"Then the clock's running. You have a minute fifty-five."

"Wait. Let's talk. There must be something else you want? How about this? I design management information software. I'm working on a new project, right now. It's going to be huge. You could—"

"A minute fifty."

"OK. What about art? I have a Lichtenstein. An original. It's worth a fortune. You can have—"

"One, forty-five . . ."

I COULDN'T BARGAIN WITH HIM. I had to concede that. Could I kill him? Knock him unconscious? Maybe. Maybe not. But what about the switch?

I needed to paralyze him. Completely. In the next hundred seconds. But how?

The answer was simple.

I couldn't. Not without help.

I started to walk away, much as LeBrock must have done earlier. But I paused when I was level with the door. The guy was standing between me and Carolyn, with the chair still behind him. Carolyn's face was pale. It was half hidden by her wild hair. A tear formed in the corner of her left eye. It defied gravity for a moment. Then started to roll down her cheek.

"Sweetheart, I'm sorry. I was wrong. About everything. This is all my fault. I should be—"

"Screw you, Marc!" More tears appeared. "You fool. You Judas!"

I took a step back, then another, until my back was touching the basement wall.

"Why are you dragging this out?" Her tears were streaming now, dripping down and soaking the front of her cardigan. "Just go!"

I gazed at Carolyn for another second then dropped my shoulder and charged, driving my head into the guy's chest and knocking him backward. The chair pivoted on its hind legs and we flew over it, crashing onto the floor. Pain jolted through my knee. And the safe room door began to close.

I pushed myself up and started to scramble away but the guy grabbed my lapel, pulling me back down. The edge of the door reached my shoulder. It started digging into my flesh. Desperate, I gouged at the guy's eyes. His grip slackened and I tore myself free, springing back and tumbling over the chair again.

The guy screamed. I leapt to my feet and saw the door had shunted him sideways. It was crushing him against the steel frame. His legs thrashed frantically. His hands clawed the concrete, unable to grip. The door motor continued to hum. It grew louder, rising in pitch. The guy's movements ebbed away. And then the mechanism was silent, locked in place, and he was finally still.

"Carolyn? Are you all right?"

She didn't reply.

"Carolyn!"

"I'm fine. Marc? What happened?"

The dead-man's switch had fallen from the guy's pocket. I picked it up. Pressed the button. It had no effect. I grabbed hold of the door and heaved, but couldn't move it even a fraction of an inch. So, conscious of the seconds ticking away, I planted my foot on the guy's chest and squeezed through the narrow gap.

I'd always imagined safe rooms to be spartan holdovers from the Cold War, full of metal shelves, canned food, and army cots. But LeBrock's was a combination of boutique hotel and industrial chic. He had leather furniture. Blond-wood fixtures. Paintings on the walls. Even a bowl of potpourri.

"Don't touch me." Carolyn's body was rigid. She wasn't crying anymore, but her cheeks were still slick with tears. "Stay away from me."

"What about your chains? You want to stay like that?"

"The police can deal with them. Just call 911, and leave."

"No."

"Just go. I can't bear to look at you. Have you got any idea—"

"Yes, Carolyn. I do. LeBrock told me everything. That's why I came back. Why I didn't leave you here, like he did. And why I'm not going now. Not on my own."

"Roger told you?"

"Last night. We talked. I know I screwed up, Carolyn. But I have a way to fix it. We can get out of this. Together."

"*You* have a way?" Her voice was shrill. "Excuse me if I'm not convinced, Marc. What's your plan? Just tell me it doesn't involve memory sticks or computers."

"Carolyn, don't be a bitch. Stop fighting me on this. Did you see where the guy put the key?"

"He didn't use a key. It's a padlock, Einstein. It pushes closed."

I stepped back toward the door, reached down, and felt for a pulse in the guy's neck. Just in case. Behind me, I heard Carolyn sob. Then I checked the guy's pockets. Found a set of keys. Fished them out. And identified the one that fit the lock on Carolyn's chains.

CAROLYN FLOPPED DOWN ONTO the Barcelona day bed that filled the corner of the room. Then she started to massage the red weals that ringed her wrists.

"What are you doing? We need to go."

"I can't do this, Marc." She clamped her hands over her face, covering her eyes.

"You have to. There's no other way out."

"Hello! There's a dead guy jammed in the doorway! A guy *you* just killed! What am I supposed to do?"

"Just climb over him. He can't hurt you."

"Can't you pull him out? Move him out of sight?"

"No. Because one, he's wedged in tight and two, that would let the door close and you'd be trapped inside with no air supply, which would defeat the whole purpose of killing him."

"But I can't just step on his corpse."

"You can. Pretend you're onstage. Imagine he's acting."

"Marc!"

"OK. Forget that. Give me a minute."

I squeezed back out of the safe room and ran to the other end of the basement, frantically scanning the shelves. One of the large plastic boxes was labeled SKI CLOTHES. I tore off the lid. Pulled out a thick, yellow parka. Brought it back to the doorway. And threw it down, covering the guy's face and torso.

"There." I gestured to Carolyn. "You don't have to touch him now."

"Did you *have* to kill him?" She made no move to get off the bed.

"It was him, or you. Would you have preferred to suffocate?"

"No."

"Well, then. Come on. We have to get going."

"Can't you call the police? Have *them* come and remove the body? They could wedge the door, and—"

"There's no time. That would take too long. And they'd ask too many questions. We need to move. Now."

"You go. I'll wait for them here."

"I'm not leaving without you."

"That's not your choice, Marc." She glared at me. "It's complicated. It's not just the body. It's . . . I don't know if I can go with you. You've changed. I need time to think."

"Time is the one thing we don't have, sweetheart. There are things I have to do, to make our escape work."

"Then go do them. I'll meet you. Give you my decision then."

"What's to decide? We need to stick together."

"Don't push this, Marc." It was the same tone of voice she'd used on Monday. Right before she walked out on me. "I'm telling you. I need time."

"OK. You'll meet me. When?"

"In an hour. At the house."

"Can't be the house."

"Why not?"

"Just trust me. Don't go back there."

"What about Zapatista's?"

"That would work."

She stood and walked slowly toward me. Took hold of the edge of the door. Pressed her other hand against the inside of the frame. And catapulted herself over the body, her feet barely grazing the coat I'd covered it with. But when I tried to catch her, she pushed me away.

"I'm going to drive around. Clear my head. And, Marc? Try to follow me, and we're done."

I WASN'T CONVINCED CAROLYN WOULD SHOW UP UNTIL THE MO-ment I saw her car pull into the lot.

I watched her park, then make her way inside the restaurant. But I didn't follow her right away. I didn't even switch off my engine until I was certain she was alone.

ZAPATISTA'S IS ON the first floor of a broad, rectangular office building. The bar takes up the whole of the right-hand wall. Behind it is a giant mirror, partially painted with scenes from the Mexican landscape. Move while you're waiting to order a drink, and your face suddenly appears from behind a cactus or a mountain. It's quite a surprise, the first time it happens. Especially if you've already had a few.

The area in front of the bar is dominated by a high, rough oak, refectory-style table, surrounded by twenty tall stools. It's always packed in the evenings, full of younger customers. But that afternoon, it was deserted. It reminded me of a time, shortly after she joined the company, when Carolyn booked it for an AmeriTel Finance department party. It had been a disaster.

The regular tables are scattered haphazardly throughout the rest of the space. Maybe a quarter of them were taken. Mostly by couples. There was the odd family. And at the far end, on her own in the restaurant's only booth, I spotted Carolyn.

"You're late." She was wearing the same dress as earlier, but had switched to a darker cardigan.

There was a *bang* behind me. I spun around, and saw a kid flinging toys from his high chair.

"Marc, take it easy." She sipped her coffee. She was drinking it black. "Sit."

"What's your decision?" I stayed on my feet.

"It's not that simple."

"It is that simple. Are you coming with me? Or not? Yes? Or no?"

"You and your damn one-dimensional universe. You're impossible. I should never have agreed to meet."

I took the seat opposite her.

"Thank you, Marc. Look—"

"Why's that guy staring at me?"

The man at the nearest table turned his head away.

"No one's staring at you. You're being paranoid."

"I'm not. But all that matters is, are you coming?"

"The truth, Marc? I don't know. My world's turned upside down so many times, I don't know which way is up. My life's been hanging by a thread. You weren't around when I needed you. And when you were around, you only dug the hole deeper. Meaning I had to do things for myself. I got money. A new identity. An escape route. And now there's a voice in my head screaming: Take it!"

"Despite what happened this morning?"

"Partly *because* of what happened this morning. I almost died!"

"And your heart? What's it telling you?"

"You're asking about my *heart*? Marc, please."

"I am asking. Because I've changed. I've made mistakes, and I've learned from them. I saved your life this morning. And with that guy out of the picture, things are different. There's nothing to stop us being together. If you want us to be. Sweetheart, please. Come with me. Right now. Let's go."

"Slow down. There's too much to process! Have you learned? Maybe. Have you changed? Definitely. But look what happened at Roger's! You've done messed-up things, Marc! Bad things. Maybe you've changed too much. I'm not sure who you are anymore."

"You said you *wanted* me to change. That I *had* to change, to be with you. At that French restaurant, on Monday night."

"Yes. I did. I meant it. But now you're scaring me, Marc. There are stories all over the Web about you murdering people. Karl's dead. And the Homeland Security agent you set me up with? He was an imposter. What the hell was that?"

"I haven't *murdered* anyone. And the guy? I thought he was a real agent. He tricked me. It's complicated. Come with me. I'll explain while I drive."

"They'll be looking for your Jag. It won't be safe."

"I'm using the dead guy's car."

"You stole a car? You see? This is insane. The Marc I married would never do that. If we're going to have a future together, we need to straighten things out. We can't just walk away and pretend nothing happened."

"Look, Carolyn, I know this has been hell for you. And I know a lot of it was my fault. But I've got it figured out now. We *can* disappear. Together. But we've got to go. Now."

"No. Not unless you can convince me the nightmare's over. I can't be running and hiding for the rest of my life. I'm thinking, maybe you could talk to someone? Like Homeland Security? Get some—"

"They're the last people I could talk to. There's a database. When they check . . . they'll find things. Records. Lies. About me. Incriminating stuff. We need to avoid them like the plague. And we need to get away from here."

"I don't think so. We can't do this on our own. We need help, to get all this weird stuff squared away. We need . . . You're late!"

Her gaze suddenly shifted to a point above my left shoulder. I spun around. And saw two men, almost on top of us.

Peever. And the other agent from the supermarket.

Carolyn may have called this *getting help*.

But I had another name for it altogether.

PEEVER GRABBED ME BY THE ARM AND SHUNTED ME INTO THE booth, next to Carolyn. Then he took the chair I'd vacated and moved in close, cutting off any chance of escape.

"You knew McKenna was an imposter." I turned to Carolyn. "How?"

"*He* told me." She pointed at Peever.

"You were working together all along?"

"No. Only after the virus came to light, and you disappeared. He sought me out."

"And you sold me out. That's why he's here. That's why you wanted an hour to *think*."

"No, Marc. He's here to help."

"He's here to bury me."

"Agent Peever?" Carolyn smiled, nervously. "That's not true, is it? You said you could help my husband set the record straight. Get out from under all these false accusations."

"Forget what I said." Peever shrugged. "I have new information. Bowman, empty your pockets."

"What?" Carolyn looked shocked. "This isn't what we agreed."

"If your husband has nothing to hide, he has nothing to worry about. Just tell him to empty his pockets."

"No. I won't. You promised to *help*."

"I *am* helping." Peever kept his eyes locked onto me. "If we do this here, and your husband's clean, we can have a different conversation. But if I have to make this formal . . ."

"Marc?" Carolyn was wavering.

I pulled out my cell phone and checked the time. Then I set it on the table, screen facing up, and took out my keys. I added the dead guy's keys to the pile. And finally, McKenna's black box.

"What's that?" Peever pointed to the device.

"Something someone gave me."

Peever drummed his fingers on the table, then took a piece of paper from his pocket, unfolded it, and handed it to me.

"From this morning."

It was a shot from a security camera. At AmeriTel's office. It showed McKenna and me leaving the node room.

"Another attempt was made to infect ARGUS this morning, Marc. Through a USB port, this time. Twenty-seven seconds before that picture was taken."

I didn't reply.

"That box you were carrying. It has a USB plug, right?"

"The box was McKenna's."

"Because you were working with McKenna. Using your knowledge of AmeriTel to help him insert the virus."

I didn't bother to reply.

"Marc?" Carolyn gripped my arm. "Don't stop. Explain it to him. Make him understand you had nothing to do with the virus. That McKenna tricked you."

"The virus is only part of the story." Peever pulled out another photograph. It showed the carnage in my bathroom on Thursday evening. "Who was *this* guy?"

"Marc?" Carolyn sounded shocked.

"I don't know."

"You should know." Peever jabbed at the picture with his finger. "You killed him."

"He slipped. Hit his head on the tile."

"And what did you do? Call 911? Get him an ambulance?"

I shook my head.

"No. You stole the guy's car and used his credit cards. Not the hallmarks of an innocent man, Marc."

"I had no choice."

"Like you had no choice when you fell out with your partner?" Peever laid a third photograph on the table. Carolyn gasped. It was of the scene in my hallway, that morning. Minus the blankets. "We see this all the time. Eliminate potential witnesses. Then disappear. Is that why you're desperate to lure your wife away? How much does she know about you?"

I turned to Carolyn, but she wouldn't meet my eye.

"You're done, Marc." Peever gathered up his pictures. "You're going to prison. For the rest of your life."

"You killed *two men* in our *home*?" Carolyn's face was white.

"There's no way out, Bowman." Peever produced an evidence bag, put his hand inside, and used it to reach for my keys. "The building's surrounded. And now that you've killed your buddy, there's no one to stage any fires. Or to ambush my car."

"What else aren't you telling me, Marc?" Carolyn's stare was piercing. "I can see it in your face. You're hiding something."

On the table my phone buzzed, and its screen lit up.

u were right. 2 agents. blue dodge. now on ice. u have the name?

Peever snatched the phone up and turned to me. "What the hell does this mean?"

"It means my wife wasn't the only one who put the last hour to good use. The text's from a woman who worked for McKenna. She knows her boss is dead. She's on a mission to find out who killed him. And she's hell-bent on revenge. I told her if she showed up here, half an hour after I met Carolyn, I'd give her a name. I figured if we were gone—no harm, no foul. But if anyone—like you—kept us here, she'd be our ticket out."

Peever grabbed his own phone and tried to make a call. He didn't get an answer. He tried a second number, and got the same result.

"My guys had better be OK. And if you think I'm going to trade *you* for this woman, whoever she is, you're crazy. You're coming with me. I'll have another team sweep her up."

"That's fine, in theory. But here's your problem. If I don't go outside in the next ninety seconds and give the woman the name she wants, she'll come in here. And I'll tell her *you* killed McKenna."

"She won't believe you. I'll show her the picture of McKenna, dead in your house. I'll tell her you did it."

"You can try. But who's the more likely candidate? The guy she knows, who was *helping* her boss? Or the agent who was trying to catch him? And who hung around to take pictures? I know which one my money's on."

"So what if she comes in?" Peever frowned. "There are two of us."

"There are five of them. And how many civilians in here?"

Peever didn't reply, so I got to my feet.

"Wait. Whose name would you give her?"

"The asshole who tried to kill my wife this morning. He's already dead, so no one else will get hurt. His body's at LeBrock's house. In the basement. I'll give you the address."

Peever shuffled his chair aside just far enough for me to squeeze past, but as I drew level his hand shot out and grabbed my wrist.

"This isn't over, Bowman. I won't underestimate you again."

I pulled free and moved out of his reach. Then I turned to Carolyn. She was still in the booth, showing no sign of following me.

"Sweetheart, this is it. Time's up. What's your decision? Are you coming?"

*B*EFORE HIS DEATH, MCKENNA HAD OUTLINED THE PATH THAT would exist for me if *I* survived. It led to prison. And that wasn't acceptable. Not with Carolyn by my side. And not with 6.4 million dollars in my trunk.

The problem was the evidence against me in the ARGUS database. McKenna said I couldn't run from it. And he said I couldn't hide from it. And he was right.

But he didn't say I couldn't change it.

CAROLYN DIDN'T SAY A WORD on the drive to AmeriTel. Her face was an impenetrable mask. It wasn't until I was about to step out of the car that her expression cracked and she finally broke her silence.

"Whatever you need to do to get away, I'll help you." She spoke without looking at me. "But beyond that, I'm not making any promises. OK?"

THE PARKING LOT WAS BUSIER than it had been at dawn, but only by a half-dozen cars. I took more encouragement from that than Carolyn's halfhearted assurance. And remembering the friendly conversation I'd had with Pete the security guard, I figured it would be safe to head into the building through the main entrance.

Pete was right there, standing behind the reception counter. He reached down and replaced a telephone handset as we walked toward him. And I could see from the way he squared his shoulders when he spotted us that something was very wrong.

"Mrs. Bowman, good afternoon. Mr. Bowman, please stay where you are."

"Pete? What's up?"

"I know."

"What do you know?"

"All about you. You shouldn't be here. You were fired. And you're wanted by the police."

"Oh, that. Don't worry. It's all a misunderstanding. Roger LeBrock and I have sorted everything out. It'll be official in the morning, but in the meantime he asked me to take care of a couple of things for him. Urgent things. And listen. I've got his home number, right here. Why not call and ask him? Put your mind at rest?"

"I don't think so." Pete stepped out from behind the counter. "Because I've just called the police. And they didn't know about any misunderstanding. They were real clear about the situation. Now they're on their way. And you had better stay right where you are till they get here, Mr. Bowman."

"The police are on their way? Great initiative, Pete. And you know what? You've done me a favor. It'll save me having to schlep down to the station house later with the papers I need to show them to clear my name. Did they give you an ETA?"

"Five minutes." He moved closer. "Ten, at the outside."

"Excellent. Although—"

"Marc!" Carolyn grabbed me, suddenly sagging at the knees. "I've decided," she whispered in my ear. "Do what you need to do, and go to the car." Then, in a loud, slurring voice: "No time. My pills. Top drawer. In my office . . ."

Pete took another step forward and Carolyn let go of me, flinging her arms around his neck instead.

"Hang in there, sweetheart." I started up the stairs, taking them two at a time. "I'll get the pills. I'll only be a second."

Carolyn groaned. I glanced down, and almost laughed. It looked for all the world like she and Pete were drunken teenagers, clumsily dancing. He was keeping Carolyn on her feet. Just. And she was forcing him to turn. By the time I was at the top of the stairs, he'd have his back to me. He'd be facing the exit. And he'd have no idea I was heading in the opposite direction from Carolyn's office.

IT WAS CAROLYN'S QUICK thinking that had bought me the time I needed to get upstairs. But when I sneaked back down and raced to meet her at the Aston, she wasn't there.

Had I heard her wrong?

Had she changed her mind, again?

Or had she been buying more time—to get away herself?

I COULDN'T DELETE ALL THE EVIDENCE MCKENNA'S PEOPLE HAD faked against me. There was too much of it, and it would have left too many loose ends. Something would inevitably have come back to bite me. So, given the amount of time available—much less than I'd hoped for, following Pete's 911 call—I had to just cut and paste.

Cut my details out. And paste someone else's in.

There's no easy way to say this, but that someone else is you. I'm sorry.

If it's any consolation, there was nothing personal about the choice. We've never met. I hold no grudge against you. It's just that yours was the easiest profile to piece together. An email account here. A credit card there. A cell phone number. A street address. A copy of your driver's license. Your details were all over cyberspace. It took no time to find them. And now, the seventh member of McKenna's web of terrorist sleepers? It's you.

Officially, Marc and Carolyn Bowman are dead. A police report shows they died in the fire at Karl Weimann's house on Friday night. I'm Daniel Abbot, now. And Carolyn is Isobel Draper. We're back together. Permanently. Offering my Lichtenstein for her life was the turning point, I think. She was only missing from AmeriTel's parking lot on Sunday afternoon when I came out because the police had arrived early, and—seeing the danger—she was leading them on a wild-goose chase. But she came back. She found me. We have a stack of cash to burn through, thanks to Roger LeBrock. We're going nowhere near computers. Or cell phones. And I'm not going to tell you where we are.

OK. That's enough of my story. You've had your warning. Now it's time to get your things in order. I don't know how long you have before they come for you. McKenna's people. Or Homeland Security. It's hard to tell them apart. But either way, the result won't be anything pleasant. So, be vigilant. Look out for anything new, or anything that changes. Like your spouse coming home later than usual from work. New neighbors moving in. An unscheduled visit from a utility repair crew. An odd vehicle hanging around your street. An unfamiliar mailman. A new guy at your job. At the grocery store. Or the gas station. You get the picture. And if you feel like something's out of place at home—if things have moved or disappeared, or doors are left open when they're normally closed—then someone's been inside, snooping around.

That means it's almost time.

But at least you know what's coming. And you know what you have to do.

RUN!

Acknowledgments

I would like to offer my deepest thanks to the following for their help, support, and encouragement during the writing of this book. Without them, it would not have been possible.

Kate Miciak, my incredible editor, and the whole team at Random House.

Janet Reid, the Queen of the Reef.

My friends, who've stood by me through the years: Carlos Camacho, Jamie Freveletti, Keir Graff, Tana Hall, Nick Hawkins, Dermot Hollingsworth, Amanda Hurford, Richard Hurford, Jon Jordan, Ruth Jordan, Kristy Claiborne Kiernan, Martyn James Lewis, Carrie Medders, Philippa Morgan, Denise Pascoe, Wray Pascoe, Javier Ramirez, David Reith, Sharon Reith, Beth Renaldi, Marc Rightley, Melissa Rightley, Renee Rosen, Kelli Stanley, and Brian Wilson.

Everyone at The Globe Pub, Chicago.

Audrey and John Grant.

Jane Grant.

Ruth Grant.

Katharine Grant, Jess Grant, and Alexander Tyska.

Gary and Stacie Gutting.

Not last, but always—Tasha.

I'd also like to extend extra special thanks to the real Daniel Peever of Ontario, Canada, for generously bidding on a character name in support of the wonderful Acorns Children's Hospice in Birmingham, England.

ANDREW GRANT was born in Birmingham, England. He attended the University of Sheffield, where he studied English Literature and Drama. He has run a small, independent theater company and worked in the telecommunications industry for fifteen years. Andrew is married to novelist Tasha Alexander, and the couple divides their time between Chicago and the UK.

ABOUT THE TYPE

This book was set in Bembo, a typeface based on an old-style Roman face that was used for Cardinal Pietro Bembo's tract *De Aetna* in 1495. Bembo was cut by Francesco Griffo (1450–1518) in the early sixteenth century for Italian Renaissance printer and publisher Aldus Manutius (1449–1515). The Lanston Monotype Company of Philadelphia brought the well-proportioned letterforms of Bembo to the United States in the 1930s.